HIS TO RECLAIM

STASIA MARS

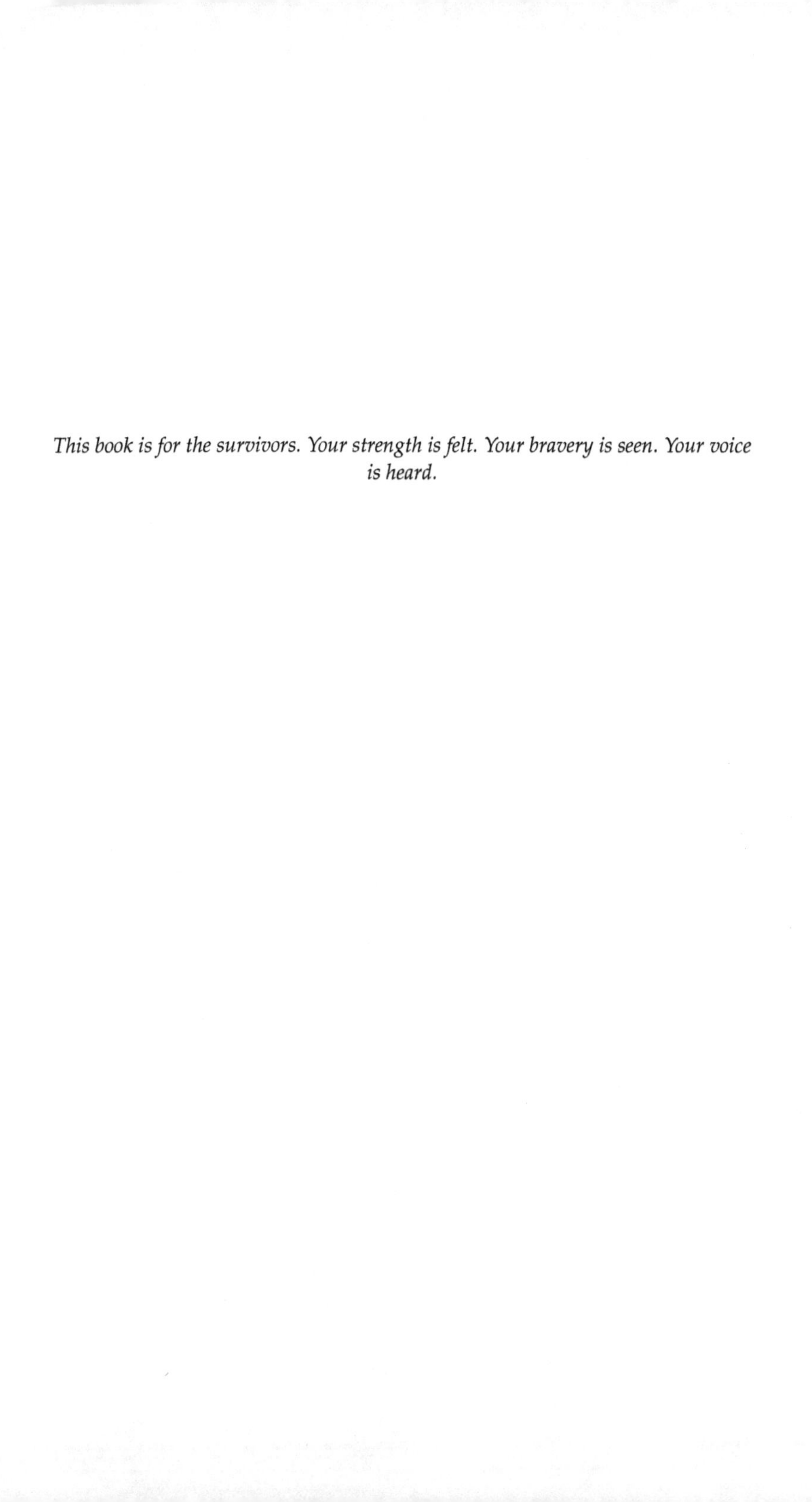

This book is for the survivors. Your strength is felt. Your bravery is seen. Your voice is heard.

AUTHOR'S NOTE

This is a DARK ROMANCE. It contains dark content and sensitive situations that may be triggering to some readers. A list of those TWs can be found on the author's website. Not recommended for those under the age of 18.

HIS TO RECLAIM

"Re-claim"
Restore, save, salvage, repair.
To claim again…

I tried to outrun the sullen cloud that had claimed me.
The one that was hell-bent on my destruction.

Determined to salvage what was left of me.
I took out a loan.
One late payment.
I was claimed by the mob.

The dark cloud flourished and festered.

Given to the Bratva heir for a night.
I thought he would take what little was left of me.
But he restored a piece of me that I thought irreparable.

I was taken to be sold like cattle.
He saved me.
Shouldering the dark cloud with me.
Claiming me as his.

But he and I were not destined for prosperity.
Never meant for a happily ever after.
Until he sacrificed everything for my freedom.

Only to end up reclaiming me.

ONE

VIVIAN

With my lungs burning and my heart literally about to beat out of my chest, I watch helplessly as the motherfucker who snatched my backpack disappears around a corner two blocks ahead of me and I finally call the quits. I chased him for several blocks shouting for someone to stop him, and of course, not one person even made an attempt to. They practically dodged out of his way giving him a clear path.

They don't call this Sin City for nothing. It's not a place for the righteous.

"Fuck," I whine. "Motherfucker!" I look around at all the passersby and want to fucking scream. They have no idea what they could've helped prevent. No idea they could have literally saved me.

What the fuck am I going to do?

I spin around as I try to wrap my head around this dire situation I now face. That man snatched my purse with every penny I had in it. And every penny of it is due to the mob. Today. *Now*, in fact.

That's where I was headed. On my way to make my weekly payment to the mob for the loan I stupidly took out with them. The mob that runs this town isn't some underground secret. Nope. Everyone knows about them and their comings and goings are all part of the daily gossip. Gossip that includes horror stories of what they do to people that don't pay what they owe.

Taking a loan from them was not at all my first choice. I tried to get a loan from an actual bank, but I was swiftly denied. I was just a young woman with absolutely no credit who was desperately trying to make a better life for myself. Yeah, why would they want to help?

I ended up in Sin City when I ran away from home at seventeen years old. I'd had enough of my mom's revolving door of scumbag boyfriends trying to sneak into my room at night, so I left in the shitty little car that I learned how to fix up myself. Haven't talked to my mother since, and it's been four years. I spent the first year and a half living out of said vehicle when it stopped running shortly after I arrived. Thankfully, you don't really need a car here. And I took any and every job I could find. Faux showgirl, cocktail waitress, club promoter, busser, the list goes on. I once even stood in for a magician's assistant.

All I wanted to do was go to college and get a job that made me enough money to take care of myself and not be the trash my mother raised me to be. I also didn't want to end up like her; constantly dependent on a man even when that man beat her and molested her daughter. After that year and a half, I began living out of dirt-cheap weekly hotels.

And because this is America, I cannot afford school, and the system is made to keep you poor. So, I eventually ended up going to the mob for financial help hoping that I could get ahead for a minute rather than continuing to survive from tiny paycheck to tiny paycheck with nothing to show for other than a long list of worthless skills. *Jack of all trades, master of bullshit.*

Surprisingly enough, getting a loan from them wasn't at all difficult. I asked around and eventually found out where to go and who to ask for. They sat me down in an office in the back of some deli, ran my ID, did some background checks, and handed me the cash I needed to pay for school. The weekly payments aren't bad at all, but obviously they added a lot of interest on top of it. As long as I kept up with the payments, it wouldn't be a problem.

Until now that is.

Now, I have to go back to the deli where I make my weekly payments and beg for mercy. I have never been a day late or a dollar short for two years with them. I've proven to be good for it. They'll show some leniency and offer me an extension, right? God, I pray so. What if they double the payment or something? No way I could swing that. Maybe I could if I checked out of the hotel I'm currently staying at and slept in my car again for a couple nights. Or I could sell my car? It's not worth much, but it's something.

Fuck.

I get to the deli with a sheen of sweat dampening my clothing and my heart in my throat. I stare at the door for a solid moment while I build up the courage to open it and step inside. The air inside cools my sweat causing me to slightly shiver. At least that's what I tell myself.

I move on autopilot from there. I approach the counter and ask the man behind it for a number seven. Silently, he nods his head and gestures for me to come around and follow him to the back.

The hallway feels darker and narrower than ever right now. I could be walking the line for all I know. I could very well not walk back out of here and no one would really miss me. I've made some friends at the casinos where I work, but nothing endearing. No one that would cause a fuss about my disappearance. Especially if they were to find out I had anything to do with the mob.

The burly man standing outside of the office opens the door for me and I walk in feeling like I'm dragging a cross behind me. Ready to be nailed to it. The same nameless man that's always behind the desk doesn't even bother to acknowledge my presence. There're no formalities or talk when I'm here. I simply give him my payment, wait while he counts it, then he dismisses me.

I wait for the door to shut behind me to move in closer. Then I swallow the large lump in my throat and lick my dry lips. "I, um…" I start with a shaky voice and the man lifts his head to stare up to me. "I'm going to be a couple days late on my payment this week." His stare remains blank. "I was on my way here with my usual payment like I have every week for over two years and some asshole snatched my backpack from me. I tried chasing him down, I swear I did. I chased him for as long as I could until he disappeared, and that was every dollar I had but I know I could make it back over the weekend in just a couple of shifts, and I will bring it right to you and never ever be late ever again. I swear," I rush everything out in one breath.

The bristled man doesn't move a muscle or tear his dead eyes away from me for even a second. It's eerily quiet in here to the point where you can clearly hear my heavy breathing. The anticipation utterly destroying my insides.

"You don't have our money," he states flatly in a thick Russian accent.

"Not yet. I mean, I did have your money, I swear. But someone stole it, and it was all I had. I've never ever been late on a payment before, and I swear I will never be late again. This was just a one-time unfortunate accident, and I will never let it happen again. If you could just give me two days, I'll get—"

"We do not give extensions."

"Please, I'm begging you. I work all this weekend and will have no problem making the money I owe you. I promise you'll have your money."

"We don't accept promises as payment."

I clench my fists at my sides and grit my teeth. I want to scream so badly right now. Why won't he fucking listen to me?! "I know, but I am good for it." I pause and try to think. "I have a car I can give you!" I blurt out. "It's not a great one or anything, but the parts are worth something for sure. You can have that, or at least hold onto it until I come back to you with the money." He remains quiet again and I'm about to pass out from all the stress. "Please, sir. I'm only asking for two extra days just this one time."

"I will allow you to pay us back," he finally says.

My shoulders drop in relief as I release the breath I was holding. "Thank you so mu—"

"You can work it off at our casino."

"Oh, I have a job, I swear. Like I said, I won't have any issues making the money."

"You work for us until your loan is paid off."

My heart sinks to the pit of my stomach and I really might faint. "I don't understand. Work at your casino until my entire loan is completely paid off?"

"Seems like you understand just fine," he says dryly.

"But...why?"

"You were late on your payment."

"But—"

"You ask too many questions for someone who should be getting the same treatment as anyone else who is late on their payment." I swallow hard, not at all willing to know what that might be. Probably a beatdown behind the deli or losing a finger. "This is a one-time clemency." *A clemency or a ruse?* "Do we have a deal?" I slowly nod my head in a daze, not aware if I actually have a choice or not. "Very good." His beady eyes roam the length of my body and I'm frozen to my core. That disgusting feeling most men give me has me wanting to puke. "You're lucky you are a pretty girl." His eyes gleam with ill and unwanted intent. The one side of his mouth curls up into a sinister grin showing off his crooked teeth. Bile burns the back of my throat and I fight to gulp it down.

I'm able to breathe when he tears his filthy gaze from me and jots something down on a tiny piece of paper. Then he slides it on top of the desk towards me. "You will show up here at ten tonight. Wear something sexy." He gives my body a perusal again. I cautiously move forward to snag the paper and stare down at it. "If anyone gets a hold of that address, I will have no choice but to mess up your pretty face."

My breath studders as I shove the piece of paper deep into the front pocket of my shorts. "I'll keep it safe," I say quietly.

There's nothing left to discuss, so I turn and leave. Thankfully, he lets me.

And thus begins my career with the mob.

TWO

VIVIAN

Working for the underground casino run by the mafia is pretty much as bad as I thought it would be. They have me cocktail waitressing in skimpy clothing four nights a week where there are virtually no rules for the scummy patrons. So, they can cop a feel and speak to me anyway they want. Not to mention I am doing all of this without being paid since it all is going towards my balance with them, which means I still have to work at my other job for actual money, leaving no time for school. Making the loan I took out with them for nothing.

I was just about to start the spring semester, but it looks like it'll have to wait till fall. And you know how that goes. Once you put off school, it keeps getting put off until you end up not going back. Meaning I will never escape this never-ending loop of hopping from job to job just to pay the essential bills.

The hours I work here vary. I start around ten at night and sometimes I'm here till the sun comes up, and sometimes I'm out of here within four to six hours. This has been going on for almost two months now. I don't dare ask how much longer I will have to do this. I'll do what I am told and keep my head down until they tell me I've been a good girl and I'm relieved of my duties with my loan officially paid off.

The other attractive women who work here walk around with a smile plastered to their face as if they're happy to be here. They must be drugged or brainwashed because who in the right mind would ever want to be working here? Or maybe they actually get paid. Who the hell knows? We're not having slumber parties or girls' night out together.

One late payment. *One!* God, I am still so bitter about it. I absolutely loathe men in power. They expect the world given to them and believe the entire female race is beneath them.

Swallowing down my sudden rage, I carry the tray of drinks to the table of loud, petulant, disgusting *pigs* I'm forced to serve. Without speaking or making any eye contact, I place the drinks down and gather the empty glasses and bottles while they all gamble and talk over each other about their dick sizes. *Bombastic idiots.*

Thankfully, no one pays me any mind and I high tail it out of there to head back to the kitchen to dispose of the dirty glasses when someone harshly grabs a hold of my barely covered ass. I stop in my tracks as a heavy breath comes over my shoulder, reeking of cigars and alcohol, immediately singeing the little hairs in my nose. Bile instantly rising.

"You're a fresh little thing, aren't you?" he mutters, intensifying the foul odor making me want to barf.

I close my eyes against the nausea and open my mouth to say something when someone beats me to it. "You will remove your hand from her ass, or I will," a deep, unfamiliar voice growls. Though grateful to whomever is saving me, his Russian accent doesn't settle my nerves one bit.

The hand releases from me immediately, but I'm too stunned to move yet. "If you want a woman, you pay like everyone else," the Russian man says, and it proves he most definitely is not my white knight.

My head instinctively whips around in offense, coming face to face with both pigs. The one who looks at me licking his chops is obviously the one who had a hold of my ass. His appearance alone makes me sick. Add in the repulsive stench and crude manners and once again the back of my throat burns with chunks ready to blow. *Oh, how satisfying would it be to puke all over this asshole.*

I look from the pervert to the asshole that first saved me from being groped, then offered me up as a whore, and my heart does that weird fluttering thing it always does when I see him. The blonde who steps in when the big boss isn't around. I've never been close enough to him to hear him speak before. He's sinfully attractive and clearly very dangerous. I should be quivering in fear, but butterflies are swarming in my belly instead. He's not at all someone I would ever think I would find remotely attractive.

"How much for her?" the pervert interjects.

My eyes widen in panic as I look between the two men. Blondie doesn't even spare me a glance. Why would he? I'm a woman. He wasn't looking out for me. He was making sure someone didn't get anything for free in his casino.

"She's not an option." A deep breath rushes out of my lungs. "Come. I will show you who is." He gives the man a grin that sends chills down my spine. It doesn't reach his eyes but it does let the gold plating on his teeth glimmer in the dim lighting. He wraps a muscular arm around the man and steers him away from me.

I don't stand and wait around for another moment. I bolt to the kitchen at a high speed and practically drop the tray down on the counter. "Hey, you okay, girl?" Claudia, another woman who works here, asks with sincere concern for me as she appears at my side.

I'm panting and trying to regulate my heartbeat. "Yeah." I take a deep breath and give her a tight smile. "I'm alright. Thanks."

"Okay. Get yourself some water before you pass out or something."

She goes to leave, and I stop her. "Hey." She turns around. "Who is the blonde guy? The one that seems to be in charge when Mr. Rogov isn't here."

She looks around and closes the gap between us. "His name is Sasha Rogov. Mr. Rogov's son."

My eyes widen. "His son?"

"Yes." She keeps her voice down. "But we call him sir or refer to him as 'the young master'." I arch an eyebrow. "Do not call him Sasha or Mr. Rogov, got it?" I nod my head, taking all the advice and warning to heart.

Of course, the first person I've found attractive in years is the son of the most dangerous man in the city. To find his unruly blonde hair, stolid look permanent on his chiseled facial features, gold crowns, and tattooed muscles at all sexy, should be the first indicator of poor life choices. To feel nervous and jittery every time he enters the room and let my eyes move with him as he refrains from drinking and gambling should be all the red flags I need to shut down my libido. He walks around as if it's all beneath him, and really, he's probably right. He's entitled, pompous, and dangerous. Literally, the exact opposite of what I should be attracted to.

I am not one of those females who likes the bad boys. No way. I watched my mother get with one bad boy after another, and that's all they are. Bad. They have rotten souls and will only treat you poorly. I am not my pathetic mother. When I feel like I am ready to try dating, it will be a nice man. One that takes care of his mom and works a regular job making a modest living.

I yank at the hem of my skimpy dress that leaves hardly anything to the imagination and get back to work. The first night I showed up here I was told to wear something sexy, so I wore a tight mini dress and thigh high boots. They accepted my outfit that night but told me to show up next time wearing less clothing. Seeing what the other women wore, I had a better idea of what they expected. So, I wore the skimpiest dress I had that fit me like second skin, hiked it up some, and I wore the only pair of heels I owned. I had zero money to buy anything else, so I had to cut up a couple of dresses to wear for the next couple of nights until I worked my other job and was able to go to the thrift store and get a few more things to hold me over. Waste of fucking money. They should've at least provided me with the 'proper attire'.

The dress I'm wearing tonight is something I would never be caught dead in, outside of these walls. It's purple, which I hate the color on me, and my breasts pour out of it. No wonder that guy thought I was a hooker. Not to mention the makeup and hair I worked hard on. The extra effort isn't to please anyone. It's strictly to blend in and keep me from drawing any unnecessary attention. I definitely do not need that from anyone here.

It's late into the night, or I guess early into the morning, when Mr. Rogov shows up. The don. At least that's what it says on the internet. The boss of the mafia or head of the family is called a don. I searched mafia lingo before starting here. I don't know if they actually use those terms or not, but I wanted to be as well informed as I could.

Sasha seems to be the only one in here unfazed by his arrival as everyone shifts in their seats and the tension in the air thickens. Unlike his son, Mr. Rogov enjoys gambling and drinking. He's also louder and obnoxious, whereas Sasha remains passive and cool.

When Mr. Rogov is here, I stay clear of whatever side of the room he occupies. He actually scares the fuck out of me. The rumors about him around this city give me nightmares. He's sick and demonic. Rotten to the core. And worst of all, he's the all-powerful overlord of everyone in Sin City. Including every cop and judge.

Bethany, a girl who has been working here for years supposedly, has no problem going right up to him. She even lets him put his vile hands on her and pull her into his lap to grope her. I shiver with revulsion as I watch her smile and enjoy his attention. It's not that he's completely unattractive. For an older man, he's quite good-looking. He has pale gray hair and perfectly groomed facial hair. Handsome features and looks fit. But his ostentatious and superior demeanor makes me sick. He actually thinks he's some holy potentate deserving of praise. It's *ugly*.

I manage to tear my gaze away from the pig and my eyes collide with dark ones. *Sasha.* I can finally put a name to his face, and a voice as well. I've been too afraid to ask any questions around here until tonight. And he's never looked at me before. Even with our earlier encounter. He avoided me altogether. Now, he's homed in on me, and I wish the floor would just swallow me up. His gaze is unwavering, sending crackles through the air. It's a look of warning and I'm wondering if he saw me sneering at his father.

Popping my shoulders back, I somehow break the stare down between us and paste a smile on my face as if phlegmatic and uninterested. When really, he affects me just by existing. I force myself to move along and continue my job.

I shouldn't have to keep reminding myself who Sasha is and that it's because of him and his father I'm here working for a debt. He's mafia. A gangster who murders and disposes of bodies in the middle of the desert on a daily basis. That alone should keep me focused on working off the servitude I've been forced into. Someone who offers up women to his customers in an illegal casino, no soul, no remorse, and absolutely no morals? I know better than to even think about getting involved.

The number of men begin to dwindle out and I can tell I am nearing the end of my shift for the night. Just as I am given the green light to leave, another man who works here stops me. "Tomorrow night you will be working a private event," he says as a command and not a request.

"What?"

"You will be picked up just before ten at night. Dress the same as you would here," the large man without a Russian accent states flatly. As if he's a robot programmed to give me instructions.

Knowing I do not have a choice, and questions only cause aggravation with these people, I nod my head and exit the building. I look up to the starry sky and beseech God, that it's not a Rogov event.

THREE

SASHA

Blyad. Fuck. I swear my father is purposely dangling this woman in front of me to taunt me. It's bad enough I have to see her several times a week at the casino, but now she's in my fucking home where she'll leave her scent everywhere.

Vivian James. Twenty-one years old. Born on June seventh at St. Mary's hospital in southern California. She moved to Vegas when she was seventeen years old and foolishly took out a loan with us a couple of years ago. Then she was stupid enough to miss a payment. Now, we own her for the unforeseeable future. If she weren't so attractive, she'd be tossed out into the desert for all of nature's scavengers to pick off the little meat she has left on her bones. But she's here, and somehow lucky enough not to have been promoted to whoring yet.

I don't know how she's been flying under the radar this whole time. She has a beauty that sets her apart from every other woman. Her brown hair shines from the roots all the way down to her waist where it ends. The slight tilt at the corners of her eyes and subtle tint to her skin points towards some kind of ethnicity in her background but her mother was listed as Caucasian on her birth certificate and the section for her father was left blank. She's taller than average for a woman and much too skinny. The only meat on her body seems to be in her breasts. I know she isn't on any drugs since we're the only ones who deal in the entire city and surrounding ones. But even with her body slightly emaciated, she's still somewhat of a beacon. Hence why she's here at the estate working our private event.

I'm expected to show up and impress tonight. Not only for our aristocratic guests, but also for my father. Always having to prove to him that I'm a worthy heir. Considering I'm his only son, you'd think it would be an easy ask. A tailored suit and a clean shave replace my usual choice in appearance. All so I can put on a show, act as if I am a part of this society and revel in its riches. What I really want to do is retreat to my bedroom and soak up the silence.

Unlike most of the other families in the outfit, I won't be coerced into an arranged marriage for more wealth and allies. My father doesn't see any benefit to it. Their only purpose for him is for one to provide a son for him.

My cousin Kazimir lucked out of an arranged marriage as well. His father made plans for him to marry a woman of his choosing, but he died, and Kazimir claimed that so did his word. There was argument within our inner circle with some backing Kazimir and some insisting he broke his word. But since Kazimir is now the head of his family and allied with Alejandro Martinez, no one would be daft enough to go against him. At least, that's what we thought. The family of the daughter he was said to marry retaliated and as a result, was wiped off the face of the earth.

Once I'm getting up there in age, I'll find some poor woman to procreate with for an heir, then most likely a couple other women to make sure I have a son, and that'll be it. I don't plan on ever settling down. It has nothing to do with an aversion to commitment or monogamy, and it has nothing to do with how my father has chosen to live his life. I simply do not have the luxury of keeping anything worth having. Any time I have found something to care about, my father has always found a way to use it to control me. To even taunt me for his own pleasures. He would do the same with a woman if I showed any interest in one. So, I have always stayed away from dating or romanticizing. Not that I'm actually capable of either.

I continue to avoid the little temptress as the night goes on. Once I feel like I've made my presence known, I slip out and call it a night. Something made me want to stick around to keep an eye on Vivian, but I talked myself out of it. She's no one to me. If my father decides to pass her around to our guests, so be it.

She is not my problem and not mine to protect.

FOUR

VIVIAN

Toshchiy-Skinny
Tselka-Virgin
Kukolka-Little Doll

"My son seems to be in surly mood tonight," Mr. Rogov heckles with the men around him at a game table.

"Perhaps the boy needs to get laid," one of the men says.

I set down the last drink I'm holding and I turn to flee. "You might be right," Mr. Rogov replies. "You." The authority in his voice has me coming to a halt and my stomach turning. I slowly spin around to find him and a couple of his comrades looking directly at me. Devouring me with their repugnant gazes. "Come here," he commands, and I think quick to obey him. I move in his direction, and he begins a thorough inspection of me from head to toe. "Yes, you'll do. Go to my son's room and fuck him." My mouth pops open in shock and I see that he is not at all kidding. He's dead serious. "Now." He turns away from me, a silent dismissal, but I'm frozen in my place. The men around him are practically drooling as they look at me with sexual intent.

I remain solid, feeling like I'm lost somewhere in space when I feel a gentle tug on my arm. "Come on, Vivian," the feminine voice murmurs and I let them pull me away. "You okay?" she whispers.

I snap out of it to see it's Claudia who has come to my aid. "No, I'm not okay," I hiss under my breath as we promptly make our way to the door. "Does he really expect me to go fuck his son?"

"Yes," she says in earnest.

My eyes bug out and my head rears back. "You can't be serious?"

She looks at me in pity. "I've been working for them long enough to know what would happen if you refused *anything* asked of you."

She pulls me outside of the door and to the side where no one can see us. "Ask of me?" I burst in outrage. "Nothing is asked of me. It's demanded."

"Exactly." She pauses and takes a deep breath for some patience. "Look. If you don't do as he says, he will surely take you for himself and may even pass you around to share." I wrap my arms around my midsection for comfort. "And believe me, none of them will be at all gentle with you."

"What about Sasha?"

She cants her head to one side. "He won't be gentle, but he isn't cruel like his father. He, most certainly, is the lesser of two evils."

I stop to try and absorb all this. "So, if I don't go fuck his son, I'll be gang raped. How will he even know if I do or not?"

She nods her head in confirmation. "Yes, that's exactly what would happen. You will be brutally raped over and over. I've seen it happen." I watch her swallow hard and do her best to keep her composure. "And there is no coming back from it."

What the fuck is wrong with these people, and how are they all allowed to get away with this? Does this shit really go on every day in this country?

My body begins to tremble and I'm on my way to tears. "I don't think I can do this."

She grasps my shoulders and looks me square in the eye. "You can and you will," she says firmly but not harshly. "The only choices you have is to either go and willingly give yourself to Sasha and pray he isn't cruel, or you can be taken unwillingly by several beastly men and leave here bleeding and wishing for death." She pauses to let the reality of her words sink in. "What'll it be?"

I stare at her in dread. Are those really my only two options? Seeing as it would be impossible to run out of this heavily guarded estate and nowhere safe to run to, the answer is yes. Those are my only options, and the right one is obvious.

"Where is his room?" I whisper with heaviness in my chest.

Claudia takes my hand in hers and I blindly follow her lead. She seems to know exactly where his room is, and I assume it's from personal experience. I shouldn't feel a tiny bolt of jealousy, but I do. I ignore the insanity and face her as we stop in front of a closed door. She remains patient with me as I stare at her.

"Do we knock?" She nods. "What if he doesn't answer? What if he doesn't want to sleep with me?"

"Vivian." She takes both my hands in hers. "If you think that Mr. Rogov will let you off because you *tried*, then you have learned nothing. *Beg* if you have to."

I nod my head vigorously and retract my hands from hers. "Okay," I say quietly.

"I am so sorry, Vivian. You seem like a sweet girl, and you do not deserve any of this, but there's no way out of it. Women are disposable to them, and once we are no good for whatever use they need from us, we're worthless. Go in there and seduce him, or you will suffer later for it."

I turn and face the door with detestation. I haven't a clue what awaits me on the other side. I don't even know how I'll walk away from any of this. But dragging it out won't do me any good. Might as well get it over with. Just go in there, seduce him, lie there while he has his way, then tuck tail and run.

I lift my fist to knock on the door and Claudia takes that as her cue to walk away, leaving me to my damnation. I knock twice, making sure it can be heard from inside, and I'm met with silence. I give the door two more knocks, putting more force behind it, and still nothing. What do I do if he left, or if the door is locked and he doesn't answer?

Only one way to find out…

I hesitantly reach for the doorknob with trembling fingers, and when it easily turns in my sweaty palm, I rejoice this tiny victory. Even if he isn't in there now, I can wait until he comes back, right?

I push my way into the dark room with the only light from the moon peeking through the curtains. I catch a whiff of the now familiar scent as I quietly shut the door behind me. The same scent that hung around after my one and only time of being in close proximity with Sasha.

My eyes blink several times to adjust to the darkness and I peer around the silent room. My gaze wanders to the large bed where I find a massive figure lying still on it.

I keep my steps light as I slink through the dark. The figure is a sleeping Sasha. Passed out horizontally on his back with his feet flat on the floor. Like he sat on the edge of the mattress and laid back, then didn't move.

His suit jacket, dress shoes, and socks are gone, reminding me that in order for this to happen, the rest of his clothes will have to come off. So will mine. The thought of it has me coming to a stop and debating on making a run for it. But we've already been through this. This is my only way out of this somewhat alive.

Only his expansive chest moves up and down as he peacefully sleeps. His blonde locks already back to their askew originality and the sleeves of his dress shirt are pushed up revealing his strong ink covered forearms. Maybe this won't be so terrible after all. If I let him do his thing and be compliant, I can focus on his physical attributes, and pretend I'm into it. Like we're two people sexually attracted to one another and let our primal desires take over. We'll rip at each other's clothing while passionately kissing and he'll show some tenderness.

Steadying my breath, I scrape up what's left of my fortitude and reach out a shaky hand. Before my hand makes contact with his knee, I'm grasped with a crushing force on both of my upper arms and pinned down to the bed staring up at a very alert, and very pissed off, Sasha.

In the blink of an eye, I go from nervous shakes to full blown tremors as he practically foams at the mouth hovering over top of me. He starts hissing in Russian and I gawk up at him in fear. "I—I don't know what you're saying." My voice comes out embarrassingly weak.

He takes a sharp breath as his grip on my arms constrict. "What the fuck are you doing in my room?"

"Your father sent me," I rush out.

"For what?" he snaps.

"To," *Oh, come on! Don't make me say it.* "To have sex with you."

He's quiet for a long moment while my anxiety only builds up. "Well, you can tell my father that I am in no mood for it. You can go," he tells me but makes no move to let me up. We remain in a standoff for a solid minute before he finally releases his strong hold on me and gets to his feet. He's well over six feet tall and uses his size to look down on me as if I'm some pathetic harlot sitting at the feet of a god.

I'm ready to jump up and run right out of here when I remember why I even entertained the idea of walking in here in the first place. "Wait. Please don't make me leave." I sit up. "Not without having sex with me. I'll make it good, I promise." Oh, my God. I hate who I am right now.

His face tenses up in a sneer. "Yeah, I'm sure you will, but I don't fuck the help or my father's whores," he spits.

I almost find myself demanding that he recant that statement, but I stop myself. I need to seduce him, not piss him off any further. "Please don't reject me, Sasha." His nostrils flare. "I mean, sir!" I quickly recover. "If you kick me out, your father will pass me around to all those men out there." The thought of him tossing me out and feeding me to the wolves has my eyes stinging and my throat throbbing. I suck back the threatening tears as Sasha remains unmoving. Both physically and emotionally.

Moments tick by as the silence taunts me, but I refuse to stand down. I'm not leaving unless he physically removes me himself. I'll cry, I'll beg, I'll plead, I'll throw myself at his feet. I. Am. Not. Leaving.

"Stand up," he abruptly orders.

With unsteady legs, I do as he says and rise. With my four-inch heels added onto my five-foot seven height, I still only come up to his chin. He isn't super bulky, but he's easily twice the width of me. His dark gaze never leaves my face as I wait for my next order.

"How old are you?" His tone is less harsh than the snarling he was doing a moment ago, but it still isn't soft.

"Twenty-one."

He scoffs as if it's something to be ashamed of and shakes his head in offense. His eyes finally leave mine to make a heated trail down the length of my body. Nothing changes in his expression while my skin breaks out in goosebumps. I shouldn't care whether or not I meet his standards, but I hope that I do. I should hate him and anticipate this all being over with so I can run home crying.

His bare feet saunter forward until our bodies are only an inch apart and he leans in. I physically shiver from his nearness, and he gently moves my hair away from my ear to whisper against it. Every cell in my body ignites, and I have the feeling of being close to fainting. "Did you know there is a camera in here?" he rasps, and I shudder from his breath in my ear and the softness of his lips brushing against the shell of it. I swallow and shake my head. "There's one camera in here, so my father will know if I in fact fuck you or not. So, I'm going to fuck you. Strictly out of pity. You're too young to be taken by my father. He would rip you to pieces, demolishing you, *kukolka*." I should be thankful for his little bit of humanity lucidly projected at me in the form of pity, but I'm also so ashamed. "Let's see what you have under this." His lips remain lightly pressed to my ear and I stifle another chill. He slips his calloused fingers under the frail straps of my dress, brushing along my pebbled skin.

This is it. This will be the first time I have ever allowed a man to touch me like this.

I brace myself when he steps back and peels my tight dress down my body. Letting gravity take over when it gets to my thighs and it falls to the floor, the cheap fabric pools around my feet.

My instincts make me want to cover myself, especially since my bra and underwear are nothing to be desired. Both full coverage and not at all matching. His gaze darkens, trailing my body, then he clucks his tongue in disapproval. "*Toshchiy*." Whatever he says isn't meant as a compliment. My body shakes even more to the point I am practically convulsing. His dark eyes dart up to my face. "I won't take you like this. If you do not want to be toyed with by my father then I suggest you find a way to relax," he seethes.

"I'm—I'm sorry," I stutter. "I just—" I chomp down on my trembling bottom lip and try desperately to calm myself. He hisses something in Russian and backs away from me, running a maddening hand through his hair. "I promise to relax," I rush the words out before he changes his mind and sends me away. "I just—I'm a little nervous because...I've never done this before."

He snorts and shakes his head, muttering more in Russian.

I realize he thinks this is the first time I've had to whore myself out like this, not that this is the first time I've been with a man. "I'm not...experienced."

He draws his eyebrows and lowers his chin to study me. "Are you saying you're a virgin?" I have no idea how to answer that. Not without letting him learn every dark secret connected to my past. So, I take the easy way out and let him decipher my silence. "*Tselka*," he curses. I'm sure another insult. "I assume my father is unaware of this." I shrug my shoulders, and he closes the gap once again. "That would be no because if he knew you were untouched, he would have sent you to his room instead of mine." I resist the urge to hug myself. The small space between us diminishes and he puts his lips to my ear again. "I am not a gentle lover, *kukolka*. But I'll do my best to take it easy on you." His tone isn't as steely as it's been, making me relax some. "Now, take off the rest."

FIVE

SASHA

Her feeble frame no longer trembles, but her smooth skin is decorated with tiny bumps. Considering she's a virgin, her nerves are more warranted. My cock doesn't drip with arousal when a woman is shaking in fear and revulsion to the mere fact of fucking me. I may be the spawn of Satan, but I am not his clone. I may not be a better man than him, but overpowering a woman does nothing for me.

I watch and take a couple steps back as she takes another soothing breath and reaches her fragile hands behind her to remove her bra. The tips of my fingers tingle as they hang at my sides. Her plush breasts are finally revealed to me and I swear my mouth waters for her. They're heavy and plump with dark colored nipples to match the natural tone to her skin.

She toes off her heels next and hooks her thumbs into the waistband of her panties before she pauses. My gaze jumps up to connect with hers and she stares back at me with a hint of mischievousness in her hazel eyes. There's still trepidation found in them, but there's more.

I hold her stare with a look of warning, and she eventually concedes, pushing the cotton fabric to the floor and finally revealing her undiscovered paradise to me.

"*Krasotka.*" *Beautiful*, I murmur and run the tip of my tongue along my bottom lip, suddenly feeling starved. Only a little stubble shadows her pussy, but it makes no difference to me. "Lie back on the bed, *kukolka*."

When my eyes roll up to meet hers, hers blaze with indecision. If she decides against this, I won't take her. The camera doesn't show my bed, so I could easily make it seem like I fucked her and not actually do it. Something I should tell her, but I'm no saint. As long as she gives in, I'm taking her.

She glances back at the bed then sits down to scoot towards the middle.

Her thighs are clenched together when she lays back, but she doesn't take her eyes off me. Brave *kukolka*. Facing her monster rather than hiding from it.

"Why are you a virgin?" I ask as I begin to peel away my clothing.

She licks her lips as her chest rises and falls rapidly. "I don't know." Her voice is almost too soft to hear.

"Is it because of religion?" I drop my shirt to the floor and her eyes bounce around my bare torso.

She shakes her head. "No."

"Do you not like men?" I pull my belt off and she carefully watches me.

She hesitates to answer, too distracted by my movements so I stop, meeting her gaze in the process. "I don't trust men."

"You shouldn't." I shove my pants down and she gawks down at my cock that is at half mass. But with the way she's looking at me, it's quickly hardening. "You want to touch it?" I wrap one hand around my cock and slide up and down my length in a teasing manner in an attempt to debauch her.

I stifle a chuckle and go to retrieve a condom from the drawer next to my bed. As I roll it on, I kind of wish I had a stiff drink right now. I don't do well with alcohol, so I mostly avoid it. But for some reason, this situation is beginning to cause me stress.

She's doing her best to keep her gaze averted when I stand at her feet, but it keeps bouncing back to me. Her little paradise is still tightly wedged between her too thin thighs. Knowing that she is pure and untouched, I decide to do something I haven't done in years.

"Relax," I say as gently as possible, but I know it still came out as a sharp command. "It's just you and me, *kukolka*. No need to be shy."

She timidly looks at me. "You said there are cameras in here."

I place my rough hands on her knees and rub the area, trying to allay her nerves some. "Don't think about it."

"Can we get under the covers?"

I release half of a grin and slowly shake my head. I see it in her eyes as she accepts her fate once and for all. My hands glide between her knees and I coax them apart. She doesn't resist, letting them spread and allowing my palms to slip down her thighs, making sure she's nice and open for me. My knees cause the mattress to dip as I climb up and she lets out a girlish squeal when I scoop her up by her ass to make more room for me.

Keeping my eyes locked with hers to help pacify her nerves, I cautiously lower myself so that my mouth hovers over her cunt. "Relax, and just feel, *kukolka*."

Her eyelids flutter shut, and she takes another deep breath to smooth away the rest of her tenseness. It does the trick because when I look down, her pussy gleams with natural juices. She might not be here by her own free-will, but she isn't repulsed nor dismayed by her present position. It could be her body's natural reaction, but I won't reject something so exorbitantly enticing offered to me on a silver fucking platter.

Not willing to delay this a moment more, I flatten my tongue against her little bundle of nerves, and I can feel dribble run down my chin from how much I am salivating. Practically frothing at the mouth. Her sapidity has my blood rushing entirely to my cock and her pungent aroma has me pressing my nose to the apex of her pussy for a deep inhale.

Her hips fly up with a sharp breath and her eyes pop open. I lock onto her and anchor her back down to feast. I suck her pliable folds into my mouth and her head snaps back with a whine. Her knuckles turn white as she fists the sheets. I'm determined to make every second of this pleasurable for her, because sex should always be enjoyed. I may not always be most generous in bed, but it's much more enjoyable when your partner is dripping with desire. That's why my head is between her legs and I'm not yet balls deep inside of her. She'll walk away from this sore and no longer pure, but she'll leave satisfied.

She whines and squirms as I release her flesh and tenderly lick and kiss, the whole time watching her every reflex and muscle spasm. She's now chewing hard on her bottom lip, reluctant to give me more verbal responses. It only provokes me as a challenge.

I work her slits and find her tight hole with one digit. Her thighs clamp around my head on instinct when I dip my finger inside. *Fucking tight.* She wasn't lying about being a virgin. I don't let up on her with my mouth and slip my finger the rest of the way in and let her adjust to the small intrusion. It only takes her a few seconds to relinquish resistance and comply. Her muscles relax, gifting me with consent.

Her cunt is going to be sculpted to the shape of my cock when I pillage my way through. Redesigned just for me. The fervid thought has me plunging my finger in until it can't go any further, making her outwardly gasp and arch her back off the bed. She's whimpering and the warm flesh sheathing my finger constricts after only a few painfully slow pumps. I'm fascinated by how responsive she is to my touch when she was more than reluctant to begin with.

I pause to watch her crash. Patiently waiting for her to steal a glance down at me. To remember who is between her thighs and who made her come so nimbly and hastily. "Open your eyes, *kukolka*," I rasp. Her eyes are sluggish when they peel open. I place a chaste and light kiss to her sensitive skin, and she twitches in response. "Have you ever had anyone down here before?"

"Not like this."

My aching cock throbs from her response. "But you have been touched…" I retract my finger and drag it upwards, causing her to quiver. *So fucking responsive.* Her head bobs up and down. "Do you touch yourself?" She looks away with pink on her cheeks, and I move my body up over hers. Gently tucking one finger under her chin, I have her look at me. "Nothing to be ashamed of, *kukolka*." She stares blankly back at me.

I hunch over some to cup one large breast and take it in my mouth. She sucks in a quick breath of air as I swirl her nipple with my tongue. I suck and grope, pushing her to give into the pleasure she obviously knows nothing about. She's resistive, but I can feel her close to surrender.

Running a hand down her thigh, I harshly grip one ass cheek and she releases that moan she's been holding back. She might be untouched, but she has a devious side. I'm betting once she discovers her sexuality, she'll find how rough she likes it.

My hand replaces my mouth, and I switch over to her other breast. Watching her become crazed with newfound desire has me ready to explode. Especially when she starts rubbing her little body against me.

My hips respond to hers and my sheathed cock slips up and down her slick pussy. She moans and twists this way and that. I continue grinding into her with her nipple in my mouth and she cries out in ecstasy again. This time not holding back. Her jaw unhinged and her voice ricocheting around the room.

In utter amazement, I act as she's still riding her high and line myself up with her entrance. I nudge only an inch in, and she sobers, the jitters trying to seep back in. I study her face for a long, drawn-out moment. Her skin is flawless, and each facial feature is feminine and petite. Those hazel eyes of hers bounce around my face in curiosity, searching for mercy, I'm sure.

Our lips are only inches away, enough to share one breath. Her soft lips are parted with short breaths coming in and out. Not capable of prolonging this any longer, I devour her mouth with mine and thrust my way inside. Her entire body tenses under me and she's slow to react. Her lips still, but she's pliant as my tongue plunders inside her mouth. After a moment she begins to reciprocate the kiss, and goddamn she can kiss. I wasn't supposed to make love to her, but I couldn't have her clamming up on me. I want this woman not only willing, but greedy.

Her arms wrap around my neck almost throwing me off kilter. She's embracing me and it's unsettling. It somehow plagues me with a sense of guilt. It's infuriating.

Doubling my efforts, I kiss her harder and grind my hips against her with every thrust. I didn't even give her time to accommodate the now large intrusion, but her body counters mine with every move I make, only pushing me to go harder.

I don't let up as I dominate her mouth, demanding her complete surrender to me. Her snugness throbs and constricts around me, making it impossible to hold out longer, as if her pussy is chiding my cock for desecrating such a pure and virtuous place. Doesn't matter though, this slice of heaven now belongs to me. My holy sanctuary to pillage and exalt in pleasure.

When her fingers find their way into my hair, her nails scraping my scalp, it forces the regimented lust coursing through me to weaken. She's taunting me, and I am more than happy to oblige. I rip my mouth from hers and pound into her, pushing her fortitude and torturing myself in the process.

The thought of this pussy being forged to perfectly fit me has me seeing stars when she clutches my cock with her inner muscles and mewls. The sensation possesses me and it's like a high I need to chase or I'll die. My muscles start locking up on me as I burst inside the condom. She moans loudly and rides out her peak while I'm literally paralyzed. I bite back a groan and bury my face into her neck to hinder her from seeing any vulnerability from me.

Goddamn.

As soon as her muscles and mine stop spasming, I'm overcome with lethargy and snapped back into reality. Her skin is moist against mine, and our heavy panting fills the room.

I lean back to look into her eyes that seem to be glazed over with the afterglow. I have no idea how I'm going to do it. To get a taste of heaven and have to abstain from ever tasting it again.

But I'll have to let her go because I'm not cruel enough to suck her into my plight of a life.

SIX

VIVIAN

Oh. My. God. What just happened is irrevocable, but I don't regret a single moment. I can only equate what I feel to an out of body experience.

I was still stuck in my head when I layed back on his bed naked, but when he looked up at me and told me to just feel, I forced my mind to quiet and my muscles to loosen.

All my life, men have taken what they have wanted from me. Touched me without my permission. Shamed me and demeaned me. Ruined me for life, or so I thought. But I don't want to allow for men to take from me anymore.

With Sasha staring up at me from between my legs, I convinced myself I wanted this. Convinced myself that I was in control. So, I closed my eyes and concentrated on his breath against the sensitive flesh between my thighs. Once I did that, my body began to react naturally, and I enjoyed every single second of it. Even when he stabbed his way inside of me. It stretched me to the point of burning, but I…liked it. A lot. I wanted more. *Needed* more, but had no idea how to tell him that. Plus, I had no idea what *more* meant.

Once we both fell limp, he pushed back for a long and heated moment to hover his face over mine. Then without a word, he removed his body from me, went to the bathroom and closed himself inside.

I'm no fool. I know he's not coming back out for post-coital pillow talk. I'm a whore to him, and I don't need to be told when to leave.

Sitting up, I try to peer through the dark to examine the space between my legs. There doesn't seem to be any blood, but there's definitely a big wet spot which is totally embarrassing. I'm still out of breath as I scoot to the edge to touch my feet to floor and begin gathering my tiny scraps of clothing.

"What are you doing?" His deep voice takes me by surprise, and I jump a little from where I'm standing. He's standing there in the middle of the room in all his naked glory. Every muscle defined and the ink and scars that cover him empowers him in stature. He's a daunting creature. He prowls forward like a black panther in the night. Stealthy and obscured.

I use my clothing to cover myself up as he nears. "I, uh, need to go."

"Not yet." He stops right in front of me. "Sit." His Russian accent makes everything he says sound harsh. I sit back down on the edge of the bed with a lump in my throat. "Spread your legs for me, *kukolka*." My eyes widen as he lowers himself to one knee, and I'm terrified he wants to fuck me again. I said I enjoyed it, even the pain, but this is all too much. Before tonight, a man's touch had always made my stomach churn. I'm not ready to—he holds something up between us and I notice a small hand towel.

Not without apprehension, I let him pry my thighs apart. When the warm towel makes contact, I flinch a little. His eyes dart up. "Are you sore?"

"A little," I say quietly.

He's tender with his strokes as he cleans me up. We're both quiet and I use this opportunity to study him up close. His eyebrows are drawn with his head tilted down in concentration as if he's hard at work. His features hold so much stress. He's the son of a mobster, not as if he volunteered to be here. Could it be he too is solely owned by the mafia?

It doesn't matter. I don't see shackles holding him prisoner here. He could leave, just like I chose to at seventeen. Sure, I'm now on the mafia's watch, but I don't have the means to run and hide. He does. Right?

"Thank you," I say as he stands. My legs snap shut and I turn my head so that I'm not staring at his large member dangling between his muscled thighs. It's hardly a foot from my face.

"Don't thank me," he mutters and walks away.

I make quick work of my clothes and wince when I slip my feet back into my neck-breaking heels. Once I'm fully dressed, he's walking back in my direction wearing black joggers low on his hips. His body is impeccable, but he scares the shit out of me. Not in the same way other men, like his father, scares me. It's a different kind of intensity.

"Wait here," he instructs and puts a phone to his ear. He fires off a bunch of words in Russian and hangs up seconds later then rests his eyes on me blankly. "Someone will come escort you out and take you home."

I frown. "I don't have to go back out there?"

"I think you've earned the rest of the night off," he says in all seriousness. He keeps his dark eyes on me, and I feel uncomfortable under his scrutiny. "My father has taken notice of you," he states flatly. "That isn't a good thing."

I swallow hard and look down at the floor. "Any advice on how to not draw his attention?" I take a nervous peek up at him.

"Keep your head down."

"That's what I've been trying to do." I sigh in exasperation. All I've been doing is trying my best to blend in and remain insignificant to anyone.

"Try harder then."

I open my mouth with a rebuttal, and for my sake, the knock on the door cuts me off. He gestures for me to follow and when he opens the door, a very large man with a shaved head and dark colored braid hanging from his granite chin stands there. Sasha rambles off in Russian, and the man replies with a single nod of his head.

Sasha turns to me, and I find myself staring at his lips. Lips that I kissed and kissed— "Goodnight, Vivian."

My stomach feels weird and tingly hearing him say my name for the first time. Gulping, I nod my head. "Goodnight."

Even though the man leading me out of this hellhole is scary as fuck looking, I stick close to him as we make our way out of the mansion to a black SUV. He holds the rear passenger door open for me, and I slip in. As the door closes and he gets behind the wheel, I close my eyes and pray no one stops us.

We take off and after about a minute I exhale, reveling in alleviation. It remains painfully quiet in the vehicle, leaving me to my own incessant thoughts. The patience Sasha showed was almost endearing, a stark contrast to the persona he usually presents. Also, very unlike his father. There was no kiss goodbye or an apology for what conspired between us, but I feel like he was gentle in his own way. Possibly as gentle as he is capable of being.

I'm too preoccupied and lost inside my head to realize we have pulled into a drive thru at a fast-food joint until the loudspeaker jostles me out of it. The driver rattles off an order as I sit silently in the back.

"Fuck," he hisses. "Do you have any food allergies?" I glance up to find him looking at me through the rear-view mirror.

"Me?" I ask in shock.

"Do you see anyone else?" he sasses with a thick accent.

"Oh, uh. No, I don't."

He doesn't ask any more questions as he completes the order then continues through to pay and retrieve the food. It's dead quiet again as we drive away, and I'm confused as to why he asked me about any food allergies. No way is he about to feed me.

The smell of the greasy food has my mouth watering and my belly gurgling as it fills the space of the car's interior. I haven't had a proper meal since this morning, and I am starved. I'm always starved though. You think my body would be used to the lack of nutrition, but it's not. The hunger pains can still be crippling.

We finally stop in front of my shitty apartment; a house that has been turned into several small condos. He grabs the bag of food and climbs out and I obediently wait to be let out of the back, like a child. The door opens for me, and he thrusts the bag of food at me. "Here." I stare down at the bag like it's going to bite. "Sasha said to make sure you have food. Take it."

I look at his rigid face, somewhat mystified. "Oh...thank you." I refrain from snatching the bag from him, afraid it's all a sick joke. I politely take it, and breeze past him. Eager to lock myself inside the safety of my cozy apartment.

With the bag concealed inside my arms as if it were drugs or stolen money, I take the stairs two at a time to the second floor. My hands are shaking as I try to jam my key into the lock. Once I'm inside, I throw the lock in place, and everything begins to settle in.

Working at an underground casino, the private event with Mr. Rogov, whored out to a mobster. It's so overwhelming my head spins and I sink to the floor with the weight of it all. I move robotically to pull out the huge burger inside the bag and I take an unladylike bite of it. Rolling over to my back, I stare up at the ceiling and try not to relive the events.

SEVEN

SASHA

It's been four nights since I defiled the vixen that goes by the name of Vivian. Knowing that I've stolen her virtue from any man after me urges on the thoughts I have to possess her. To take her and keep her for myself. Let her be the one and only good thing in my life. Something made just for me.

Which is exactly why I won't. Caring for her would be her death sentence, along with the death of what's left of my soul. And not a quick one. It would be a long and drawn-out life of torment and pain.

I'm supervising the underground casino tonight where she's laboring away for free, completely oblivious that her debt will never be paid off. She'll eventually discover that she'll be serving drinks until she either ages out, or my father decides to put her to some other use. Either way, she'll walk away penniless, a chunk of her soul missing.

I'm due to return back to Russia soon with some new recruits for the whorehouse, and the thought of leaving is worrisome. Vivian will no longer have any kind of protection. If my father already singled her out, even only to throw at me as a plaything, that means she in some way has caught his attention. He's diluted himself to think that he can have anything he wishes, and that's exactly what women are to him. *Things*.

Ever since I experienced a moment in nirvana, planted deep inside the sweetest cunt, that tiny feeling of guilt eats away at me. I constantly have to remind myself she is nothing to me. No one. Just another casualty that found themselves imprisoned by the mob.

But goddamn, when she walks into the casino wearing hardly anything, her legs looking a mile long with the heels she's wearing, I want to snatch her up and run away with her. Keep her as my precious sparrow locked inside a gilded cage, only allowing her to spread her wings for me.

These feelings will soon fade. Fascination always does. Once she's gone from my view, she'll be forgotten.

Forbidding myself to look anywhere in her direction, I watch as my father gambles and entertains the lowlives clothed in lavish suits and adorned with gaudy accessories. Tossing money around as if there will be no repercussions. Most of them will end up indebted to us if they're not already.

Out of the corner of my eye, I see Vivian make her way around the room. Avoiding my father and remaining reticent. It almost puts a smile on my face knowing that she absorbed my words to her about keeping a low profile here. Such a good girl.

Typically, I go to great effort to tune out my father's conversations, but I overhear him discussing the new shipment of unfortunate women we're collecting. My father has gotten so confident he no longer does background checks for the women he takes. He holds no concern for who they may be or if anyone with any power will come looking for them.

What snags my attention is the mention of a few last minute additions... And that his son was able to sample one already...

My tolerance wavers slightly as my gut binds in knots. It chisels away at my austerity, testing the confines I trapped myself in years ago. I remain aloof as if too consumed with surveilling the room. It's a test. And it will not be the last. His ever-present foresight and prudence would be impressive if I didn't detest the man. He already suspects my fondness of Vivian. Meaning he plans to snuff out any future happiness I might think I am entitled to.

Imagining her strung out on Rapture, begging to be fucked by different men— It grinds my teeth and has me murderous.

Rapture is our most profitable business venture. A designer drug, and it lives up to its name. Exceeding it actually. Its effects are a strange combination of Viagra and what one might say is the opposite of the date rape drug. Rather than being incoherent, the user is sex-crazed and delirious with lust.

It won't matter if his suspicions are confirmed or not. He'll poke and goad until he finds satisfaction. Meaning Vivian will be going home to Russia with me. I'll be forced to watch her thrown into the shipping container with the rest. Helpless to do a fucking thing but hope she doesn't die before I come up with something.

My sliver of kindness was the catalyst for her damnation.

EIGHT

SASHA

"You're extra prickly today," Artem mutters beside me after we take off.

"I wasn't ready to leave for home yet," I reply, matching his tone.

"No?" he questions. "You're always looking forward to going home. Specially to get a break from your father," he says.

There's no response from me because he's right. I'm always looking forward to being in a different country than my father. Whether it's me in Russia and him in Vegas, or vice versa. To not having him breathe over my shoulder every moment of every day is a welcome reprieve. Though, I feign oblivion, I know he has eyes on me always.

The reason for my thorny mood is knowing that Vivian was indeed one of the sorry souls to be snatched, drugged up, and placed inside a shipping container and loaded onto a boat headed for Russia. Along with about a dozen other women in the same condition, they will all wake up disoriented and terrified, forced to live off crackers and share a bucket to relieve themselves. They'll arrive reeking of vomit and ammonia, filthy and emaciated. All so that when they're taken to the whorehouse to be bathed, fed, and 'cared for', they'll be grateful. They'll see our men as their saviors. It's all thanks to Bash that the women are treated like human-beings and not trash. He's long since earned respect working for us for almost twenty years, and he abhors this part of the job more than anyone. He'll crack heads if he finds any man using unnecessary force with the women. Not only has he shown reverence, but he's also the most intimidating man physically. Close to seven feet tall, and twice the width of most men, but he holds a soft spot for the opposite sex.

I've never been comfortable treating young women like cattle, but this is my life. I am in no control over it. Going against my father in any aspect is treason. That includes any disagreement I may voice.

"You know what has his balls in a twist," Artem says in amusement. He, Bash, and Trip are the closest thing I have to friends and the only ones I tolerate any kind of jest or teasing from.

Artem and Bash have been with me since I was a young teenager. They were always stuck 'babysitting' me. But as I got older, we grew closer. I know exactly where their loyalties lie.

Since knowing me most of my life, they see things my father, or anyone else, would never notice. They know that Vivian was sent to my room the other night, and they know how I made sure she was safely relieved and taken home. Even made sure she was fed. Bash was the one to do so for me.

"Fuck off," I grunt and lay my head back to close my eyes.

Vivian's face pops up in my head. Her face, already so familiar, that I can vividly remember each feature. Her hazel eyes with corners that kiss the sky. The beautiful color of her skin and lips. Those delectable breasts of hers. It's hard to imagine the state she will be in when I see her next.

Knowing that she was captured and laid dormant inside another man's arms, then disposed of in the pile of other faceless women. It'll be at least a few more days before the ship arrives, where they'll be drugged and knocked out again for safe transport to their final destination, where I will see Vivian for the last time. I'm only there to ensure transport runs smoothly. And if it doesn't, I'm there to handle the problem.

Rest doesn't come for me. Instead, I had Artem get me a glass of whiskey to help take the edge off. I've never felt so jittery and restless in all my life. Anxious for the ship to arrive.

The three days it took for our shipment's arrival were excruciating. Over a dozen cargo ships sink every year. Some even go missing without a trace, containers sometimes fall off due to negligence. Anything could've happened, and I wouldn't have known until the ship either arrived or didn't.

Now, it's the middle of the night and we're entering the warehouse where most of the containers were unloaded. Knowing exactly which container is ours and where it is placed, we make our way swiftly through the maze. I lead with Artem and Bash flanking and several other men following behind.

We're quiet as we stop in front of the ordinary looking container. The only difference is the Rogov symbol hidden in one corner. You'd have to search to find it. I gesture to Artem and Bash approving them to begin and they start to bark out orders to the other men. I step aside and rigidly stand there with tension in my head, neck, shoulders, and back.

As soon as they go for the twist locks at the corners, the metal against metal sound causes the women inside to stir and begin to panic. Probably hoping and praying that it's someone here to rescue them.

The screaming and pounding of fists grows louder as the lock is removed and the men surround the entrance, prepared for runners.

As soon as the doors are cranked open, the foul smell from inside hits. Then it's chaos.

Women begin running out while others scream and huddle together. Our men quickly round them up and knocking them back out with a syringe to their necks, but my focus is on one pair of dark eyes. She's the only one just standing in the container. She neither ran, nor cowered. Her piercing gaze stabs at my insides, causing my teeth to grind and my head to spin with irresolution. Our eyes remain glued as a needle penetrates the side of her neck and her eyelids begin to droop. She stumbles and quickly gives in to the torpidity that is already consuming her. She leans against the side of the container and wilts down to the ground. Never once taking her haunting gaze off mine, until the moment they fall shut.

Aware that I have too many eyes on me, I turn and leave to wait at the truck where they'll be loaded into next. Not worrying about who will take Vivian's fragile body in their arms and whether or not they'll be careful with her.

About an hour later we're back on the road to the whorehouse, which is a few hours away. The entire time I stay silent in the back of the SUV with only Artem and Bash occupying the front. They know when I need the silence.

Unrealistic and rash thoughts conjure up inside my mind. Tempting me. Daring me. Dominating me. I take pride in my self-restraint and self-discipline. It's the only thing I feel like I have total control over. My fortitude being tested has me agitated. Resentment burgeoning for the woman.

I practically jump out of the vehicle as soon as it comes to a halt. All too ready to get this over with so I can go home and move on with my life. Let the memories of her existence deteriorate until they vanish all together.

The men are unloading the truck with limp and slowly awakening bodies, but when someone goes to pick up Vivian, I cave. "Stop," I bark sharply.

"Mmm," she groans and tries to move but is still too drugged to do much.

I easily scoop her up into my arms and my nostrils flare. Not from the pungent smell that doesn't even seem to bother me. The fumes of urine and mold should repulse me, but it only encumbers me with penance. She somehow weighs even less than she did before. The greasy food I had sent home with her the other night was all for nothing.

Promptly moving all the women into a couple different heavily secured rooms, I place her frangible body next to the others and steel my spine. My feet don't seem to want to move as my eyes blaze over her. Her brown hair, dirty and sprawled around her like a halo. The drawing power she seems to possess pulls at me. Claiming me as I unavoidably claimed her.

"Sasha," Trip says lowly in his southern accent for only me to hear. I'm 'sir' to everyone. "What's going on?"

I'm still incapable of moving from my spot. Only my head turns, and I see Bash standing there unconcerned and waiting. I don't need to verbally communicate with him as he can read me with lucid comprehension. He gives an imperceptible dip with his head and disappears.

"This one doesn't stay," I utter under my breath as I bend down to hoist her back up in my arms.

Trip knows not to question me, assuming Artem and Bash will most likely fill him in later. So, I don't say a word as I walk right back out of the house with her officially in my possession. I may not ever be able to have her in the way I wish, but no other man will have her either. I'll have to be tactful with the excuse I give my father as to why I took one of the whores as a maid back at the estate.

I know she won't ever see me as her liberator, but maybe she can eventually appreciate me as her protector.

NINE

VIVIAN

Nausea was the first thing I felt when I came to. Then the smell, the headache, the terror, the swaying. It all had me sick and woozy.

It took me some time to remember what had happened. I was in bed in my apartment when I heard someone breaking in. I barely had time to become fully aware when three men came into my room and pinned me down. There was no time to scream or run as a hand clamped down over my mouth to silence me and I was immediately powerless. I tried fighting. I really did. I strained every single muscle in my body and screamed until my lungs burned. Then I felt… tired. They drugged me.

I woke up ready to puke and my head muddled with confusion in what we soon discovered was some kind of shipping container. It didn't take acuity to come to the realization that we were all women being trafficked. All of us delirious with nausea and befuddlement.

After the haze of disorientation waned, the panic began to set in. A frenzy of hysteria and maniacal fear broke out. The only light was a tiny sliver coming in from the outside, and the only sound other than our screams, cries, and fists pounding on metal were the crashing waves outside. Which explained the swaying.

Whoever put us there was generous enough to provide us with saltine crackers and water, and humane enough to leave a large bucket for us all to piss, shit, and puke in.

Once the adrenaline from the initial panic wore off, we clung to each other for comfort. As we tried to wrap our heads around our fate, I found myself in some kind of comatose state where my mind numbed itself. I don't think I was the only one.

Then the second round of panic began. This time it was rage driven.

Some of us pounded on the sides until our fists bled and our voices grew hoarse. I knew the effort was futile, but I would have been disappointed in myself if I hadn't tried.

After What had to be days later, the ship finally stopped moving. The anxiety of what awaited us was crippling. More so, who awaited us and what we would have to endure as our fate was sealed.

Our prison was moved, and we all seemed to be on the same wavelength. None of us made a peep, knowing that whoever was on the other side of the doors were not our rescuers. All of us strangers hugged and cried against one another, and hours later we were released.

Some of us tried to flee, running for our lives, and some fell into the fetal position. I was planning to run when I caught the eyes of someone who had infiltrated my dreams. He might not have been cruel to me, but he damn sure was not my hero. He'd given me pleasure and cared for me afterwards. Even shown a glimpse of kindness in the way he arranged for my safe passage home. I almost believed that he was as much a prisoner to the Bratva as I was. But it was all a ruse, and I wouldn't forget the betrayal.

The women around me were collected and drugged. I stood there patiently awaiting my turn, never once straying from the man who beguiled me with false hope in humanity. He stared right back at me, bereft of emotion. All the while I brimmed with enmity and vengeance. So done with being taken advantage of and treated like garbage. The ramifications would be gruesome if I was ever given the opportunity to exact my revenge.

I calmly let one of the deplorable men approach me and prick my neck with something that quickly warps my vision. Right before it takes me, I curse Sasha Rogov.

The familiar feeling of waking from a drug-induced sleep is no less overwhelming. My mouth is dry, my head aching, and my memories are jumbled. It takes my eyes several attempts to pry open, and when I do, I take in my unfamiliar surroundings.

I find myself in a small sterile room, void of any decoration. Unlike anything I expected to wake up to. I thought I'd be in the same room as the other women, still reeking of excrement, curled up on a cold and hard floor, not cozied up on a clean and soft bed. The sheets, blankets, and pillows all luxurious and pure.

Pushing myself up into a seated position, I examine the room some more. Two doors. One large and heavy looking, and the other cracked open.

Groaning, I rub at my temples and try to clear my head. Something out of the corner of my eye steals my attention. A small side table next to the bed displays a bottle of water and two white pills.

I snatch up the water and practically rip off the cap to chug. The coolness soothes my throbbing throat and momentarily allays the thumping in my head. I gasp for air and eye the pills. I pick them up and study them in my open palm. No engraving or symbols to signify what they are. It may be foolish, but the pain in my head is too much to bear.

No longer contemplating, I swallow down the pills and lay back to wait.

I don't know if it's from the pills or the water, but soon I'm feeling a little more human and ready to explore.

Finding purchase with the ground, my feet land on plush carpet. My bare toes wiggle on top of the creamy color and I realize my feet are clean. In fact, all of me is clean. Including the large t-shirt I'm dressed in. It's white and comes down to the middle of my thighs. Lifting the fabric to my nose, I smell laundry detergent and the hint of a man. No undergarments though. But the cuts and bruises from pounding my fists for hours have been tended to and dressed with bandages.

I decide to investigate the one door left ajar and enter a bathroom. It matches the bedroom in its blank appearance, but I'm surprised by the jack-and-jill style doors.

I bolt for it and try the knob. Locked. I give it a few bold knocks and press my ear to the door to listen for any signs of life on the other side. For someone who might be able to give me some kind of answers. But I'm met with silence.

Looking around, I debate on my next move. Falling to my knees, I open the cabinet doors under the sink and search for anything I might be able to use to my advantage. But there's nothing. Not even an extra role of toilet paper.

Making my way back inside the bedroom, I look at the closed door. I presume it's pointless, but I have to try. I go for it and when I twist the knob, it doesn't budge even in the slightest, feeling like it's reinforced with something on the other side. The weight of it feels almost like a fire door, heavy and insulated.

Not having a clue of what to do next, I go back over to the bed and sit down on the edge of it to chug the rest of the water. I wipe my mouth with the back of my hand and search the room again for anything I may have missed.

It's no easy feat for the condition I'm currently in. The lack of nutrition and the amount of stress I've been under, I can no longer fight it.

Questions swirl inside my head as I allow myself to doze off.

Where the hell am I?

Who bathed me?

Why?

Where are the other women?

My questions will have to wait, because right now, I need rest.

TEN

VIVIAN

With no windows, I have no idea what time of day it is or how long I've been asleep for. But my stomach is screaming in hunger.

I go to use the bathroom and wash up when there's a knock on the door to what I assume leads…well, out of this room.

I'm torn between running out to answer the door and getting some answers, or finding some place to hide. The choice is made for me when I stand in the center of the room frozen as the sound of locks grinding comes from outside. There's nowhere for me to hide and nothing to arm myself with. I'm defenseless.

The door opens and reveals a woman. She looks almost old enough to be my mother wearing what looks like a maid's uniform and carrying a tray of food that beckons me. Fuck escaping. My stomach feels like it's caving in on itself with hunger.

She enters and begins speaking in Russian. I huff in exasperation, "I don't speak Russian. I can only speak English." My voice is gravelly and hoarse.

She blatantly rolls her eyes at me and switches to English for my sake. "You need to eat. I will be back with clothing and necessities."

I lick my lips, eager to inhale whatever food she brought me regardless of what it may be. "Where am I?"

"Food first." She thrusts the tray at me and although I am famished, I'm also cautious. I have no idea who this woman is. For all I know she could be the warden of this place. "Take it," she orders.

It's all the coercion I need. I'm too hungry to be overly wary. I accept the tray, and barely have it balanced in my hands when she steps back and slams the door shut, locking me back inside. Losing all self-regard, I plop back down on the bed with the tray and begin stuffing myself. No thoughts about whether or not I should be preserving anything in the event that this is my only meal for a while. My head is once again killing me, but my stomach no longer screams in agony making me want to keel over.

My stomach has shrunk in size from being starved for so long that I can't even finish the surprisingly delicious food. I have to stop myself before I burst. The blood all rushing to my stomach makes me once again somnolent and ready to pass out. I have to lay back and rest some more. Telling myself only long enough for my food to fully digest and regain some strength.

I wake startled, shooting up from my horizontal position. The sound of metal on metal announces a visitor. The same woman appears, handing me two brown, paper bags.

I stand to go to her and take the bags. "What's this?"

"I told you. Clothing and necessities." She's curt with me. Obviously not here to befriend me. "I'm Greta. I will give you time to wash up and get dressed. Then we start work."

My heart sinks and I gulp. "Work?" I make another perusal of her uniform and try to understand what she means by work. I thought I was being sold as a sex slave.

"We clean," she snaps, her aggravation with me clear. "I'll be back soon. Don't dawdle." She leaves just as swiftly as she came, and I'm left here paralyzed in some sort of state of shock.

I'm here to *clean*? To be a *maid*? They went through all that hassle to abduct us, drug us, ship us like animals to have us *clean*? It doesn't make any sense!

Needing answers more than I have time to stand here and process all that I have learned so far, I go into the bathroom with both bags and do as she says. Wash up and get dressed.

The gray and white dress is a little short on me. If I were to bend over, it would reveal the undergarments I was provided with. Greta said I was here to clean, but with the scandalous matching bras and underwear I found in one of the bags, I think I'll be doing more than just cleaning. Why else would they provide house maids with expensive lingerie? And that's all they gave me too. A uniform with white tennis shoes and undergarments. No pajamas or lounge wear or even jeans. The other bag consisted of the 'necessities'. Meaning toiletries, towels, toilet paper, etc.

Greta comes and gets me not too long after. She permits me to leave my confines and explains that she will be showing me around and training me. It could be from being drugged and carted around like cattle, or the fact I feel like I'm in the twilight zone, but I cannot seem to comprehend anything she says. Everything goes in one ear and out the other making everything spin like a vortex.

I know wherever we are currently, we traveled far since I had to be transported by sea, but I still expected to be inside the Rogov's estate. It was naïve of me to think so, but I'm still completely thrown off kilter and feel like I'm going to puke when I look out the window to see snow.

Any and all sound is drowned out as my feet move closer to the window. "I don't understand," I say quietly and peer out the window to see an endless frozen desert. "I don't understand. Where am I?" My eyes bubble up with tears, distorting my vision. "How did I get here? What is all this?" I'm on the verge of hysteria. My breathing is uncontrolled and shallow. *This cannot be real. This cannot be happening to me.* "What is going on!" I whip around and almost scream.

Greta has the audacity to shush me as she clears the space between us and stands close. "You need to calm down, Vivian," she says firmly.

My head vigorously shakes. "No. Not until you tell me what the hell is going on! Where am I?" I demand, the panic rising, choking me.

"Please, Vivian." She suddenly looks a bit remorseful as her eyes dart around in paranoia. "I need you to calm—"

"No! How the hell do you expect me to calm down?!" I shout.

"That's enough, Greta." The familiar voice ricochets off the walls, and stills my heart. Greta casts her eyes downwards and steps away from me. "I'll take over from here. You may continue with your own duties."

I ignore Greta's exit and turn to face Sasha. I can feel my cheeks wet with tears and my hands shaking at my sides. His head is tilted slightly down like I see him do a lot. And no matter how much hatred I have for the man, I still find comfort in seeing his familiar face. He's dressed in his usual dark jeans and black shirt with sleeves pushed up his forearms to reveal ink and muscle. His blonde locks thrown this way and that.

"Where am I?" I ask the question I already know the answer to after too long of silence.

"Russia," he simply confirms.

"Why?"

"Because my father wanted to sell you as a whore," he states ever so casually. "Instead, you will be a servant here."

"Here? Is this…?"

"This is our estate in Russia."

"I don't understand…" I shake my head and rub at my temples.

"My father will be under the impression that you are here as my own whore." The air rushes from me. "If you don't want to go back to the brothel where you will be sold to many, I suggest you play along and behave accordingly."

His whore? Play along? Behave accordingly? What the actual fuck is wrong with these people!

"I want to go home." My lip quivers and I angrily wipe away a new tear. I've never wanted to go *home* before. Never felt like I ever had one.

My tears unfazed by him. "This is your home now, *kukolka*."

"No." My head shakes and I know I'm about to have a panic attack. My eyes begin seeking out my nearest exit as they dart around the room frantically. *I can't stay here. This can't be happening. This is beyond a nightmare. This is hell. What did I do to deserve this?*

I don't even see him move, but he's suddenly in front of me and I trip over my own feet trying to leave space between us. He's quick on me as he grasps my upper arms firmly to hold me in place. "You will harness your emotions, Vivian. There are eyes and ears all around us." I gape at him in pure shock. "I'm warning you. One false move and you will be shipped off back to where you belong."

"Belong?!" I shriek indignantly.

One hand releases my arm to slap over my mouth and I'm being shoved back until my back hits the cold glass of the window. "Yes," he hisses an inch from my face. His eyes ablaze. "Your life belonged to my father the moment he decided to take you. If you do not adhere to the words I am telling you, you will go right back to the whorehouse where you will be pumped full of Rapture and fucked by as many men as they provide you with until you either age out or die. And believe me, you will want to kill yourself."

Rapture?

"Do you understand me?"

I frown and my teary eyes bounce around his face as we have a standoff. A lock of pale hair has fallen over his forehead making him look out of control and I drop my gaze to his dark eyes. I swear he rapidly blinks his eyes as if his vision is impaired like mine.

"Vivian," he says my name more calmly. Then he drops both hands from me. "Tell me you understand."

I take a few breaths before answering. "Please, Sasha. Please let me go. I don't care where, just let me go," I beg, remembering to keep my voice down. "I swear I won't tell anyone, and I'll disappear. Please."

The only change in his face is the muscle in his jaw that flexes as he stares down at me. His eyes don't soften or waver. "There's no way out of here other than in a body bag or back to the whorehouse. You may have the rest of the day to yourself in your room. I suggest you get some rest. Tomorrow, your new life begins."

My head is caught inside of a fog as I shuffle my feet behind Sasha as he leads me back to my room. Have I not suffered enough my entire life? Was it not enough that I had a mother who found it necessary to remind me that I was a mistake? To be molested by her many repugnant and disgusting boyfriends since I was in training bras? To feel so unsafe, I had to run away when I was seventeen and live out of my junk of a car for years? I know taking out a loan with the mafia was my own doing, but getting mugged so that I'd be late on a payment was not. I thought that being compelled to visit Sasha's room would be the low point of my life. That things could only go up from there. I had no idea how much worse it could get.

Lost inside my inner turmoil, I almost run into Sasha when he stops. It looks as if we're back at my room. I study the door from this side. It opens to the outside like a prison cell with three large latches to lock me inside. That I already knew, but to see it with my own eyes, it makes it all the more real. I cannot seem to wrap my head around it all. How much can one person really handle?

He stands there motionless, chin down, dark gaze locked on me. I step over the threshold and turn back to him. "Are you that man at all?" My voice is soft, a complete contrast to his granite features.

There has to be some truth to the man that was somewhat gentle with me.

Or is he just the man that stood by while women were abducted, drugged, and sold?

Moments tick by at a snail's pace, and just when I think he's not going to answer me, he opens his mouth and says, "I can't be." His words are depressing yet he remains apathetic.

Accepting his answer, I back up and let him close me inside. Leaving me to my life in solitude and unfortune.

ELEVEN

SASHA

The phone conversation with my father went well, but I won't know if he bought the ruse until I see him in person. Telling him that I decided to keep one of the whores as my personal toy wasn't so simple. To be convincing I had to give him crude and intimate details about the sweetest cunt I've ever had. When he asked who caught my eye, I told him it was the one he had sent to my room, then I thanked him for the gift.

Whether he believes me or not, I'll have to make sure they do not cross paths.

I've done my best to be scarce and managed to keep myself from Vivian since I escorted her back to her room. I know eventually I'll have to face her and the consequences of my impulsive feelings. The way her hazel eyes bored into me with accusation and emitting vulnerability, it almost broke through my impregnable fortress. I was close to feeding her lies.

Greta is in charge of the staff here. She's been here the longest and never sticks her nose where it doesn't belong. I gave her strict orders to keep Vivian away from my father when he arrives and she was prudent enough not to question it.

I'm sitting down at the dining table waiting on my lunch. The only other thing I can think about other than Vivian is the situation with my cousin, Kazimir. Ever since he moved back to Russia full-time a few years ago, we've grown to be stronger allies. Him being several years younger than me, we were always in different stages of life. Now that he's older, the years doesn't seem to be much of a gap anymore. Especially because he was forced to grow up sooner than most. He's lived through much more than people three times his age, so when his father was killed at the hands of

Alejandro Martinez, Kazimir was competent enough to step up as the head of the Kalashnik family at only twenty years old.

His estate was recently invaded by the Semenov's, and when my father was informed about it, he didn't seem perturbed in the least. Something about it doesn't sit well with me. His sister is Kazimir's mother, and although they are not close, family is sacred. It's an insult to offend related families. Declaring war on one's family is declaring war on the family as a whole.

My father's nonreaction could be because Kazimir took immediate action in wiping out the Semenov's himself, or he's that much of a soulless bastard. To have no loyalty even when it comes to your own blood… It's unthinkable.

Someone enters the dining room, and my eyes jump up instinctively to clash with hazel ones. She falters in her steps and has to steady her tray. Composing herself, she continues forward and carefully sets the plate down in front of me. She's close enough to smell, and even though the scent from her body wash is different, I can still make out her natural aroma and it's just as intoxicating.

I find myself speechless as she silently retreats back through the doorway in which she entered as I stare at the empty space, willing her to come back. My self-restraint is hanging by a thread. The consuming hold she has over me without any effort at all it's something I need to combat and learn to bear, or I'll lose my shit when my father comes home.

The food I shovel into my mouth might as well be sand, for it lacks taste and real substance. My mind is bursting with overwhelming thoughts. Thoughts like getting rid of my father. It would take intricate and flawless planning to devise a plan with any hope of success. Even thinking of such a scheme has me paranoid my father can somehow hear my thoughts.

Vivian enters the room again, this time with her eyes averted. She's now fully aware of her current situation and her doomed fate, yet she seems more radiant. As if there's a sheen of resilience on her skin that she wears with pride. It's easier to live with false hope that freedom will come rather than living in self-pity and defeat.

The thought of my father or his men taking notice of her drives me mad. When she comes to retrieve my empty plate, her scent scrambles my thoughts and I pounce. Using a firm grip on her thin wrist, I yank her into my lap, and she lets out a mousy squeak.

She freezes with one hand clutching the front of my shirt and her other arm braces herself on the table. Too stunned to speak. Her fear is irresistible.

I thread one hand through her brown, silky hair and the other rests on her bare thigh. "My father will be here in a couple days. You will tell me if he or anyone else tries to touch you." My eyes cannot stop fixating on her tempting lips and I watch her throat work hard to swallow.

"Why do you care?" she asks softly, and my gaze is broken from her lips back up to meet her eyes.

I wait a moment before answering. "You will tell me."

"What if you aren't there?"

Picking my phone up from the table, I look down for only a second to hit the contact I want and then glance back up as I place my phone to my ear. I lean forward and pull her to me, invading her space until our lips barely touch.

"*Da*," Artem answers after the first ring.

Changing to Russian, I say, "I need you three here. Now." My lips moving against hers the entire time as she remains deathly still. After I hang up, I place the phone back on the table and rest my hand on her smooth thigh again.

Her eyelids struggle to remain open, and I lazily pull away some. I hear their boots hitting the hard floor and her eyes bounce around then widen when they stop. I take another moment with my eyes on her before turning to my men.

"This is Artem, Bash, and Trip." I gesture to each one as they stand several paces away shoulder to shoulder. "One of them will always be nearby. If *anyone* tries to touch you, you tell them if I am not here." They've already been given strict orders to keep an eye on her. Discreetly, that is. Bash was the only of the three to not look at me as if I had lost my mind.

Knowing that's all I needed from them, they leave just as stoically as they came. Vivian remains stunned as she peers back at me with childlike eyes. "Why?" she finally says after a while.

Good fucking question. One I still do not have an answer to. Why does she stand out to me? Why is she so alluring? Why the fuck can't I seem to detach myself from her?

"I can't answer that," I say in earnest as my hand begins to caress her skin. "All I know is that the thought of someone else touching you…" I rasp, and her breath hitches when my hand creeps up her thigh further, "It swells my chest with rage." My hand disappears under the fabric of her dress, and she doesn't swat me away or ask me to stop, so I appropriate her docile demeanor.

My hand makes its way to the apex of her thighs and when my thumb brushes against the fabric of her panties, I find them warm and growing damp. Her thighs begin to quiver, and her eyes shut of their own accord. She hesitantly parts her knees, granting me access and giving me approval. Always sensitive and pliant under my touch.

"You've already put on some weight, *kukolka*." Her dark eyebrows deepen some and I realize how my words could have been taken out of context. The corners of my mouth draw up slightly as I study her pretty frown. I draw lazy circles over top of her moistness and lean in to brush my lips across her cheek making a path to her ear. "It's a good thing, angel. You were withering away on me. I need you with more meat on your bones." My thumb drags up her slits and she parts her legs even more for me.

"With how much food you send to me a day," she pants, "I'll have too much meat on my bones."

I grip the back of her hair and give her a good yank to keep her locked in place. "And I'll still find you most tempting," I murmur with my mouth pressed to her ear.

The fist she still has tangled in my shirt tightens and she's full-on panting. Her neck relaxes when I boldly push the fabric of her panties to the side and my thumb runs through the wetness underneath. She's instantly a mess.

"*Blyad. Iisus Khristos.*" *Fuck. Jesus Christ.* My voice is rough as I swirl around her clit, and she pants. I've hardly begun touching her and she's already on her way to her climax. I'm in complete fascination with how damn responsive she is to me. I've never had trouble pleasing a woman, but not like this. Not to the point of them nearly combusting from one small touch. It's like I'm able to press a button on her and she's in euphoric ecstasy.

Watching her face closely, I study every little muscle twitch. She's already close and I haven't even entered her, but she's about to explode. It's fucking bewitching.

Right before she does, her mouth comes crashing down onto mine and I still for a moment. She comes to realize that I've gone lifeless and stops moving her lips and goes to pull away.

Curling my hand that's still in her hair into a fist, I hold her close and kiss her back with ferocity. My tongue plundering into her mouth and my thumb working her again. Moaning deeply, she ravishes me with her mouth before she falls limp against me. Trembling with every last stroke.

I break apart the kiss and find myself breathing just as heavily as she is. As if I too have combusted.

I'm fucked. Staying away from this woman will be the worst torture I have ever had to endure in my thirty-one years of the hell I was born into.

TWELVE

VIVIAN

I've been here for twenty-six days that have crawled by. I only know because one of the digital clocks in the kitchen also says the date on it.

When I'm not doing chores, I'm locked inside my room. Greta is the head servant for our department and is the one to let me out of my cage each and every morning and the one to bring me my meals and lock me back inside when my chores are all complete. She's all business, but I catch her giving me looks like she is trying to figure me out.

But there's this girl Nastia who isn't much older than me that seems friendly enough. She hardly speaks any English so it's difficult to communicate with her, but we both try. It'd be prudent of me to learn some Russian before formulating some kind of escape plan.

I haven't completely lost hope of getting out of here. I've been inspecting the place as I am tasked with cleaning it. Inconspicuously memorizing where they have cameras placed and where they have guards stationed. So far, I haven't seen any easy gaps. Also, I don't see anything past the snow. Though even without the guards, cameras, and snow, I'll be completely lost and most likely freeze to death. I'm in a foreign country I know nothing about, I don't speak the language, nor do I have anything other than undergarments and a maid's uniform to shelter me from the cold.

I have yet to run into Mr. Rogov, and Sasha has been absent for the last couple of weeks. He should terrify me, and I should be repulsed by his affection, but he doesn't and I think that's the most terrifying thing. He gives me chills, but in an exciting way. I shake under his feel, but in anticipation. Yes, he's incredibly sexy and the whole bad boy vibe he has down to perfection, but it's something more. Am I so desperate for attention? So desperate to be loved that I remain daft to obvious danger?

I know I have no experience when it comes to real intimacy, but it was embarrassing how fast he had me convulsing on his lap. Only one swipe with his thumb through my panties had me melting.

And anyone could have walked in and seen us, yet I didn't feel humiliation. I even thought about someone seeing us, catching us with my legs spread for him and his hand up my dress, and it wasn't mortification I felt heating my cheeks. It was a rush of arousal.

He helped kidnap me, planned to sell me to the sex trade, then decided that keeping me here as his little whore maid was mercy. He's in the mob for crying out loud. He could let me go if he really cared, right? So, why did I spread my legs on instinct? And why the fuck did I initiate a kiss? It's because I'm fucked up with daddy issues. I obviously don't know the difference between right and wrong when it comes to relationships or whatever you would call this. But why have I always been repelled by a man's touch until him?

I have been doing my damnedest to avoid thoughts like these. But when I'm in his bedroom, changing his sheets that reek of him, I find myself wondering if he has other women visiting his bed. I haven't seen any women around the estate that aren't staff, but I'm also confined to my room at night. He can definitely get any woman he desires without much difficulty. And just because he has some sort of attraction towards me doesn't mean he has any attachment. I could be one of several women he's fixated on.

I'm finishing up his bed, which is the last chore in here, when I hear the door click shut behind me. Knowing that I'm trapped in here with someone has me incapacitated. Sasha told me to tell his men if anyone tries to touch me, but what if I'm stuck inside a bedroom with them with no escape?

Seconds tick by and I'm still frozen to my spot as silence engulfs us. Goosebumps break out on my arms as the temperature seems to drop. I hate how much of a coward these people make me. I'm constantly on edge and jittery. Afraid Mr. Rogov will soon find me and send me back to be a whore hooked on *Rapture*. The Viagra for women that men use as the new date rape drug, slipping it in their drinks. And the fact that Sasha has to have one of his friends, or whatever they are to him, keep watch of me at all times like I'll be plucked right up without supervision gives me all the more reason to be skittish.

A chill slithers down my spine when I feel the heavy presence close behind me, somehow lessening my fear but feeding my anxiety. I don't know if it's my wishful thinking or my gut telling me, but I know it's him. The air feels like it's being sucked out of the room, and I steel my spine to slowly turn and face him.

He stands only a few feet from me like a beautiful and mighty sculpture, perfectly created. All brawn and solid muscle. His dark gaze pulling at me. There's some stubble on his chiseled jawline and his hair isn't as tousled. I can still remember exactly how it felt with his heavy body splayed over mine. His weight securing and comforting me. And how he moved inside of me… He was confident and aggressive but not cruel. He used his might to show me the power of pleasure. I had no idea I could ever enjoy intimacy and crave more.

We both stand there motionless as the tension visibly builds. The dire consequences of this fatal attraction are unequivocal and inevitable. It'll end badly…for me. He'll walk away unscathed. I could easily give in and enjoy this while it lasts, or I could guard myself from the pain.

"You should stay away from me," he says after the painful drawn-out silence. "You should run. Hide. Fight."

I swallow. "Would it matter?"

One side of his mouth twitches. "Sometimes."

"Sometimes?" I parrot back.

"Sometimes I'll let you." He steps forward. "And sometimes I'll give chase."

Blood rushes to my pussy and I shiver with desire. The thought of him chasing me, it extracts this primal need from me that I didn't even know I possessed. "I should be afraid of you." My voice shakes.

He closes the gap, his body lightly touching mine. "You should be. And you're not." I look up into his dark eyes and shake my head. He shakes his in disappointment. "You're dense and have a terrible judge of character." I feel like he's trying to repel me with insults, but I don't know what it would take to make me revolt. "Why do you so easily break my resolve? I'm trying to stay away." His voice dips low and our chests are both rising and falling in unison. He reaches up and tucks some of my hair behind my ear causing my breath to stutter. The simplest touch from him has my skin crackling and sizzling with heat, ready to melt me into a puddle at his feet. "My willpower is shit where you are concerned," he rasps and leans down some. I don't dare move. "Last chance to run out of here, little cat," he whispers over my lips.

"I can't," I reply as his mouth crashes down on mine.

The kiss is so rash it becomes violent and sloppy. Our teeth clank together and it's as if we're trying to swallow each other whole. Neither of us seem to care, only driven by carnal and reckless urges. No thinking about the potentially catastrophic ramifications. No dissecting this magnetizing attraction. Just going with it. Acting on our basic instincts. As if it would be life or death trying to abstain.

This is all so wrong, but I don't give a fuck. It feels good and I'm going to chase these good feelings because goddamnit I deserve little moments of happiness in my life. If this is my fate, imprisoned here in Russia always looking over my shoulder, then I can enjoy being Sasha's 'plaything.' Especially because it makes me feel more alive than I ever have before.

He holds all the control as he roughly strips us of our clothing and backs me up to the bed. I let his body pin me down on my back, sprawled out for him. Our naked bodies already moist with sweat and writhing together as we continue to savagely ravish each other's mouths.

Something long and hard probes at my entrance and instead of getting shy and clenching up, I arch my back and moan, begging him to enter me. The intense desire for him turns me wanton and greedy with salacious thoughts. All I want is him inside of me, rutting and stretching me to the point of pain.

He reaches between us and swipes through my wetness making me desperate and indignant. When he lines his cock up with my entrance, something inside screams for me to think straight. "Wait." I break away panting, and he stills. "I'm not on birth control. I mean, I was, but I was taking the pill and well, I didn't get to take them with me," I rush out, panting.

Two lines appear between his brows with a deep frown, then he looks down between us where we were about to become one. "*Blyad*," he spits and backs up.

I'm almost afraid he's changing his mind when he stomps over to the night side table next to his bed and yanks open the drawer. He plucks a golden square wrapper from it and slams it shut before stomping back over to me on the bed. Tearing the wrapper open with his teeth, I watch in fascination as he rolls the condom over his thick length and he's climbing back over me.

His mouth finds mine again and he doesn't waste any time as he prods at my entryway again. With him kissing me so deeply, I stay relaxed and pliant under him. I still have to stretch to accommodate, causing the muscles surrounding him to throb, but it's almost as if I've memorized him. It's tight, but my body welcomes and conforms to his size and shape. Almost like a strong embrace.

He begins moving inside of me and starts muttering in Russian against my mouth. The word *kukolka* stands out, and I still don't understand what it means. It could be some derogatory name that would taint everything, so right now, I'd rather not know. If this is the only good thing left in my life, I want to keep it as pure as possible.

I gasp for air when he removes his mouth from mine and kisses his way down my body as his hips continue to rock. Journeying down my neck, he sucks on the flesh making it tender. He makes his way to my breasts. His back hollows out to take one of my nipples forcefully into his mouth and I feel a zap of heat go straight to my core. My head rolls back and my mouth pops wide open on a cry.

More foreign muttering comes from him as he replaces his mouth with his fingers to pluck the hard bud as he takes my other nipple into his mouth, and I can't take it anymore. Heat explodes from every cell of my body, burning the hottest out of my core, spewing like hot lava. I can feel every muscle wind up, my insides squeezing him. He growls as he starts pounding into me, his hips slamming against my thighs, bruising them.

I let out the faintest whimper as my muscles involuntarily twitch and convulse with his continued movements. His mouth is slack when he removes it from my breast. His hair a mess and his eyes sleepy.

"This pussy is made for me, *kukolka*. No one else will fit inside of you like

I do. It's all for me. You waited for me, didn't you?" He slams in harder as if trying to force the words from me. "You waited for me to make this mine. Tell me." He leans back to hook his arms under my knees, using the hold to fuck me harder.

I have no words. My tongue tied and my throat dry. When he presses his thumb down on my clit, I try to push him away. Unable to take much more stimulation. He refuses to remove his thumb and begins circling it against the oversensitive bundle of nerves.

His chest vibrates with a growl as he quickly withdrawals and flips me over onto my knees. My chest and face pressed into the mattress. He makes quick work of gripping both wrists behind my back with one hand and he's shoving his way back inside of me. I cry out from the abrupt intrusion, and he gives me absolutely no time to accommodate him, but it's all the same. It all feels good. I like the tinge of pain. I want more of it.

With my hands restrained and his body draping over mine, I don't feel trapped. I feel comforted. Like a warm and weighted blanket. The control taken from me is refreshing. I don't have to think. I can just exist.

His fingers begin rubbing the delicate flesh between my legs. "Sasha," I whine and spasm. "It's…it's too much. I can't…"

"You can," he pants. "Your cunt is fucking dripping, *kukolka*." His fingers abandon me, giving me a slight reprieve. Then something wet is smeared across my mouth and the smell is exotic and vulgar. "That's all you, angel." He presses his fingers between my lips, and I automatically let my jaw go slack. "Taste your juicy cunt. Know that this is all you." His three fingers fill my mouth, gagging me, and I let the taste from my own body burst on my tongue.

He hisses behind me and fucks me even harder. Then he gives my ass a good smack. "That's enough, *kukolka*," he commands, and I release the suction of my mouth.

His fingers find their way between my legs again and this time I relish the way my body spasms and twitches. His hips ram into me harder as he tries to go as deep as possible. His Russian is thick and murmured in my hair sticking to my shoulder blade. "Yes, my little doll. Only for me."

I moan and bite down on the blanket under me. My pussy ready to combust. Stars dance behind my eyelids as the orgasm smacks into me fast. *Yes.* If this is the one and only good thing in my life, I will not forsake it. I will embrace it with everything I have. I have more than earned it.

He's grunting and growling behind me as his movements become more jerky and rigid. The thought of him coming has me convulsing with an aftershock, rolling into another climax. His hips slow and I can feel his cock throbbing and swelling until he collapses on top of me to pull us both onto our sides.

I wilt in his embrace as spots dance around my vision. Both of us torpid and clinging to consciousness. The smell of sex and sweat is intoxicating, challenging me to keep a grip on reality.

As actuality begins to seep in, the post-orgasm haze recedes, and I'm left with realistic thoughts. It seems like he comes to at the same time. His body heat leaves me, and I wait a moment to roll over to see where he's gone.

I catch him disappearing into the bathroom, closing the door behind him. I don't know what to do from here, but my muscles are not at all willing to move right now.

He exits the bathroom a few moments later and doesn't look at me or speak. Picking his clothing out of the pile on the floor, he robotically puts them back on. I scoot off the bed and begin to do the same. The silence stretches between us as we dress until I find the courage to speak.

"Sasha, I—"

"You need to go," he snaps.

I frown at him, and he won't even look at me. His eyebrows are knit tight with tension and his jaw muscle bounces. "What? Why did—"

"I told you," he says darkly, finally meeting my eye. "You should run from me, Vivian."

"How the hell am I supposed to run? Where can I go?" He doesn't answer and the tension only escalates. *How dare he give me whiplash like that!* "Then let me go," I demand.

"I can't."

"Why not?"

"Because there is no escaping him. Believe me, I would have done it a long time ago."

And just like that, he disarms me and pulls me in again. I catch a glimpse of the vulnerable man beneath the cold facade. A man incarcerated inside a large prison cell with plenty of exits, but no escape.

He's done talking, and I won't reduce myself to being wholly pathetic and beg for him to.

THIRTEEN

VIVIAN

I must be a gluten for punishment. Sasha told me to run, but all I want to do is seek him out. To taunt him and goad him until he breaks and shows me that boorish yet tender man again. I need it. I yearn for the only affection I have ever welcomed and enjoyed. The only contact that doesn't make my skin crawl and my insides churn.

I'm still pretty much left in the dark when it comes to conversation amongst the other staff. I've picked up a few phrases in Russian in the several weeks being here. Nastia teaches me little things here and there, and I help her with her English. Definitely no easy feat. It amazes me how people used to learn languages from each other without a translator to help. It's a slow process, but I'll be fluent someday.

I see Nastia getting instructions from one of the cooks and all I catch is the title they use in reference to Sasha. Supposedly it means 'the Young Master'. Then I notice the tray she picks up. It looks like some kind of bland soup and a pitcher of water. I heard that there's a stomach bug going around the estate and I'm wondering if Sasha caught it.

I act before I contemplate my thinking. I follow Nastia out of the kitchen and stop her. "Hey." She whips around and gives me a friendly smile. "Are you going to the Young Master's room with that?"

She nods her head. "*Da.*" *Yes.*

I step in closer so I can keep my voice as low as possible. "Could I take it for you?"

Her smile drops. She starts murmuring in Russian and I'm able to catch a few words. She's worried she would get in trouble.

I give her a reassuring smile. "I promise. It's okay." I hold her gaze and it seems to convince her. She hands over the tray and I don't let her second guess it as I retreat from the kitchen.

His door is tightly sealed when I approach. I place an ear to it first, and I'm met with silence.

I knock twice and wait for approval, but nothing comes. I try the knob, and it effortlessly grants me entry. I cautiously slip inside the dark room and am immediately hit with his familiar scent.

I scour through the shadows and check the bed first as I discreetly shut the door behind me, trying not to make a sound. The bed is empty, but it's unmade.

I white knuckle the tray and step further into the room. "Just leave the tray," he says hoarsely from somewhere near the window making me jump, almost spilling the soup everywhere.

The curtains are cracked, only allowing a sliver of light from the day inside where he sits in a sitting chair with his back to me. Steadying the tray, I approach him. Before I close the distance, he snaps his head in my direction with a glower.

"What are you doing here?" he says grumpily.

"I'm bringing you soup and water," I say stopping next to him. His hair is messy and he looks so pale in his all-black t-shirt and joggers. "You're sick."

"I am. And you will be too if you don't put the damn tray down and get out of here."

I roll my eyes and place the tray down on the coffee table in front of him. I pour a glass of water and turn to him. "Drink," I say holding the glass out to him.

He scowls at it and doesn't move. Of course, he's going to be a horrible patient. *God forbid anyone see him as anything but a scary mobster.* "I said leave." He puts more strength behind his words, but they're still not at his potential magnitude.

"You need to drink water. A lot of water. It's important."

He huffs like a child and snags the glass from me. He takes two large gulps with his sleepy eyes on me and hands the glass back. "You can go now."

I glance down at his outstretched arm and see the goosebumps causing the hairs to stand. "You're cold." I put the glass down and step away to retrieve the duvet from his bed.

When he sees me coming at him with it, he shakes his head and tries to shoo me away. "I don't need that."

I narrow my eyes down at him. "You're cold. Probably the chills from the fever."

"I don't have a fever," he grumbles, looking away.

I place the back of my hand to his forehead and feel the abnormal heat before he's able to swat my hand away. "Yes, you do. You need medicine, water, soup, and—" I hold out the blanket. "This."

He keeps his eyes averted and doesn't move. Sighing, I start to wrap the blanket around his shoulders. "Sit up," I instruct, and his eyes snap up to mine, offended I would give him any kind of order. I don't falter, locking horns with him.

He doesn't look pleased as he relinquishes and sits forward a little so I can tuck the blanket around him. "Thank you. Now you can go."

"Not until you get some medicine and some soup in you. When was the last time you ate?"

He sighs and sinks down in the chair. "I don't know," he mutters.

"Have you been able to keep anything down?" He doesn't answer. "Well, let's start with some medicine."

He has no qualms about displaying his agitation at my attempts to care for him, but he doesn't tell me to leave again. There were some fever reducers in his bathroom, and I was able to get him to drink a full glass of water. I found the end of his patience when I tried to spoon feed him. He spluttered his appeal in Russian raising his voice with me slightly. Not wanting him to pass out from exhaustion, I backed off.

I watch as a bead of sweat rolls from his hairline and down the side of his face. His eyelids flutter and he looks like he's about to keel over or blow chunks. He abruptly pushes himself out of the chair and makes it to the bathroom to slam the door behind him. I cringe when I hear him heaving on the other side.

I take the time to tidy up his room some. Making his bed and filling up a glass of water to place on the bedside table.

After a few minutes I hear the toilet flush and the faucet running. He comes out after another few minutes looking much better than before. It looks like he put a comb through his hair and splashed some water on his face. And the fact that he removed his t-shirt, I chastise myself for ogling him at a moment like this.

"You should lie down," I say quietly as he walks at a steady pace.

"I don't want to lie down," he mutters, heading back for the chair.

"You won't get any better without a lot of rest and—"

"I do not need you taking care of me," he snaps as he stops next to the chair.

I swallow down the melancholy lump in my throat, feeling hurt by his abrupt rejection. "Then who will?"

His nostrils flare as I see his shoulders visibly sag. Seconds tick by as we stand there, both stubborn with pride. "Come. You can sit with me." He plops back into the chair leaving no room to argue.

Taking his glass of water with me, I join him in the chair adjacent to his. I can't help myself; I push the water at him, and he gives me a half of a smirk.

"You know, you will probably get sick now," he muses.

I stifle a smile. "I was probably doomed anyways with how rapidly it's going through the house. I am the one cleaning up after everyone who has it."

He sips his water and stares at me contemplatively, the attention making me squirm in my seat. "Why did you leave your home at seventeen?"

Although the question seems random, I'm not at all surprised he knows that about me. I clasp my hands tightly together between my knees, something I habitually do when I get uncomfortable. "My mother and I didn't get along." It isn't a lie, but it's the most vague version of it.

"You didn't have any family to go to?"

I snort and stare down at my clasped hands. "You tell me."

"I'm asking *you*," his voice dips and I peek up at him to find him watching me intently.

"No. At least no one that would take me in."

It pleases me to see him take another sip of his water. "Why Las Vegas?"

I shrug my shoulders and avert my gaze again. "It wasn't far, and I knew it was somewhere I could make fast money at my age. Didn't intend to stay long."

"What changed?"

"I didn't make nearly enough to go anywhere else. Figured I could stay put and go to school. Then with a degree I could go anywhere." I know it's never as simple as that, but at least with a degree, a whole new world of options would open for me.

"For social work." I look at him in surprise. I wasn't officially majoring in it yet, but had planned to switch my major. "The classes you were taking and the fact that you left home at such a young age," he states as if it was no mystery to him.

I'd love to somehow make a living by helping young women get out of bad situations. To have a shelter for teens close to aging out of the system. To help young mothers escape abusive relationships. I wish I had felt like I had somewhere safe to go instead of having to run away and end up homeless for a while. How many of the women who were taken with me had similar upbringings? None of us asked for this life. We didn't ask to be brought into this fucked up world.

"Yeah." I nod my head and study his face. His eyelids look like they weigh a ton as he tries to keep them open. "You should really get some rest, Sasha. You'll feel much better."

He stares at me blankly, as if unsure of what to say. To argue or to succumb to what his body is begging for. He may not take himself to his bed, but he makes the smart decision in leaning back and closing his eyes.

Nothing more is said, and I sit there to study his profile a while longer. Though I can't seem to tear my eyes away, I feel like I'm exploiting his vulnerable state.

As soon as he seems at peace, I refill his water and take the tray with me to leave.

FOURTEEN

SASHA

It's hard to separate the monster I must be with my father and his men from the man I truly am. Sometimes I'm not sure which one is the fraud or who I truly am because it's getting more difficult to turn off. The subliminal messages my father has instilled on me has me constantly thinking like him, or with him in mind. Not able to ever be my own man and think for myself.

Except when I'm with *her*.

She makes it easy to drop the act. The desire to lower my shields and discover who I am at the core is most enticing. To let her dig deep inside of me, unearthing a man I am unfamiliar to, only has me solidifying the decision I made to keep her.

But when I'm sitting with my father at the dining table and she comes through the door with my lunch, I'm fucking livid. She stops in her tracks, her eyes wide and bouncing between me and my father.

Greta knows she is to be nowhere near my father. She will most certainly be punished for this, regardless of the excuse. When my father is here, Vivian is to stay out of sight either in the kitchen or assigned to guest rooms and other lesser used areas of the house.

My father has yet to heckle me about my new pet, but with her sudden presence, I know he'll seize the opportunity to assert his dominance and remind me of my place. That I, like everything else, belong to him.

I recover quickly and give Vivian a smirk. "Come, my pet. Don't be shy," I muse. I watch her throat bob as she lowers her gaze and comes to me.

"I'm surprised to see you still have her around. It isn't like you to keep something for so long," my father says in Russian as his eyes indulge on the only treasure I possess.

"She took longer than I anticipated to train." My father and I both laugh.

I switch to English when I say, "Come, sit." I yank her into my lap after she places my food in front of me. She's fearful and goes still when I reach up and drag the backs of my knuckles down her smooth cheek. "Such a good *kukolka*," I coo.

My father chuckles and I gleam at Vivian. Forcing the devil inside to surface. She must see it clearly because she starts to shake against me. That's good though. My father must not sense any sort of comfortability between us.

"She is something to look at," my father says in the language Vivian thankfully still does not understand. When I look away from her and see the hunger in my father's gaze, my fists practically shake with rage. "How old is she?" He sits back in his chair.

"Young." I grin.

"The young are typically easier to train. Either she's a firecracker in bed, or you've gone too soft with her," he provokes, and I see right through him. I know his games all too well. Doesn't make it any easier to power through them.

"She's a fucking firecracker." I look at Vivian and take one large breast in my hand. She lets out a tiny gasp when I squeeze hard, giving it a good jiggle. My father's cackle in the background makes me sick to my stomach. "Isn't that right, *kukolka*?" I murmur in English.

Her wide eyes turn to my father, and the anger I feel is not at all forced. I grip her jaw harshly and turn her face back to mine. "What did I tell you about eyes on me and me only?" I warn with darkness rimming my vision and mental state.

I need her out of here. Out of sight of my father, and out of my presence so I can think straight. I want to rip my father's eyes out of his fucking head and spank Vivian's pretty little ass till it's a brilliant crimson for giving him any attention at all.

Plastering my lips to hers, the simmering rage abates and I'm able to momentarily clear the haze. She's unresponsive as I kiss her hard, not at all deep or affectionate. This is for show, not to pacify or quell her nerves. So, I thrust my tongue vulgarly inside her mouth and grope her.

My mouth rips away from hers and she gapes at me as my lips curl into a conniving grin. I turn back to my father and give her breast another good jiggle and his eyes light up. "Why don't you go run along, my little pet," I say smugly and thrust my hips forward to jolt her upwards.

She doesn't hesitate to jump up from my lap and bolt as we chase her out of the room with mocking laughter.

I begrudgingly force her out of my mind and continue with the character I'm expected to play. The performance seemed to be plausible enough to keep my father from suspicions for now. The ploy to demean and belittle her was loathsome and I detested every second of it. To cause her fear and disgust.

The day seems endless. I feel the overwhelming need to go to her and explain my actions. I want her to know that this is what I have to do to keep her safe from the real vileness of our world. She doesn't understand the evil he's capable of.

I should let her think the worst of me. That I'm that crude bastard that sees her as nothing but a toy. One that will one day lose its shine along with my interest. Prove to her that I am my father's son. But I can't.

I'm entitled to one good thing in my life. I thought that men like me would never get to be happy. But my cousin has proven me wrong, and now I crave the one thing he's found.

Vivian James is that one thing for me.

The only camera in my room here is pointed at the door, keeping my bed and the secret passageway out of shot.

This estate was built by my family several generations ago, and the passageways had been abandoned before I was born. I'm sure my father knows about them, but I don't think he knows that *I* know about them. In fact, I made sure of it.

I discovered them when I was a little boy and have used them to explore ever since. No cameras and never any activity other than my own. The dusty footprints have only ever given proof of my own activity. I've even scattered flour over the ground throughout the entire passageway and stairwells to let me know if there has been anyone but me in them and nothing. Ever. My first secret ever worth keeping. Until now, that is.

It's past midnight when I maneuver my desk to gain access to the secret door. Pressing firmly on it, it pops open giving me a small ledge to curl my fingers into. I'm all too familiar with moving through the shadows, but the motion sensor lights I've equipped ease my way of travel as well as allow me to check for intruders.

As always, none are detected as I make my way to the spiral staircase and descend to the next floor. Vivian's room assignment was not made at random.

The servants that come here either have a debt to be paid, or have aged out of the whorehouse. None are given a full wardrobe, not to be confused with a human-being with basic human rights. Another way my father projects his power. Preying on the defenseless.

The passageway leads me right to her.

I was informed that she went to her room hours ago. All the while I have been counting down the minutes until I could safely go to her.

Giving the door a good nudge with my knee and my fist, it cracks open. Stealthily, I push it the rest of the way open into the dark room. Not a single light on, but my eyes adjust and I can make out her sleeping form on the small bed. Her brown hair dusted with hints of gold sprawled out around her pillow and her hands tucked under her cheek as she lays on her side facing the wall. The covers are pulled up to her shoulder as her breathing remains steady.

She's an angelic looking thing. Peaceful in her slumber and so pure and innocent. She was those things before she slipped into my bedroom. Then I defiled her and stole her virtue, lacking any contrition for my transgressions. I find pure pleasure in the fact that I have been her one and only. And it will remain that way.

Approaching the side of her bed that isn't shoved against the wall, I lift the blanket in no hurry at all. Tonight, she's wearing the cream and pink matching set of undergarments, and she fits them to perfection. She was alluring from the start and now with her healthy curves finally filling out, she is beyond delectable. I want to bite into the soft flesh of her thighs and breasts.

With the lack of weight from the blanket on her, she begins to stir. "Mmm," she moans and tries to wrap the blanket back around her, but I still have it in my clutch. Her brows furrow and she tries again to cover herself.

Those long lashes of hers begin to flutter as I stand there over her, watching and waiting. Anticipating her reaction. She flips over to her other side and tries to pull at the covers again.

Slowly coming to, she looks around and when she notices me, she jolts to an upright position with her back against the wall. Cornering herself like a scared little cat. I release the blanket when she indignantly yanks it from my grip to cover herself up.

FIFTEEN

VIVIAN

I'm sound asleep when I feel my blanket being stolen. It takes me some time to differentiate between a dream and reality. But I open my eyes to find Sasha standing over me.

I jolt upright and rip the blanket from him to cover myself while I press my back against the wall. Not at all a pleasant way to be awoken.

"What the hell are you doing in here?" I chide with malice in my tone. Still reeling from earlier.

His lips twitch as if this is all so amusing to him. And why wouldn't it be? This is all one big game for him and I'm not even a player. Not even a piece. I'm only one of his many moves. I suppose I should have known, but I still wasn't prepared for the shame I felt at the blatant disregard for my feelings.

I have never felt so small and worthless in all my life. To once again be used and shamed at the hands of men. And to a man I had willingly given myself to. A man that didn't make my skin crawl and proved to me that I wasn't completely dead inside. And the whole time he was this monster with a beautiful veneer.

The look on his face while he violated me with his crude behavior, the performance too realistic to be fake. The two men heckled at my expense and ran me out of there, cackling at my quick departure and humiliation.

That revulsion to touch crept in and I had felt sick the whole way back to my room. The degradation overwhelmed any other feeling for him. Its presence hadn't dissipated with his arrival.

"I want to show you something," he says and then offers his hand to me. He might as well be holding a grenade, because I do not trust him. I abstain from speaking and make no move to go along with whatever he has in store. "Come, *kukolka*."

The word has me narrowing my eyes at him and breaking my resolve. "What the hell does that even mean? *Kuk*—whatever it is," I demand.

"What do you think it means?" he teases.

"I don't know." I tighten the covers around myself. "Whore?"

"Is that what you think I have been calling you?" He looks crestfallen as I shrug my shoulders. "Come." He keeps his hand out.

"Why?"

"Because I'm asking you to."

"Are you really asking me, as in I have a choice?"

He doesn't answer, and my curiosity has me putting my hand in his. I'm not surrendering, I'm only playing along. It'd be completely asinine for me to put my trust in him.

I rise from the bed, wrapping the blanket around me like a toga. "You can't wear this." He tugs at it, and I clutch it tighter around me.

"What do you mean? I'm not walking around out there in just my underwear."

"We're not going out there." He pulls on the blanket again, and I reluctantly let go.

He keeps his eyes on me as he tosses the cover back onto my bed. I suppress a shiver as he rolls his gaze down the length of my body, his eyes oddly stopping on our joined hands.

"Why don't I have any clothes? Like pajamas or something."

He looks back up at my face. "Why do you need them?"

My face tenses into a scowl. "I don't know. Maybe for moments like this?" I sass.

He curls one corner of his mouth up. "Still don't see your reason. Come, *kukolka*." He tries tugging me along, but I stubbornly stay rooted. "Trust me, Vivian."

I scoff as my mouth pops open in shock. "Trust you? Coming from the man who degraded me publicly? Who treated me like trash?" I raise my voice.

"I told you. In order for you to stay here as a maid, I have to convince my father that you were my personal...*pet*."

What he really means is his personal *whore*. "So, you're telling me that was all for show?"

"Yes."

"How can I believe you? And am I really here to be your little sex doll, because I—" He places a finger over my mouth to shush me. I can feel my nostrils flaring but I don't retaliate. Only because I'm afraid of my own actions right now.

Silent and compliant with my hand still in his, he leads me around to the head of my bed and stops in front of the empty wall space. He presses a flat hand to the wall, and I gasp in shock when it pops open.

He pries it open with his fingertips and I'm still in shock when he pulls me through the secret entry, that I go without any protest.

When he closes us inside, I tighten my hand in his and cling to his side in the dark. "Where are we?" I whisper.

"Secret passageway," he vaguely states and begins to pull me along with him.

As we make our way forward, subtle lights automatically turn on to light our path. My bare feet shuffle along the dusty floors as I pray this isn't a trap.

We come to a stop at the foot of a spiral staircase, and I look up into the darkness that cloaks its landing. "Up leads you to my room. Never go down."

I glance down where the stairs spiral into a black abyss that I hadn't noticed at first. "Why not? What's down there?"

"The catacombs. You do not want to be seen down there."

He pulls me up the stairs with him, the metal beneath my feet chilling me to the bone. We arrive at the top and hang a left. The sensor lights continue to light our way. We walk down the dark hall until it ends with what looks like a wall.

He pushes through it and pulls me through the hidden door before shutting us inside his bedroom. Still trying to wrap my brain around the most recent series of events, I'm completely taken aback when he sweeps me into his arms that I release a small yelp.

A smirk hints at his lips as he briskly carries me towards his bed. "What are you doing?" I hiss.

"Your feet are dirty," he says in an even tone then places me on the edge of the mattress with such delicacy, you would think me made of glass. The affection toys with me.

He walks away to disappear inside his bathroom without closing the door. I hear the water running for only a couple seconds before shutting off again and he's exiting with a hand towel in hand. My cheeks heat at the memory of him cleaning me up after our first encounter. The thought not unwelcome, but also not helpful to the conflicting emotions I feel where Sasha is concerned.

My heart stills when he bends to one knee and lifts one of my feet to clean the bottom. His eyebrows drawn together in deep focus, making sure he doesn't miss a thing. How his calloused hands can be so damn tender has my mind flooding with overwhelming perplexity.

I remain reticent as he picks up my other foot to repeat the actions there. "I'll get you some slippers," he mutters then gets up to dispose of the dirty towel.

I don't move an inch until he comes back and I ask, "What am I doing here?"

An eternity passes by before he says a single syllable. His eyes speak volumes though. They make a scorching path all over my face and body. My resolve already completely dissolved.

"You can use the secret passage when you feel the need to. I don't have to tell you to never speak of it to anyone though, do I?"

I shake my head no, and he stands over me silently again. The room dead quiet. My heart pounds so hard I feel the thumping at the base of my throat. "Why are you doing all this, Sasha?" I pause to lick my dry lips. "Why save me from being sold off? Why the ruse with your father? Why show me *this*?" I gesture to the secret doorway and around his bedroom.

"If I told you that I cared for you, would you believe me?" I can't quite place the emotion he's trying to show me, but the depth in his gaze is so poignant I can physically feel it.

"I shouldn't," I admit.

He shakes his head slowly. "No. You shouldn't. It would be naïve of you to believe me so easily."

I look down at my bare knees and rub them with my palms. For warmth and for comfort. "But I have a feeling it wouldn't matter." I look back up at him and his face hasn't changed. He's patient and serene. "Whether I believe you or not. Whether I trust you or not. I'm under your rule. You'll humiliate me in front of your father or anyone watching. You'll seek me out in private and muddle my head with tenderness. You'll tell me you care about me and that you saved me from being sold as a sex slave. And I just have to accept it, don't I?"

"You can believe me or not. You can trust me or not. You are under my rule for your own safety. Yes, I will humiliate and demean you when I deem necessary." He steps forward so we're toe to toe. "The better our act is, the safer you will remain. But I will always make up for it."

A lump forms in my throat as heat expands in my chest. "What do you mean you'll make up for it?"

His long fingers thread into my hair to cup the back of my head, cranking it back to look right up into his eyes. "Meaning I will muddle your head with tenderness..." He leans down, so close I feel his lips brush my ear. "And worship your body with greed..." He fists my hair making my breath hitch. "I'll protect you from real harm..." He leans in more causing me to recline back so we don't clash. "I will fucking erase every bad feeling with pleasure so vulgar your innocent little mind couldn't even imagine," he rasps and continues to advance on me. "My words or intentions may not be of value to you yet, but I will show you insurmountable pleasure, *kukolka*. You'll drip from just the sight of me, even when I have to be someone else."

All I can do is gawk up at his handsome face and search for the truth. I can't even remember why I was so angry with him.

SIXTEEN

SASHA

It isn't my motive to fraught her head with hopeful thinking or romantic dreams. When I made the slightly impulsive decision to take her home, it was a temporary fix. I didn't have any grand scheme of getting her to safety. I only hoped that I would be able to come up with something that would release her from my father's clutches. Even if it meant hell for me.

I've wracked my brain trying to find a solution that ends with her getting her life back, but so far, I can't find a way.

Until I stumble upon something, I'm going to cosset my little doll. Spoil her with pleasure because that's all I am capable of giving to her at the moment.

As always, she's unresponsive at first when I grip her hair tightly and bring her lips to mine. Her body stills only for a moment, then it's as if she melts under me. Her lips become pliant and her body is tense with desire rather than rigid with fear.

I flinch under her tentative touch at my sides. Her smooth fingers slipping against the skin at my ribs. Over the random patches of mottled flesh and scars that I've earned from my love of fighting. Her touch is angelic and somehow so erotic.

I pull back, and she's slow to open her eyes. They've glazed over and her cheeks are burning fuchsia. I start to slip the straps to her bra down her shoulders when she has me tense with shock. "I want you to do what you want to me," she says so innocently I don't believe the words coming out of her mouth. She blinks several times as if she's fighting to keep eye contact. "You don't have to treat me like I'm fragile. I've had pieces taken from me, but I have yet to break." She swallows hard and I don't trust myself to move. Her hands slide up from my torso over my chest and rest on my shoulders. "I want you to show me what you like."

How the fuck can she still look and sound so innocent and pure when she says things like that? Words that make my cock throb and my mouth water.

"No, *kukolka*." I pause. "We're going to find out exactly what *you* like."

I back up a few steps. I'm going to ease her into this. If I do precisely what my urges want me to do to her, it'll scare her away. And again, sex should always be about pleasure. Pain can heighten the experience, but I don't want her to fear me. Not here.

"Take it off," I order. Her eyes light up slightly telling me she likes it when I give her direction. She's timid, but she obeys as she unclasps the back and lets the material drop from her breasts to the floor. They've plumped up with the rest of her. Her new curves delicately appetizing. I need a woman with something to grab onto.

She pushes her matching panties down, her heavenly region hidden between plush thighs. I go and sit down on the edge of the bed, and she rotates her body around to watch me. "Come sit, little cat."

Her approach is hesitant, but her eyes are still brimming with curiosity. My little curious cat. I pull her into my lap, her back against my chest. "Tell me, angel." I spread her legs wide for me, using my spread knees to hold them in place. I cup her breasts gently and place my lips at the shell of her ear. "How did you feel when I touched you that day?" My reference back to the day I touched her in the dining room, where I pulled her into my lap and slipped my hand up her little skirt and had her creaming all over my fingers.

Her nipples harden and her breath hitches. I rub my thumb over the taut mounds. "Were you afraid someone would see us? See you coming in my lap? Hm?"

She shudders making me smirk. "I was. I was afraid of someone walking in, but..."

I pinch one nipple, and she gasps. "Tell me."

"It excited me...a little."

I hide my grin, zealous to discover her most inner desires. "Good, *kukolka*." I give her breasts a good squeeze and grind my erection against her ass through my pants. "Never be ashamed of what arouses you. Never with me. You understand?"

She doesn't answer right away, so I give the same nipple another harsh pinch. "Yes!" she blurts out. "I understand," she pants.

"Good. Now, tell me what you want." I lightly play with her nipples and kiss the spot behind her ear.

"I don't know how."

"Yes, you do. Just use your words."

"But what if I don't know what I want?"

"Your body will tell you exactly what you want."

Her head leans back against my shoulder and her eyes close while her chest rises and falls with heavy breathing. "I want you to touch me."

"Touch you where, *kukolka*? I'm touching you right now," I tease. Coaxing her into demanding what she wants.

"Between my legs."

"Call it your pussy," I order. She hesitates for too long, so I pinch both nipples and hold onto them. "Say you want me to touch your pussy."

She grits her teeth and takes a sharp breath through them. "I want you to touch my pussy."

"Good, *kukolka*."

I breathe into her ear as I make my way down with one hand. Sliding along her soft skin, loving every inch of it. My fingers land on her wet pussy and she jumps a little in my lap, her head rolling back harder. I massage her with little pressure, and she starts riding my hand and biting on her bottom lip.

"Is this what you want?"

She nods her head vigorously. "Yes," she rasps. "More."

I feel a bead of pre-cum drip from my cock. It's almost painful at this point, but it'll be most satisfying to wait until I have her soaked and covered with a sheen of sweat from overstimulation.

I shove three fingers inside of her, knowing it'll hurt. But I'm quickly learning what my little cat truly desires. She tenses and jumps in my lap again. I still my hand to see what she does. Her mouth pops open and she sinks back down on my fingers, taking what she needs from me.

My mouth latches onto her neck and I begin pumping my fingers. I'm not slow or gentle. I push in as deep as possible with violent thrusts. She moans and undulates her body, rolling it with serpentine grace.

I speed up my brutal pace, slapping the heal of my palm against her and curling my fingers inside. She starts twisting this way and that, crying out and gasping for air. I apply even more pressure and she screams. A clear liquid squirts out of her, splashing against my still-moving hand. Her back arches and her voice turns hoarse as her legs try to close on instinct. I use my knees to spread them wider until she rides her climax out.

"Sasha," she whines and continues to contort her body, trying to squirm away but also trying to resist it. "Oh, my God," she pants, and her body begins to relax some. I slow down my thrusts and she twitches from each one.

I kiss her neck and watch her face. She's still feeling the aftershock and I don't still my hand until she relaxes, giving me all of her weight and trying to catch her breath. But we're not pausing. The short reprieve was for my own selfish reasons.

Before she can open her eyes or speak, I begin to rub her drenched little pussy. "No," she rasps and shakes her head. "I can't."

I pinch one nipple and apply more pressure to her pussy. "You can, *kukolka*. And you will. You'll fucking come over and over again for me. I will sap you for every drop your cunt has to offer. You'll squirt and cream until you beg me to stop. Then I'll fuck you. And I'll make you come for me one more time right before I paint your beautiful face with my cum." She shudders and moans, her hips rolling to find more friction. "You'll wake up with a swollen pussy, won't you, *kukolka*?"

"Yes," she hisses.

"Then I'll take you again, and it'll burn. You might even bleed. Would you like that?"

"Yes," she rushes out with short breath.

"Such a good little doll," I coo, and she moans. My praise arousing her more. "I want you to touch yourself with me."

She removes a hand from my thigh and slips it between her cunt and my hand. We play with her together and I watch the pleasure bloom across her face and chest, painting it a bright pink.

Hooking my fingers, her fingers mold to mine and we both enter her. She sucks in air through clenched teeth and arches her lower back to find a better angle. My pants are soaked, and her pussy only gets creamier. The soft substance makes lewd noises while we both fuck her pussy with our digits in tandem.

I let her take the lead and follow her movements, rubbing her pussy with her palm then thrusting in sharply. I watch in pure fascination as she brings herself to orgasm. When she begins to lose her strength, I take back control and move our hands together with more force.

Her breath hitches, and her body locks up. Her head tilts towards me and I smash my mouth against hers. She moans against me and rides our fingers while our tongues sloppily tangle. The creamy juices flowing from her.

She screams out and I don't give her time to come down. I give her pussy a good slap then I flip her onto her back on top of the bed.

Shucking my dampened trousers off, she watches me through heavy lidded eyes. Her legs are unabashedly open, her cunt glistening and dripping. Already soaking the sheets.

I get down to my stomach and inhale her cunt into my mouth. Naturally, her hips rise off the bed, and I use my brute strength to anchor her down. I hook my arms around her thighs, immobilizing the lower half of her body. She heaves with labored breath as I engorge. Pulling her already puffy pussy into my mouth and sucking the palatable wetness from her.

Using two fingers, I spread her pussy lips open so I can reach every area with my lips and tongue, tasting every inch inside and out. Flattening my tongue, I swirl it around her puckered hole and drag it up languidly, making sure I'm thorough with expanding her sexual horizons. There aren't enough hours in one day to explore everything—Maybe not enough in a lifetime. But I will spend every minute I have to let her get a taste of everything I can.

When I feel like I have her teetering the edge again, I shove three fingers into her channel, my free arm holding her down over her waist and hips as she digs her heels into the mattress.

"Ah!" she yells and throws her head back as her pussy ejects that sweet liquid. Squirting all over my hand and arm and splashing off my palm.

Removing my hand, I line up my cock and invade her cunt with one violent thrust. Slamming my groin into hers. I lean on one forearm near her head while I use my other hand to grip her ass brutally, fully intending to leave marks.

Her fingers find their way into my hair, and she pulls me down on top of her, asking for the weight of my body. I'm already close but I hold back, waiting for her to give me one more.

I slam into her over and over, her breath hitching from the jolt of the impact. She mewls and whines and I can tell she's about to combust. Three more thrusts and she's convulsing. I speed up with gritted teeth and we both get lost in a drunken haze of insurmountable pleasure.

After she's enjoyed the full effects of her climax, I pull out and straddle her upper body. I vigorously stroke my cock over her. "Open," I demand. She immediately obeys. Keeping eye contact with me the whole time.

The tingle at the base of my spine works its way into my balls and spurts out of my cock like a cannon. Painting her pretty face and open mouth. Her eyes remain on mine, waiting for instructions. I give her a daring look, telling her exactly what I want.

Her lips seal shut, and I watch as her throat works to swallow me down.

"Good, *kukolka.*"

SEVENTEEN

VIVIAN

I wake the next day still in his bed, but I could tell I was alone. No weight or heat for comfort.

I rapidly blink my eyes and search the room, but it's as empty as it is quiet. Then I catch a glimpse of the clock and my eyes pop wide, and I shoot up out of the bed. Giving me zero time to lay here and think about last night.

"Fuck," I mutter and try to find my bra and underwear. I'm going to be late! What will happen if Greta comes to let me out of my little cage and I'm gone?

Unsuccessful at finding my undergarments, I literally sprint into his closet and throw on the first t-shirt I can find. I only have about ten minutes to get back to my room and throw myself together for the day. Not like I have any makeup to wear or anything to do my hair with. But I did want to shower. Obviously, it'll have to wait.

Thankfully, I paid attention to Sasha's instructions and I know where to find the hidden door and where to go once inside the passageway. I shuffle my feet quickly along the cold, dirty ground and wish I had stolen a pair of his socks too. I can't full-out run because of the delay of the sensor lights, and I won't be able to see if I'm about to run into a wall.

I'm too worried about Greta discovering my absence to worry about how creepy this all is. Of course, these Russians would have secret passages and hidden doors inside a mansion that's more like a gothic castle. It would be really cool if not for its occupants. I would actually love a gothic style castle of my own. *Hah! Listen to me. A castle of my own…*

I slip inside my bedroom and double check to make sure there isn't even the slightest hint of a crack visible. Knowing I'm running out of time, I dart into the bathroom and rush through my morning ritual.

I'm just pulling my hair back into a ponytail and sitting on the edge of my bed to put my socks and shoes on when the sound of the locks on my door click. My eyes widen when I see the bottom of one foot and how dirty it is. I promptly throw both socks on just in time for Greta to appear in the doorway.

"Just getting my shoes on," I rush out with ragged breath.

She makes no comment on my disorderly composure as I exit the room and fall into step with her. I hope she doesn't notice the potent smell of sex still clinging to me.

Breakfast isn't served to my room most mornings. I'm expected to grab something quick in the kitchen on my way to do my chores for the day. Every single day since I've been here.

Cleaning toilets and changing sheets that haven't been slept in doesn't seem so wearing today as I reminisce about last night. I should be walking around in a state of dysphoria for all that has happened to me, but the soreness of my body and the fact that it burns when I pee brings me back to the carnal pleasure Sasha showed to me. He promised I would beg him to stop, and I wanted to, but I lost all ability to speak.

And oh, my God. He made me squirt. I wasn't sure if that was even a real thing. I may have seen it once in a porno one of the few times I indulged in my curiosity. But I honestly didn't think it was real. But my body burst with warm liquid when he brought me past my limits. Past the ecstasy and into a state of euphoria. It was unimaginable.

Then he fucked me until I was braindead. My body stiff with paralysis and my brain unable to make any thoughts. I don't remember much else but his body blanketing mine.

My head remains in the clouds drifting through in a daze the rest of the day. Hours fly by and I'm anxious to run into Sasha. He made good on his promise to paint my face with his release. But one promise he has failed to make good on is fucking me again while my pussy is raw and sore. Making it hurt. I have to squeeze my thighs together just thinking about it.

The morning pep talk I had with myself while rushing to get ready did absolutely nothing to my vulnerable fortitude. I told myself not to dig too deep into what happened between us. That I'm not as fucked up as I sometimes feel, and that it was still only sex to Sasha. My warped brain tries to tell me different though.

I'm heading into one of the many sitting rooms that doesn't get put to any use when a familiar voice accompanied by an unfamiliar one causes me to pause. The room I'm assigned to clean is across from the room that Sasha is sitting in cozied up to a beautiful blonde. Both of them smiling and conversing, his arm slung over the back of the couch and her body is turned in towards him. Her slender legs crossed while she laughs about something and touches his chest. He smiles down at her and doesn't remove her claws.

To think that I was woman enough to be the only one warming his bed is so juvenile of me. I'm his pet, and his dirty little secret. I'm not his girlfriend, and this isn't some kind of illicit love affair.

Stupid stupid stupid.

I manage to get myself back to work, I can berate myself later. I won't run out of here crying like I really want to. I'm going to be strong and feign indifference. I need to remind myself that all men are the same. They're lying *pigs*.

My resolve won't so quickly evaporate with sweet words and sensual touches anymore. No. I am a strong woman with morals and courage and —

"Vivian." *Oh, shit.* His deep voice paralyzes me in an instant and my stomach flips. "Would you come here, please?"

Squaring my shoulders, I take a deep breath and turn. Purposely staring over his head, I walk into the room and stop in front of him. "Sir?" I say flatly.

"Could you get the lovely Rada here a drink?"

And she has a name. My heart plummets to the pit of my stomach and on instinct my eyes catch on his. He stares back at me with a blank look, and I want to ask him why I deserve this. Why do I deserve to be played with and mocked? He said he would continue to mistreat me in front of his father. He never mentioned he would treat me this way in front of *everyone*. Putting on a volatile show with my body and having a girlfriend I knew nothing about are different playing fields.

"I would *love* a red wine, darling," The beautiful woman next to him purrs in a strong Russian accent. My eyes move over to hers and I see amusement dancing in her light ones. Her lips are slightly tilted up at the corners as she too mocks me.

"Yes, ma'am." I swiftly move out of the room with my head held high. No one is worth the pain I am feeling inside right now, nor the tears stinging my eyes.

I grab a bottle from the cellar located in the kitchen and pour her a glass. I stare at the crimson liquid, tempted to pour bleach in it. But it's not her that I am spewing hatred towards. It's Sasha. He's the one who deceived me and her.

My rational thinking doesn't overpower my tantrum unfortunately. Hovering my mouth over the glass, I sneak a peek around to make sure no one is watching, and I drop a nice wad of spit in her glass. Then I take my finger that I haven't washed and have been cleaning with and stir it up to hide the bubbles.

Balancing the wine glass on the silver tray, I walk out of there feeling pretty proud of myself. It's a small hit, but it's what I have to work with.

Keeping my composure, I walk back out with the serving tray, and I place the glass of wine on the coffee table in front of her. Not waiting for a thank you or any acknowledgement, I leave the room and forget about my duties for the time being. I need to put some distance between us and scream into a pillow or something.

EIGHTEEN

SASHA

I watch as Vivian takes purposeful strides out of the room and away from me. "She's jealous, Sasha," Rada muses.

"Who?" I tear my eyes away from where Vivian disappeared.

"Don't try and lie to me. I saw the way you were looking at her. So, tell me. Are you fucking her?" She sips her wine and watches me with a twinkle in her eye.

"It's none of your business," I grumble, and she chuckles.

"I'll take your refusal to answer as a yes. Since when do you fuck the maids? I always thought you were too *sanctimonious* for that," she teases with a roll of her eyes.

Snorting, I shake my head. "You mind your business, you little rat."

She giggles and playfully hits my chest with the back of her hand. "Come on. I'm your sister. You can talk to me about this. Do you like this woman?" She pauses, watching me carefully. "Because it seemed like you do."

"I'm fucking her. That's it." I hate the sound of those words leaving my lips. I trust Rada, but it's best that she doesn't know these things.

"Mhmm." She sips more wine, still observing me. "Well, whether or not you like her, you definitely have some explaining to do."

"I don't need to explain anything to anyone, Rada," I say little too harshly. My father is the only one I am obligated to explain anything to. Only because he'll find out anyways, and he'll be suspicious if it doesn't come from me.

"You don't have to be like him. You're *not* like him."

"Don't confuse my generosity towards you and Vera as endearing. I'm not a man capable of more."

"That's bullshit, Sasha. Do not act like you have taken care of Vera and I out of pity or obligation. You've taken care of us because you care and you knew it was the right thing to do. You're not *him*. You are so much better." She pauses for a moment after her rant. "You're allowed to care about others, Sasha." She softens her voice.

I whip my head around in her direction. "You know damn well that I cannot. Father looks past my attachment to you and Vera because he chalks it up to a weakness for family relations. A weakness he has no problem exploiting. You know what happens when I care for someone or something. He hangs it over my head, always taunting me with it." To try and break me. "I can only care for two things in my life. Family and myself."

"Sasha, you can't live like that." Rada has been sheltered from the ghoulish truth of my life, and it's my fault. She knows our father to be a vile tyrant, but she has never had to suffer at his hand.

"I can and I will." She opens her mouth to argue, and I stand up. "I think our time is up today. I'll have Bash take you home."

I walk her towards the door and call for Bash to meet us there. Rada turns to me with a solemn look on her face. "Sasha. Don't deny yourself happiness. You are more than deserving of it." She cups my cheek gently. "Letting him keep you from it is what is destroying you. Don't let him. He won't live forever." She gives me small smile.

"Careful what you say," I murmur and lean down to kiss her cheek. If anyone were to overhear her, she'd be punished.

I watch her leave with Bash and try not to let her words fill me with fantastic notion. She means well, but she doesn't fully understand the father-son dynamic. Avoiding happiness is less miserable than if my father were to use Vivian against me in some way. Like kill her. Or sell her. That would be my undoing, and any piece of my humanity would be obliterated.

Thinking back to Vivian and the way she tried her damnedest to suppress her hatred towards me when she saw Rada, leads me to want to seek her out. To maybe poke and prod a little more and see how far I can get her to go. See how deep her passion goes. To feel this burgeoning energy we seem to naturally create.

And to fulfill one more promise to her.

I find my pissed off little pussycat in an empty sitting room, angrily and aggressively fluffing pillows. Most likely picturing my face on them as she punches them and curses under her breath. I stand and watch with a smirk on my face. Enjoying the display.

When she turns and finally takes notice of me, she gasps in surprise. Then her shock morphs into anger and she ignores me to go back to her chores. "Can I help you, Mr. Rogov?" she says sweetly, and I feel my molars grind.

Closing the distance, I abruptly spin her around and shove her down on the couch to sit. She glares up at me as I seethe down at her. "Do not call me that." At first, she seems confused, but then realization shows in her expression. She knows she's hit a nerve and it seems to please her. My father is Mr. Rogov and I do not want to ever be confused with that man.

"Then what should I call you, *sir*?" Her smile and tone are saccharine and aggravating.

"You can call me, *dorogoi, lyubimiy, moi sladkiy, meelyi moy, malysh, ty mayo fsyo.*" *Dear, my love, my sweetness, my darling, baby, my everything.* I smirk. "Any of those will suffice."

"Well, unfortunately I don't speak fucking Russian," she growls.

I choke down a chuckle. "You might want to learn, *kukolka.*"

"No, thank you. Now, if you don't mind, I have a job to do." She stands but I don't give her any room, pinning her body between mine and the couch.

"You can take a break."

"I don't need a break." She stares at the base of my neck, avoiding my gaze.

"I'm pretty sure I have a debt to collect."

This makes her glower at me. "You mean another one?" she sasses.

I respond with a twitching smirk and one arched eyebrow. Taking her by her hand, she tries to resist, but her strength is nothing compared to mine.

"Let me go," she snarls and tries to pry her hand out of mine. Her distain will make a good show for any prying eyes. Wouldn't want anyone to think she's my plaything willingly. Ignoring her, I continue to tow her with me towards my bedroom. "Sasha." She tries digging her nails into my skin, but they don't break the surface. "Please don't." Her voice is less threatening, but it doesn't deter me.

We arrive at my bedroom and I pull her inside, quickly closing the door and throwing the lock into place. Looking like a frightened cornered animal, she starts backing herself further into my room. "You seem upset about something, *kokulka.*" I tilt my head down and begin stalking her.

"No. I'm just finally seeing things clearly."

"Clearly, huh? And what is it that you see?"

"I—I don't—you made me..." she stutters and backs herself right up against the wall.

"I made you what, Vivian?" I'm closing in on her.

"Nothing. It was more my fault than yours."

I stop and frown at her within arm's reach. "And what is that?"

"I thought that...it doesn't matter." She shakes her head. "It was foolish of me, and I won't let it happen again."

"Tell me." I continue forward again until I'm caging her in with my arms.

"No." She purses her lips in defiance.

"Then how can I fix it if I don't know what the problem is?"

"Fix it?" Her voice hitches.

I trail a finger down the side of her face. "You are obviously upset with me, but if I don't know why, then what can I do about it?" I rasp and stare down at her lips.

"I…I didn't know you had a girlfriend," she whispers weakly, and my eyes snap up to hers.

"And you're upset about that?" She looks away, so I turn her face back to me. "Are you upset that I have a girlfriend, or that you didn't know?"

"It doesn't matter. You're a pig either way."

I unleash a full-on grin and she tries darting her eyes away from me again. Leaning in, I brush my lips against the shell of her ear. "Rada," I pause for effect, "Is my sister."

"Sister?"

"Yes, *kukolka*. Rada is one of my sisters. I have two, they don't live here at the estate, so they sometimes come for a visit."

"So, she isn't your girlfriend?" she asks quietly as I nuzzle her ear with my lips and nose.

"No, little cat."

"Do you have a girlfriend?"

I smile. "Would you care?"

"I would feel bad for her if you did."

Chuckling, I pull back some to look at her. "You are a horrible liar, Vivian." I thread my fingers into her hair and pin her against the wall with my body.

"I don't deserve to be mocked, Sasha."

An emotion abruptly lodges itself in my throat. "You don't deserve any of this, angel," I say softly. Then I throw her a bone and tell her the truth. "I do not have a girlfriend."

She looks up at me with eyes full of meaning and Rada's words ring inside my head. Vivian is my first little slice of brilliant light since I found out about my sisters. I know I should be happy with what I got from her already and end it now, but I can't seem to walk away. Not until I am somewhat repleted, even if only momentarily.

"How's your pussy?"

Her cheeks instantly light up with vibrant color and she tries to avert her gaze. "It hurts," she mutters.

"Good. Then this is going to hurt even worse."

Ignoring the augury of what's to come, I spin her around, pinning her face-first to the wall. Thrusting her skirt over her hips, I yank her panties down too abruptly and end up tearing them and making her yelp.

Pulling my cock out, she hisses when I run two rough fingers through the lips of her swollen cunt. My cock twitches against her ass from the contact. "How did it feel when I fucked you raw, huh?"

She moans when I move my fingers and grind my cock into her backside. It nestles nicely between her rounded flesh. "Good," she weakly pushes out.

"And now?" I glide my fingers down to her entry and push three inside of her. She tenses and tries to fight the intrusion.

"It burns," she pants and squeezes her eyes shut.

I pump my fingers. "And?"

"And I like it," she rushes out and shutters from the pain.

I grin. "Good, *kukolka*." I kiss her cheek and her inner muscles relax some.

She's wet, but I want her soaked before I fuck her again. This time painting her ass with my release. Maybe I'll make it so her ass matches the flaming cheeks on her face.

She's still holding too much tension in the rest of her body, so I give one of her ass cheeks a good smack. The sound ricochets off the walls and drowns out her cry. I raise my hand and bring it down again to leave my handprint and she cries out in pain again, but she tilts her hips up to me. I speed up my fingers, and she's now a sopping mess. A lude response to the spanking.

Not wanting to push her past the point of unenjoyable pain, I replace my fingers with the head of my cock. Gently pressing in. Her wetness slicks up my cock, but the swelling of her cunt makes it even snugger.

She gasps then sucks air through her teeth as I encase myself with her tender heat. Pulling out slowly, I ram my hips forward, crushing her hips to the wall and stealing her breath. I find purchase with her hips and squeeze encouraging her to tilt them again for me. She obliges and I fuck her with short and hard thrusts. Punishing her pussy.

"Sasha," she cries on a shaky breath. "It...I can't..."

"Tell me to stop." I give her shoulder a good nip with my teeth. Not enough to pierce through the skin, but enough to leave a mark. She moans louder and drops her forehead to the wall. "Tell me it's too much, and I'll stop." I keep my relentless pace.

"It's too much," she murmurs, then quickly follows with, "But don't stop."

I crush my lips against her ear. "My good little doll," I rasp. I lean back to give her reddened ass another good swat. Hitting the same spot a couple more times to be sure it'll remain vibrant for the rest of the day.

Once I'm satisfied with one round cheek, I work on the other one. Her pussy constricting and her yelping with every contact. The sight of it has my balls jumping up. I grit my teeth to hold back as her own orgasm shoots through her. Her pussy squeezing me and her muscles spasming.

I abruptly pull out and decorate her inflamed flesh with my cum. Ropes if it shoot out and cling to her tender skin. The contrast of colors is a beautiful sight to see. And when I see smears of blood on my shaft, my cock jumps inside my palm in an aftershock of pleasure. Blackness rims my vision and I lean into the wall around her to remain upright.

The goal was to help her find her own sexuality and deviant desires. I didn't anticipate her awakening mine.

NINETEEN

VIVIAN

I toss and turn in my bed for hours begging for sleep to take me. Anxiety fuels the shame I feel at my feelings for Sasha. This can't be normal, right? I mean, nothing about this is anywhere close to being normal, but the things I like…

He seems to be less restrained with trying to stay away from me. He struggled before, but he seems to be giving in. Giving me permission to sneak into his room when I want. Not holding back when we touch.

Every moment I spend with him is exhilarating. And after every encounter, I find my carefully constructed walls less strenuous. As if I can slightly lower them and rest for the first time ever.

Just as he profanely pulled my partially torn panties up and over his cum, covering the throbbing flesh of my backside, his phone rang with a call that seemed urgent. He kept the brief conversation in Russian, but I didn't need any translation to feel his entire demeanor change after he spoke to whoever was on the phone.

He seemed remorseful for having to run out on me, but said he would find me later and kissed me with heated passion, lighting up my arousal all over again.

I'm startled into full consciousness when I'm weighed down to my mattress. A very large warmth blankets me as my eyes pop wide open with a squeal. His gold teeth glimmer in the dark when he lazily grins above me with his hair a mess. Something is off about him. His eyes look sleepy and glazed over, and there's this playfulness to him.

"Angel," he rasps and tenderly brushes back my hair. It's hard to enjoy his touch when my nostrils suddenly burn with the potent smell of alcohol coming from him in waves. I may not have known him for very long, but I know he doesn't drink often. His entire disposition displays intoxication.

"Are you okay?" I ask quietly and search his face for any changes.

His smile drops some. "I've had an eventful evening."

I lick my lips and it's impossible to miss his eyes darting down to my mouth and his eyes visibly darkening. "Do you want to talk about it?"

His eyes bounce back up to mine and he chuckles. His body vibrating against me. "It's not something talking could help with."

"But sometimes it just makes you feel better."

He looks at me like I'm an innocent child and it makes my cheeks heat with embarrassment. *Here I am, asking a mobster to talk about his feelings.* "It's best you not know anything," he almost whispers, and before I can ask any questions, he covers my mouth with his and kisses me so deeply my head spins.

I open my body for him to fit against. My knees widening and my arms wrapping around his shoulders. He grinds into me, and I flinch at the pain.

"You're still sore," he rasps.

"I am," I pant regretfully.

"Let me make it better."

He scoots down my body, peeling my panties down along the way. The cool air feels good when it hits my overly sensitive area, cooling the burning pain. The hotness of his breath over it when he wedges his shoulders between my thighs has me sucking in air and stilling in my lungs.

"I'll be gentle, little cat."

It stings at first when he kisses the apex of my thighs, but when he delicately licks me, it begins to soothe the throbbing pain.

He remains gentle, and while I enjoy his rough side, the one that pushes me to my limits, I can't help but appreciate seeing the tender man behind the mobster that has me shaking with salacity.

He pushes me over that edge, and I fall hard and fast.

He groans in satisfaction and sits to pull his shirt over his head. Using the fabric of the shirt to wipe his mouth, he tosses it to the floor and climbs back up my body. He kisses me slowly, only deepening it enough to leave me light-headed with the taste of myself in my mouth.

Not another word is spoken as he curls his body around mine and falls fast asleep. It takes me a while to fall asleep myself, but once I do, I do so with a smile on my face.

TWENTY

I've managed to steer clear of Mr. Rogov since being here, aside from the one incident at the dining table. I'm starting to wonder if Sasha is overly paranoid about his father and his supposed suspicions of my importance to him. Or maybe he has his father completely fooled and I'm officially off his radar. Then there's always the possibility I am the one being played, and our intimate moments are the ruse. It's hard to make the wheels in my head stop spinning when there's not much else to do and there are always games being played with these people.

There's an event going on tonight in one of the entertainment rooms, and everyone is working it. So far, I've been kept inside the kitchen helping with plating and resupplying fancy hors d'oeuvres. But the men eating them are far from fancy. They're despicable and ignoble pigs that binge on expensive liquor and unwilling young women when they should be served potato chips and peanuts like the low-class they truly are.

There's some kind of commotion between one of the cooks and one of the maids. I don't understand what they are arguing about as she holds one tray and he's trying to thrust another one at her. She looks around then stops on me and rambles off some more in Russian and the cook's eyes go to me as well. He responds to her, and she leaves. Next thing I know, he's stomping over and shoving the tray of fresh appetizers at me.

I try rejecting it, but he keeps pushing and telling me to go. I scan the room for Greta, but unfortunately for me, she's not here.

Gulping, I take the tray and shuffle my feet out of the kitchen and in the direction of the party.

I take one more panicked look around for someone to save me, but there are only a few large and stoic men I don't recognize standing outside of the large entryway. Two of them mutter to each other in Russian while ogling me with their beady eyes, practically drooling. My stomach turns in disgust, and I cast my gaze downwards and take a deep breath.

I enter the room and I'm blasted with heavy smoke and the stench of alcohol. The plan was to keep my eyes averted and make one lap of the room then leave, but the scene has me gawking. My eyes roaming in every direction.

It's disturbingly provocative and obscene. I may have been a prude, given my traumatic past up until recently, but I've been living in Vegas for four years. I've seen everything. But nothing has prepared me for this.

There are about a dozen or so young women in here. Some are naked, some are almost there. Some are being fucked by a man, some are being fucked by two. But the most bizarre thing of it all, is the fact that none of the women look upset. They aren't crying or begging for help. No one screaming 'no' or 'stop.' They're enjoying themselves.

Rapture.

The room tilts in front of me as I'm witnessing what could've been my life. This is why I was kidnapped from my apartment and tossed onto a ship headed for Russia. This is what Sasha saved me from.

I watch in outrage as a woman gets on her hands and knees and crawls seductively towards an older man with a big belly and stained teeth. She sits back on her heels and rubs her hands all over her body, looking for some kind of stimulation. I can't bear to watch any longer.

My wide eyes stop on another woman. One I recognize as one of the women who was trapped inside the shipping container with me. She looks to be around the same age as me, possibly younger. To see her strung-out on Rapture and serving men sexual favors while I'm serving food and drinks has a guilt-ridden lump forming in my throat and melancholy burning my gut like acid.

I am in no way fortunate or 'better off,' but I was dealt better cards from the same deck. In some way, I should be grateful.

A heavy aura surrounds me, breaking me from my stare and I spin around to find a pair of dark eyes shooting through me. Sasha sits with a few other men as naked women entertain them with a sensual dance to the beat of the music. His chest visibly rises with every inhale and his nostrils flare with every exhale. He's livid, and I'm sure it's from my presence.

Tearing my eyes away from his burning ones, I get my feet to move and stop at the nearest table. They're in the middle of some card game I don't care enough to know and offer the tray to one. He pays me no mind as he snags something off it and I quickly make my way to the next man. I try to just assert myself enough to blend in, but not enough to draw any kind of attention.

I can feel Sasha's eyes following me the whole time. When I begin to head over to the next table, I catch sight of Mr. Rogov and I swiftly switch directions to approach another group. Hopefully, they're distracted by the naked women entertaining them enough not to care about the plain maid with clothes on.

I sigh in relief as I walk away unscathed and head to the last table I plan to serve before high tailing it out of here. Just as I'm about to offer the very last item on my tray, I feel the sudden energy shift in the air. The men are all speaking in Russian, but I can tell in the tone that the conversation has redirected, and most eyes are on me. Someone mutters something making the men chuckle and then a hand is up my dress causing me to freeze. Calloused fingers slide up my thigh until they reach the fabric of my panties and I feel my stomach turn and the back of my throat burn with bile. Vivid memories of my past are thrusted to the forefront of my mind, stilling me in fear.

I'm shaken from the paralyzing fear when a beastly roar fills the room and I find myself at Sasha's back with my arm practically being pulled from the socket. He looks larger than ever right now with raging heat radiating out of him like hades himself. The men laugh despite Sasha's foul temper. Mr. Rogov appears behind the jeering men and says something making them all snicker like little hissing snakes. I hate not having a clue what is being said. But also thankful for the reprieve and able to feign ignorance.

"Selfish little bastard, my son," Mr. Rogov says in English. I dare take a tiny peek around Sasha's arm and see him grinning right at me. The look gives me the chills and Sasha tightens his grip around my forearm making me wince in pain.

"Or maybe the boy has caught feelings for the whore," another man taunts, and my eyes dart down to the floor. I have been referred to as a *whore* more times in the last few months than I have in my entire life. I know I'm no whore, but it still never feels good to be constantly labeled as one.

It grows quiet aside from the music in the background and I glance up to see Mr. Rogov raising a questioning eyebrow at his son. "You know I do not like sharing my *things*," Sasha says smugly, but I can feel the threat behind his tone.

This is all an act. He has to. He's protecting me.

The urge to touch him, to wrap myself around him for comfort is practically suffocating. It would instantly calm me and bring me relief, reminding me this will all be over soon. That he will make up for it later. But I refrain from doing so. It would only entice the pigs more.

"Then at least show us how you like to play with your little pet," Mr. Rogov challenges and the bile again burns my chest and throat.

Considering we have a larger audience and based off the energy of the room, he's not going to get away with groping my breasts and sloppily kissing me this time. But Sasha will find us a way out of this. He'll grope and demean me, he'll pose possession and haul me out of here like a ragdoll over his shoulder.

"I'll give you a tiny glimpse," Sasha shocks me. Then I'm yanked in front of him, my back to his front so that I have to face all the men that are watching us. Watching *me*.

One of Sasha's arms bands around my waist as the rest of the room focuses on us. I can feel his breath on my neck as it distracts me from the jeering men and their discursive chatter. I wish he would tell me it's all going to be okay. Tell me not to worry and that he'll always protect me. Give me some kind of reassurance or put my panic at ease. But when his other hand makes its way to the hemline of my dress and starts to slip it upwards, my heart begins to palpitate with terror.

He wouldn't take it that far, would he? Maybe he's just going to give them a peek or something. A flash or whatever. Enough to give them something to laugh about and then use it as a distraction to slip us both out of here.

My eyes widen as his arm tightens around me like a restraint as he forces my dress around my hips, his fingers boldly heading south. Closing my eyes to shut out the heckling that imbues me with humility and disgust, I pray that this is only a tease for them. He's going to tell them to go fuck themselves and drag me back to his room where he'll be sweet and gentle to me. Profusely apologize for having to yet again humiliate me.

My body begins to quake as his fingers tease the waistband on my panties and the boisterous men grow louder.

Please, Sasha. Please don't do this. Please.

His hand dives in until he's cupping my bare pussy in the crudest manner, and I shake even harder. I'm not wet at all for him. I'm repulsed and petrified. I have never been so mortified and degraded in all my life. This is worse than any of the times my mother's boyfriend have touched me. They hurt me, but they never put me on display to mock me, and they could never get close to my heart.

"Oh, come now, Sasha. Show us that sweet little pussy of hers," a man says, and I squeeze my eyes shut tighter.

I hear Sasha make a growling noise low in his throat and the cold air hits my most private part as my panties are shoved down. I whimper some, but I don't dare open my eyes. I numb myself to the pain of embarrassment.

As his fingers are placed over my crotch, he presses his lips to my ear and rasps, "I'm sorry, angel." It's barely audible and possibly just my mind playing tricks on me, trying to offer some self-comfort.

His fingers toy with me and he whispers again into my ear. "I have to." Then he shoves a finger up inside of me and I tune out the noise of the repugnant men. I concentrate on my own breathing and hold onto the feeling of the steeliness of his body pressed against mine.

He works my pussy, and although I started out dry, his touch begins to bring out some of my natural wetness making it bearable. The thought of someone walking in on us like this would excite me, but being vulgarized and disgraced brings me no joy.

"Just fake it for me," he whispers after a minute or so of this heinous act. His words only cause me to clench up in revulsion. He nibbles on the shell of my ear, yet it has no effect. "You have to work with me, Vivian." I want to scream at him. Take a fucking machete to every abhorrent motherfucker in this room. Going from absolutely horrified to murderous.

"That's it, angel," he rasps, curling two fingers inside of me. Between his voice in my ear and the way he's fingering me, it dissuades the animosity boiling inside of me. Setting it aside to stew on later. "Concentrate on your pleasure." The background noise tries to threaten the bubble I am putting myself in, but Sasha's voice again grounds me. "It's just you and me, angel."

The blood all begins to rush between my legs leaving me hot and light-headed. Then he pulls his lips from my ear to speak to whoever in Russian making them all give their obnoxious plaudits and praise. Before I have the chance to lose it, he dives his tongue inside my ear and doubles his efforts with his hand on me.

It's just us two in this room. Just us two. Only us.

Beguiling myself with the lie, I come apart in his seize. My knees wobble and my lungs still. In the peak of my climax the background noise doesn't even faze me. All I can do is quiver and ride the wave until reality seeps in, hitting me like a ton of bricks.

Sasha's hand slowly retracts from my sensitive flesh, and he slowly pulls my panties up into place. I still don't have the courage to open my eyes just yet. "Is that all? I thought she sucked a good dick or something." The now familiar and gut-turning voice of his father goads him to deprecate me even more. Leveling every single thing Sasha and I have begun to build. There will be no exonerating him from this. If he pushes this further, abates me and grinds me down to nothing but dirt, I will hold nothing but hatred and revulsion towards him. There's always a choice. He can tell them the show is over and pretend to haul me away with gluttony.

"You got your little show." Sasha's voice is tight behind me, and for a second, I heave a sigh of relief.

Someone shouts something in Russian making the men cackle. "What's wrong, son? Can't rise to the challenge?" My eyes pop open to the provocation coming from his father and I find him gleaming right at me. It chills every bone inside my body. I can physically feel the tension coming off of Sasha in tendrils that coil around me. Between him and his father, I feel like I might faint or just flat out drop dead. I can't handle much more. I have never been so petrified and nauseated. My blood pressure boiling to a break point.

"Get to your knees, *kukolka*," Sasha orders and I snap my head back to gape at him. He's stone-faced as he looks right through me. His jaw ticks right before he takes my hair in a tight fist and jerks me to the ground as I bite back a whimper when my knees hit hard. "I said, get to your knees," he seethes, and I swallow back the tears as I stare up at the face I still find dauntingly beautiful.

The men continue their high praise and continue to chip away at the tiny bit of dignity I have left. As I'm forced on my knees facing his crotch, I know exactly what he's about to make me do, and I don't have the stomach for it. I might actually get sick. Again, painful memories surge forward, and I begin to hyperventilate.

I've only done this one other time, and he too forced me to my knees. No matter how much I cried and begged, he choked me with his disgusting cock and threatened to kill me if I bit him. I ended up puking and he didn't stop. It turned him on more and he finished in my mouth. Made me swallow it down along with my own vomit.

I make one last ditch effort to find some piece of the man I know inside him as I look up at him with tear filled eyes and whisper, "Please. Don't do this."

His nostrils flare as he pulls harder on my hair pulling a cry out of me and he undoes his pants to pull his cock out. It's barely hard as he coaxes it towards my face. "You know what to do, pet." His voice is empty, lacking any hint of emotion or remorse.

Knowing what will happen if I end up puking again, I take a soothing breath to allay the nausea in my stomach. My lips and chin tremble as I sluggishly part my lips and he shoves his cock inside without pause. I don't move. I'm frozen solid. "Suck my dick, or I'll shove it in your ass and fuck you so hard you won't be able to sit for a week," he sneers, egging on our audience with the performance of me being defiled and violated. Watching me become utterly worthless.

Flattening my tongue around his cock, I begin bobbing my head with my eyes squeezed shut, concentrating on not using my teeth and not gagging. His fist remains tight in my hair, and I try to pretend that none of this is real. That it's just him and me in his bedroom after I snuck in through the secret passageway he introduced me to. We're just two lovers messing around, and after this, he's going to make sweet love to me. He's going to be gentle and loving and tell me everything that he loves about me. Tell me that he's going to find a way for us to escape together so we can live happily ever after.

I feel his cock growing hard inside of my mouth and it makes me falter some, but he isn't having it. He uses the grip on my hair to fuck my mouth. I hold my breath as he rams the back of my throat over and over. I blink open my teary eyes for a moment to glance up at him and I see that he has his eyes shut too. It doesn't look like it's from pleasure though. It's almost as if he's praying, or maybe confessing his sins. I squeeze my eyes shut again so I can focus on not puking.

After a minute of him literally choking me with his cock, he stills at the back of my throat cutting off my airway and making my head feel dizzy. I begin clawing at his thighs as he coats my throat with warm fluid, and I have no choice but to let it go down or I'll suffocate.

Still using the firm grasp in my hair, he rips me off of his cock and I gasp for air and sputter. He yanks me up to my feet and I desperately try to blink through the tears to see. I don't get the chance to get a look at his face as he puts his mouth over my ear and speaks lowly, but loud enough for others to hear. "Now, go clean yourself up and wait for me in my room. I want you naked and touching yourself." He releases the fist from my hair with a jerk, and I stumble and run out of there trying not to trip over my uncouth steps.

With my heart in my throat and my vision unclear, I wheeze trying to hold back my sobs making my way to my quarters. Not caring if I'm allowed to or not.

I had held such a reverence for this man only moments ago, now, all I see is a didactic conclusion. He's just a great actor. I had thought this was his great act, but the man he lets me see is the real academy winner.

With a heavy heart, I enter my room. Resolute now with my condemnation and loathsomeness. I was wrong about this place breaking me. *He* is the one breaking me, but not if I don't let him. I thought he was worth saving, worth sacrificing myself for, but he's just another sanctimonious asshole with the power to do whatever the fuck he wants.

I close the door on myself and curl up into a tight ball in my bed and let the tears fall. Feeling malevolent yet utterly disgraced. Two strong emotions fighting for the upper hand tearing my heart in two and locking in the conviction I should have given him from the start.

TWENTY-ONE

SASHA

Everything Vivian and I have built has been torn to shreds and demolished. Just as I had set the plans in motion. I wanted to teach her to embrace sex and pleasure, but I used it to degrade her and bring her down with shame.

A few days earlier…

"*Da*," I answer the phone after it rings for third time. My hands still roaming Vivian's growing curves.

"Sasha," my cousin Kazimir's familiar voice greets me.

"*Da*?" I spin Vivian around and pepper her neck with kisses.

"I need to see you." The severity in his tone gives me slight pause. "It's urgent. Can you come to me today?"

"*Da*," I say with no lightness to my tone and hang up.

Looking into Vivian's glossy gaze, I regret having to leave her, I wanted to relish in the sight of her squirming in her wet panties as my cum slowly dried to her ass. Her cheeks are still pink with lust and her lips are swollen from my brutal kisses. I could ravish her for hours. But it'll have to wait. Kazimir wouldn't deem something urgent if it weren't.

"I have to go, angel," I breathe out on her cheek.

She looks up at me with those innocent eyes and nods her head in complete understanding. It isn't easy to tear myself away from her, so I spend a few more minutes kissing her, with plans to come back to see her later.

Rounding up Artem and Bash to go with me to my cousin's, I leave Trip to keep an eye on her.

Kazimir had called me not too many days ago asking for the whereabouts of my father, saying he's been avoiding him. Typically, our fathers met with each other quite often, along with the head of other

Russian families. And again, since the attack on the Kalashnik estate, my father hasn't shown much concern for the personal insult. So, for my father to be avoiding Kazimir in a time like this, it only raises brows.

The sun is just beginning to set as I arrive at the Kalashnik estate. The setup here is much the same as it is with ours. Iron gates, guards scattering the perimeter, the obnoxiously long drive leading up to the ostentatious doors. Where my father made our home look like an emperor lived there with all the gaudy décor, Vladimir Kalashnik made theirs look like a haunted mansion inside.

I'm surprised to see how much the inside has changed when I'm allowed entry. It seems brighter in here. I don't doubt it has everything to do with the woman in Kazimir's life, Marta. She's a beautiful blonde with kind blue eyes that can soften any man in her presence. She's good for my cousin. He deserves her.

My father may have enjoyed taunting me and constantly reminding me of my lower status, but he didn't find pleasure in physically torturing me like Vladimir Kalashnik liked to partake in. My father wasn't as physically cruel, not because he cared about me, but because he knew he would be creating his biggest threat in doing so. Someone who would take the first chance to usurp him. He demands respect from me, not hatred, though I do abhor the vile man.

"Maksim," I say with a smirk when I'm met with Kazimir's righthand man. I don't think there was ever a time in my life when I didn't see him at Kazimir's side. Even when he was a small boy.

Maksim dips his chin in an unflappable manner then turns for me to follow him further inside. "I like what you've done with the place," I muse, as I spot a vase of bright-red roses and shake my head with a smirk. Never did I think I would find flowers in or around this place.

The amusement only swells as I enter Kazimir's office and see the other changes. I look around and release a low chuckle. "Am I in the right place?" I tease my cousin and look around in delight.

"Funny," he grumbles from the chair behind his desk. Always a surly little sod.

I continue to badger him and pluck the framed picture up from his desk and grin. It's a picture of Kazimir, Marta, and Kazimir's son, Grisha. And I'll be damned, he has the hint of a smile on his stony face. "Look at you. A family man," I say, grinning at him.

"Put that shit down," he mutters and snatches the picture from me to put it back in its place, perched on his desk.

"Where is the lovely Marta?" I plop down in a chair.

"She's around." He sighs and leans back in his chair. I swear he went from a sixteen-year-old boy to a forty-year-old man, so many years stolen from him.

"So, what is it you so urgently needed to speak to me about?"

He looks over my shoulder for a moment and I hear the door being shut behind me. He looks directly at me then rests his elbows and clasped hands on his desk. "Your father."

I nod my head, suddenly sobering. "I figured as much." I pause. "Tell me the truth. Do you think he had something to do with the attack on you?"

He doesn't answer nor does he break his stare.

"Accusing my father, your uncle, of treason is bold, Kazimir."

His nostrils flare and I feel a shift in the air as tension quickly rises. "And withholding any information that has to do with the attack on me is foolish," he counters.

Now my nostrils flare and I too am seething. "Are you accusing me of knowing something?" He knows I couldn't betray my father or it would be my head.

He takes an audible breath to tame his temper. "I know I'm putting you in a bad position."

"You are."

"We can help each other, Sasha."

"We can? And what do I need help with?"

"Your father."

"Meaning?"

He sighs and leans back in his chair. I'm still not used to seeing him sitting behind a desk. But it suits him well. "Meaning you could be sitting where I'm sitting." I raise a questioning eyebrow, curious where he is headed with this. "You know…" He gets up and buttons his suit jacket. Heading over to his mini bar, he pulls a bottle of chilled vodka out of the ice box and pours us each a glass.

He hands me one of the glasses and leans back against the edge of his desk. "If your father had something to do with the attempt on my life, I have ample reason to retaliate." He raises his glass and I salute him with mine before tossing back half its contents.

"You do."

"Like Alejandro Martinez had ample reason to retaliate with the Petrofski's and my father." I nod. "He was the one to wipe them out leaving my hands clean. All it took was a little bit of useful information. Something vital enough to be worth loyalty."

I sit forward in my chair, resting my elbows on my thighs. "Do I know where this is headed?" I don't say it outright, but he understands what I'm implying.

"I think you do, Sasha." He pauses. "If you have some useful information for me, I will give you my eternal loyalty. And I can easily orchestrate it so you can have exactly what you want."

The thought of betraying my father and being rid of him is tempting. But if I were to be caught scheming behind his back, the punishment would be worse than any death.

"Do you not understand that your father would betray you just the same?" I look at him, offended. "If you were standing in his way of *anything*, he wouldn't hesitate. He would take you out."

My heckles snap up. "And what is it you think I want?" I snap, paranoid of what he might know about the angel I keep hidden from the world.

"You have to want for something."

I study my cousin wondering what he really knows. Suspecting he might have eyes inside. I realize he's only speculating, assuming there's something I want that my father prevents me from having. Given his personal experience. "If I find you the information you are looking for, you would need to do something for me."

"If you find the information I'm looking for, no matter the outcome, I will owe you. You have my word." He knocks back the rest of his vodka. "It's time for a change, Sasha."

We're all silent in the car as we pull away from the estate, heading for home. No one dares break the silence until we are cleared from the gates and have put some distance between us. "I need you two to do me a favor." Both and Artem and Bash remain silent, waiting for instructions. "I need you to find any information you can on my father's whereabouts leading up to the attack on Kalashnik."

"The attack from the Semenov's?" Artem questions from the passenger seat.

"What other attack would he be referring to?" Bash sasses from behind the wheel.

"Uh, I don't know. Maybe the attack from Alejandro Martinez?" he sasses back.

"That wasn't directly on the Kalashnik's. That was on the Petrofski's for taking his wife, and Vladimir Kalashnik just so happened to be there because he was secretly colluding with them."

I roll my eyes and pinch the bridge of my nose as they continue to bicker like a married couple. They sometimes give me a headache. "I am talking about the recent attack on Kazimir," I raise my voice with exasperation, making them both shut up and listen.

"What kind of information are you looking for?" Bash asks.

"Anything and everything my father was up to before it. Where he's been? Who he spent time with? Any large transactions. You find any leads, you follow them. And I do not want to know anything until you have found what you're looking for."

"And what exactly is that?" Artem asks.

I lock eyes with Bash through the mirror. "My father's possible involvement."

Bash gives me a subtle nod and looks at the road ahead of him. "You got it, sir," Artem verbally confirms his loyalty.

If I find proof of my father's involvement, it would give Kazimir the right to retaliate. And I wouldn't hesitate to take full advantage of it like Kazimir confessed to doing. An opportunity was bestowed upon him. An opportunity to free himself of his father's clutches and make it safe for him to be with his woman.

Snooping around is a perilous risk. It's near impossible to have anything go unnoticed by my father. Kazimir's father was bombastic and almost completely oblivious to his son plotting against him. He thought he was untouchable and that no one would even dare try to take him out. That his son was a silly little boy that feared him, not a powerful man with the means to dispose of him and get away with it.

My father is not only paranoid, but he's overly perceptive. He can sniff out betrayal like a bloodhound. He raised me to be an heir he could be somewhat proud of. Who wouldn't embarrass him or drag the family name and empire through the mud. But I too have the means to usurp him. I'll have to be just as evil and cunning as him to pull it off, and never have I wanted so badly to do so.

If it could make it so that I could have Vivian in the way that I want her, the peril would be worth it.

If we survive.

TWENTY-TWO

SASHA

As I make my way back to my bedroom hours after she fled in tears, I'm being torn at with indecision.

I had made plans with Kazimir, for him to take her in and keep her safe for me. At least, until I found out whether or not my father was involved. If he was, it'll easily set Kazimir up for requital and no one would condemn him for his just actions. But if I find my father's innocence, I will have to let Vivian go either way. Set her free and give her a life she well deserves.

Then the other part of me is unwilling to give her up. She's mine whether she wants to be or not. The tear-filled gaze she gave me will eat me up inside and make me bleed with guilt for years to come, but we'll get past this. She needs to hang on a little while longer for me. I might have to be her monster in the meantime, but one day she'll see the reasoning behind the madness. That I only ever did what I had to do. But until then, I might have to learn to live with being her nightmare.

The selfish part of me wins just as I reach my door. My resolve swayed completely to one side. I will not loosen my grip on her. Vivian is *mine*. I didn't risk everything just to let her go.

I'm shocked yet relieved to see her sitting on the edge of my bed waiting for me. The lights are all off and she's silent. I have the strong urge to pull her into my arms and never let her go, but I'm not sure what good it would do at this point.

"Which way did you come in?" I ask as I loosen my tie and cufflinks. Wearing a suit will never befit me. No matter the position I uphold.

"Your door." Her voice is scratchy, most likely from crying. I'm prepared for her anger, but she sits there, meek and docile. My *kukolka*.

I walk in her direction, slowly pulling more pieces of clothing off as she tries to avoid eye contact. "I don't want to talk." She rubs her arms and my head cants to one side. "I don't need to hear any explanations or—or—excuses or reasoning," she says. "Just don't," she snaps, and her watery eyes bring me to a halt. She's still in her maid's dress, her socks and shoes already kicked off. "Whatever you need to do to me, just do it. I don't need to hear your fictitious words or empty apologies. This is obviously the fate I was dealt, so just carry it out. No more lies," she spits then jumps to her feet with her small fists clenched at her sides.

"No more zeal or—passion. You pretend like you're better than your father, like you don't have a choice, but you and I both know that there is always a choice. *Always*. And you choose to be like him. A disgusting pig. An entitled, Russian—*bastard*." The air rushes from my chest as the rage boils to the surface. No one has ever spoken to me like this.

"I hate you," she hisses, her face turning red with anger. "I hate your touch. I hate your voice. I hate your fucking country. It's ugly and cold, just like its miserable people."

Her bitter words sting, and I have the strong urge to throttle her, make her understand how much I hate the life I was given. That she and I are not so different. She's a servant during the day, and I'm a mobster, but we're both prisoners.

I manage to restrain myself as we both stand there loathsome of everything we have been given, and for everything being taken from us. For neither of us having control over what happens to us and the choices we're forced to make. Because regardless of what she says, I do not have a choice. At least not in the way she thinks.

My forbearance can no longer withstand. Not when the fervent emotions inside of me threaten to liquefy me from the inside out like acid. I lurch forward without warning and have her pinned to the bed with her fragile wrists bound in my grasp above her. She starts thrashing and growling with spitting rage, so I maneuver her wrists into one hand so I can grasp her slender neck with the other.

The hold causes her to still, but the malevolent fire in her gaze is no less scorching. She has no idea how painful it was for me to do what I had to do. To feel her body shaking in authentic fear and to be the one causing it. For letting those bastards see what belongs to me and spoil the intimacy we have shared. It gutted me.

It was either put on a provocative display or smack her around some. The former was my only choice because I would rather die than to ever lay a hand on her like that. She doesn't comprehend all the risks I am taking by sneaking around with her.

"You're upset, but you need to understand what my father is capable of. Anything I care about will be used against me. Not just as a threat, but as a taunt. A vicious reminder of who holds the power. That he can take everything away from me with a snap," I gnarl, fuming. "Anything I have ever loved he has destroyed. If he knows what you mean to me, he'll destroy us both. He'll destroy *you* to destroy *me*." Her face drops and a look of remorse takes over her angelic face. But it does nothing to quell my rage. I only feel deranged more than ever. "What happened back there is *nothing* compared to what he'll do to you if he knows you are of *any* significance to me." Her eyes bounce all over my face. "Please," I say tightly. "Please understand. I tried so fucking hard to avoid this. I swear, I tried to come up with ways to get you as far away from him as possible. I didn't anticipate him wanting to ship you to Russia until it was already too late."

Tears roll down her cheeks in an overabundance and it deteriorates my fucking soul. "Why can't you help me disappear?" Her voice is thick with tears. "Get me to a different country, under a new name. I can dye my hair and—"

I'm shaking my head gravely. "It isn't that easy." I'm not sure if it's smart of me to tell her about the plan yet. "I can't do anything without him knowing. Why do you think he made me do that to you? He was testing me because he already has suspicions. He knows *everything*. He's a despicable man, but he's seemingly omniscient where his business and family are concerned." My hand around her throat squeezes a little more making her eyes widen in fear. "And I'll someday be just like him."

"No," she rasps.

"I will. He won't let me have anything to keep me from turning into a monster like him." I squeeze harder and she begins to flounder under me. "He'll be sure to rip the humanity right out of me. I can feel it. I can feel it being torn from me, Vivian. It'll end with you, I know it. He'll use you to extract the small humanity I have left. Leaving me empty and I'll eventually fill that void with wrath and horror. Never again to be the same man. Hardly a man at all." I expose my most vulnerable fears.

She somehow goes even more still as she stares up at me, fat tears still raining down her reddening face. This look takes over her as if she's fully yielding. Surrendering herself to me. Making peace with the life she now has and trusting me with little hope of some comfort along the way. That she could bring me some kind of peace in return. What she doesn't understand is that if she were taken from me, I will never find peace again. She is my sole serenity.

Releasing her, I back away as she splutters and coughs. I hate myself. Almost as much as I hated myself for the scene I forced her to play out, derogating her integrity and pureness.

She continues coughing and props herself up on her elbows. I have to avert my gaze from the pity-filled look she gives me. The hatred she momentarily had was more bearable because I deserved it. I don't deserve her softness, and I don't need her pity.

"You can go," I say backing away, so she doesn't have to get near me to leave.

"Look at me, Sasha," she says with a scratchy voice making me internally cringe. "Sasha." I can see her sitting up all the way. "Look at me." I slowly turn my head to meet her gaze. Her face is still pink and blotchy from crying and from being deprived of air. Her cheeks are still wet, and the tip of her perfect nose is pink as well. "You're not like him. You'll never be like him."

"You don't know what you're talking about," I murmur.

"Yes, I do." She scoots off the bed, and I swallow hard as she cautiously approaches. "You know how I know? You don't *want* to be like him. You don't *want* to lose your humanity. You realize that it's at stake and you don't want to lose it. Sometimes evil is just born. Sometimes evil is created. And sometimes…" She stops right in front of me looking up. "Someone is stronger. You might feel the evil your father created in you trying to surface, and maybe sometimes it will, but it will never *be you*. I can only imagine what that man has done to you your whole life, and here you are, still *you*. Still hanging on to the humanity inside of you. If you haven't lost it now, what makes you think you will?"

My nostrils flare as I stare down at this angelic creature who was so unfortunate to stand out to me. To be connected to my soul in some fucked up way. "I've never cared so much about something before." I gulp around the throbbing in my throat. "I've come close to breaking, and you might be the thing that finally does it."

She practically jumps forward to close the gap between us. "I don't want to be the thing that breaks you, Sasha. I want to be the thing that makes you stronger than ever. To become utterly unyielding and impossible to pierce."

"You shouldn't want that, Vivian. You shouldn't want anything to do with me. I might not be as heinous and evil, but like you said, that villainy inside of me surfaces, and you seem to be its trigger."

She steps in even closer and reaches up to brush away a lock of my unruly hair. Her touch, so tender and sincere. "Because you care about me." I snatch her wrist up in my hand on its way down. To my surprise she doesn't flinch or wince. As if she expected it.

"I don't know how to care for things." I've avoided it for so long.

"You seem to care about your sister."

"Again." I bring her hand to my mouth and kiss the inside of her wrist. "You don't know what you are talking about. You hardly know me."

"You hardly know me, yet you seem to care an awful lot about me already."

One side of my mouth fights to remain stoic. "Do I?"

"I think so," she whispers.

The tiny amusement I felt promptly drains. "You should go," I say trying to disguise the grievous lie.

"Why?"

I drop her hand. "Why? Maybe because I just violated you in front of a bunch of those fucking shit sucking bastards," I snap vehemently.

"You had to." She crosses her arms to hug herself. "I blamed you for it at first because I was hurt. But I now see that you didn't have much of a choice."

"Why are you doing this?" I demand. "Are you that stupid? Do you hate yourself that much?"

She looks at me indignantly and drops her arms to clench her fists at her sides. "Maybe I am stupid, but at least I'm not stupid enough to push away a good thing."

I chuckle and shake my head looking at her incredulously. "A good thing? Did you listen to anything I just said? All the warnings I have been giving you? And again, what I fucking did to you out there?" I throw my arm out gesturing towards the door.

She steps forward and goes to place her hand on my chest, but I angrily swat it away and step back. Her fists clench again, and her lips thin as she advances and tries again. When her hand flattens over my chest where my heart should be beating, I stop and this time I don't push her hand away. Her touch instantly taming me. She reaches to place my hand over her own heart where I can feel it rapidly beating.

"Maybe I am stupid and maybe I am a glutton for disaster and pain, but in here it feels good. When you touch me, not only does my body respond, but everything inside me does too. I should be afraid of you. I should be angry, hateful, and repulsed, but the man you have shown me glimpses of has a stronger pull. A pull right here." She presses her hand against mine still resting over her heart. "It's worth letting you take pieces of me to help keep you whole."

Cupping the back of her neck, I bring our foreheads together. "My angel," I rasp. "I promise you will not have to endure this much longer," I whisper as I bring my lips to hers.

Showing her my gratitude for being my Godsent angel.

TWENTY-THREE

VIVIAN

My arms loop around his neck and I'm kissing him as deeply as he kisses me. If I have to sacrifice pieces of myself to save him, then so be it. This place is bound to be where I meet my end. Might as well gift him the parts of me not yet broken. I've learned to live with cracks and fractures, and I can continue for a while longer. His goes beyond minor wounds and breaks. He's already in pieces and barely hanging on. I have enough to give him to make sure that he doesn't crumble. I'm not ignorant enough to know that there will only be one of us who survives this. And it won't be me.

My desperation matches his hunger as he backs us up to the bed and we go tumbling down. We're fumbling with our hands trying to remove our clothing, impatience and passion driving us both mad.

I have no idea how our clothes are completely removed without having to take a breath from each other, but we're finally skin to skin. His body hot against mine. His cock is long and hard as he rocks his hips and butts against my heat. The ardor in his kisses never let up and all I can think about is him moving inside of me and the slight pain it brings me.

His cock begins penetrating me and I almost lose my head and welcome him, but I seem to possess some kind of cognizant thinking. "Sasha." He kisses my cheek and then nips at my neck. "We need a condom, remember? I'm not on birth control." I throw my head back and moan when he inches his way inside of me. "Sasha," I whine, my body totally betraying my head as it arches, offering every part of myself up to him.

He rains down kisses all over my face and neck until he makes his way to my breasts as his body continues undulating on top of mine. Inch by slow inch inside of me. He mutters something in Russian and then smiles as if remembering that I don't understand him. "I'll pull out, angel."

My body makes the decision to acquiesce and continues writhing, and when my mouth opens, only gasps and moans escape.

My legs wrap around his hips, begging him to fully plunder me. He obliges and sharply jerks his hips forward to sheath himself with my heat. I gasp and he attaches his mouth to mine again. Swallowing up my sounds and moving with more precision on top of me. His entire massive body covering mine, and my body rocks slightly with his.

He breaks away to mutter Russian against the skin on my cheek and then he buries his face into my hair. My hands are all over the taut muscles on his back and the black ink on his skin. My hands brush over raised skin from the scars he has scattered, and I have the urge to dig my nails into them. Reopening them and claiming them.

I demanded some kind of elucidation for everything he's doing for me. I didn't expect him to openly admit that he cares about me. I don't know what I expected, but it wasn't that. It had me handing over my absolution instantly.

His father is the villain here. Sasha is just as much a victim in all this as me. I know there's danger lurking under the surface with this broken man, but maybe I can somehow be something to mitigate it. I'll absorb it from him and replace it with empathy. Restore the goodness inside of him that his father tries to extract.

The fire he has stoked inside of me turns into hot lava. He pushes me to that place that still kind of scares me. He's told me to tell him what I want, but I am still unsure of what it is that I need.

His motions begin to quicken and intensify, and I know I'm close to that amazing carnal sensation that only he can unleash from me.

"You were made for me, *kukolka*. Right here." His words are choppy and breathy as he rasps them against the side of my neck. "Mine."

"Yes," I rasp. "More, Sasha. More."

My fingers rake through his hair, and I pull his head to get his lips back to mine. I inhale deeply when they meet and moan when our tongues touch. My body arches into his, needing him somehow closer.

Sasha growls and chomps down on my lip. I yelp and I'm a little stunned by it, but when he kisses me deeper and I taste blood inside my mouth, my nipples tingle and my pussy pulsates.

He grips both ass cheeks, squeezing them roughly and spreading them wide. He rams into me, jolting my body and hitting me deep.

"Sasha," I whine his name and pant as I feel the scorching heat making its way towards the center of my core to explode. He so easily has me combusting, but this build-up is being drawn out, and I can't hold on much longer.

"Yes, my angel." He grunts and thrusts harder and faster. Reaching between us he pinches my nipple and I cry out as my orgasm hits me. My head cranked back and when he sucks hard on my other nipple, it augments my climax making it last forever.

He pulls out and I think he's going to come on me, but he rolls me with him so I'm now on top. He gives my ass a good smack and grins. "You're going to come sit on my face." My eyes widen in excitement and apprehension. "You're going to fuck my face until you come again." He gives my ass another harsh swat when I hesitate. "Now, *kukolka.*"

I get my ass in gear and crawl up his body and go to straddle his face. He tsks and twirls his finger around, silently telling me to turn and face the other way. The thought of my ass being so close to his face is slightly disturbing, but the thought of rubbing my pussy on his face until I come has me turning around and straddling his head.

I almost gasp at the sight of him stroking himself. The way his strong hand moves up and down his hard length, pleasuring himself while I'm sitting on his face.

He spreads my cheeks and uses the grip to force me to sit. When his tongue darts out and he licks me, my hips react on instinct. I moan and rub myself on him. He has a slight stubble rubbing and scratching me. It'll leave my skin raw and pink. The thought has me grinding on him with more pressure. He groans against me making me twitch and I gawk at his hand still moving up and down his cock. Watching him touch himself, I'm now so close to coming again.

Planting my hands flat on his defined abs, I roll my hips letting him taste and devour every inch on my pussy. Not once taking my eyes off his cock. My breath hitches when I begin riding upwards, and his hand speeds up on his cock. I'm eager to see him explode. I can't come until he does.

Groaning and biting my tender bottom lip, I grind harder, and he strokes himself faster. "I need you to come, Sasha," I whine.

Grunting under me, he speeds up more and I watch in amazement as white fluid starts spurting from him. My orgasm detonates, rupturing and shattering me to pieces. His hand on his cock stops and he grabs a hold of my breasts with both hands. The hand that was covered in cum smears it all over, making me a sticky hot mess. My hips become immobile so he makes sure to prolong it with licking and sucking until I can't do it anymore.

I collapse over to the side and roll to my back. I can smell him on me as I breathe heavily, trying to regulate my heartbeat. I'm sticky with cum, and so is he, but I am too dazed to care.

Sitting up, I crawl over and wrap my arms around him tightly for a searing embrace. He stills against me for just a second then slides his arms around my body to hug me back. Our faces buried into each other's neck and our limbs entangled. Torpid, content, dirty.

I've never been in love before. I've had crushes, but nothing like this. Nothing that made me feel more than tolerable or less like a pest for existing. Maybe it's because Sasha is the first person in my life to show me care and affection, or because of the situation I'm in. All I know is that I've never felt so safe with someone before. Like I might have a place in this world. Like maybe my life is worth something.

He grunts and sits up with me, then scoops me up into his strong arms effortlessly.

"What are we doing?"

"Taking a shower," he murmurs with his eyes forward as he carries me bridal style.

My cheeks burn with abashment and I'm suddenly feeling shy. He's literally seen every part of me, but something about getting in the shower with him feels so much more intimate.

I try to conquer my nerves and concentrate on the protective hold he has on me, and the arousing smell coming off his chest. I watch the tense look on his face, studying his handsome features. Even though his muscles are hard, his fingers are calloused, and he has gold crowns on some of his teeth, his face is smooth and blemish free.

He catches me watching him and I dart my eyes downwards. His gaze too intense at this distance.

His bathroom is obviously lavish and several times bigger than mine. One that I thought I would be sharing with someone else since it has another door to it. "Can I ask you something?"

He sets me down to my feet and leans into the extravagant glass enclosed shower to turn the water on. "Hm?"

"Did you purposely put me in that room? The one with the secret passage and no one to share the bathroom with?"

He snorts and tugs my hand to pull me into the shower with him. "No. Just lucky," he says with sarcasm.

I narrow my eyes up at him. "Liar."

Suddenly, I'm aware of my vulnerability. No longer cloaked in darkness or tangled up in the sheets. He can see all of me, and I can see all of him. His body is impeccable. The scars only add to his painful beauty and the tattoos he has match the bad boy persona. Never thought I would be so attracted to his type. But I am.

"You keep looking at me like that, *kukolka*, and I might have to do something about it," he says darkly, but there's playfulness inside of his words and his eyes twinkle with delight. Eyes that show little slivers of gold in their dark orbs.

"Are you ever going to tell me what that means?"

Amusement is still adorned on his handsome face. "I'll let you sit on it for a little while longer," he teases, then comes at me with a soapy loofah.

I smile up at him and he glances down at my lips as the suds get massaged over my backside. "Can I ask you something else?" He arches both eyebrows. "And you actually answer it? Truthfully?"

"I make no promises." His accent is usually intimidating, but right now I find it cute.

"My undergarments. Did you have anything to do with them? Or do all the maids have ones like mine?"

One side of his mouth tilts up and he moves the suds to the front of my body. "I may have had something to do with that." He's once again being evasive. I'm sure opening up isn't exactly second nature for him.

He's so tender and nurturing as he washes me from head to toe. I'm going to smell like him until the next time I shower and something about that gives me a sense of comfort. It'll feel like he's with me even when he's not.

I step back into the water to rinse off as he begins washing himself and I watch his hand making circular motions all over his defined muscles leaving a soapy trail. When he washes his groin, I stare in fascination at how it's growing larger by the second. That too I haven't really seen like this. On display in all its glory.

"What did I tell you about staring, *kukolka*?" His gravelly voice makes me look up at him as I run my hands through my hair. The threatening look in his eyes has tendrils of heated chills running down my body. His eyes dart down to my chest, I'm sure because my nipples are now taut.

I gulp when he steps back under his own sprayer, eyes on me, and starts washing his hair. The muscles in his biceps flexing and his abs stretched and sculpted. He's the sexiest thing I have seen in my life. How many women has he gotten looking the way he does? Did he look at them all with the hunger he has in his eyes now?

His lips curl up into a sinful grin and he leaves his sprayer to come join me in mine. His body now flush with mine and his erection stabbing me in my stomach. "How old are you?" I blurt out of nowhere, but a question I've wanted to ask him for a while now.

He snorts and bends his head down to kiss my neck. My hands grip his biceps as my head falls back. "I'll be thirty-two soon," he murmurs. Pretty close to what I had assumed. I knew he was younger than he seemed.

He continues caressing my neck and jawline with his lips and tongue. "Now, it's my turn to ask you something." I'm quiet as I wait. "Why were you a virgin?" He doesn't pause to wait for my answer, and I have to close my eyes to focus on the conversation.

I was hoping this subject would never be brought up. "I don't know." I go with the same non-answer I gave him last time.

He starts coercing me with his body until my back is pressed against the cold tiles. "You'll give me a better answer than that, little cat." His fingers snake down my belly making the muscles twitch and then slide in through my wet folds. "Tell me. Why have you held out on so many men?"

"What makes you think there were so many men?" I pant as he languidly strokes me.

"Because you're beautiful," he says so casually and then dips a finger inside of me, stealing the very breath right out of my lungs. "And sexy." His hand fists my hair to crane my neck back and he kisses my throat. "So fucking sexy," he rasps heavily. "And so goddamn angelic."

Between his touch and compliments, I can't find it in me to lie to him. "I had…some things happen to me when I was younger," I say quietly. "It took me a while to be…comfortable being touched."

His fingers and lips still, but his fist in my hair tightens, stinging my scalp. Slowly, he pulls back only enough to be able to look me in the eye.

"Who," he quips, his jaw tense making his cheekbones look more prominent.

"Who what?" I wince from my scalp burning.

His nostrils flare. "Who. Touched. You."

"It was a long time ago, Sasha," I rush out, praying we can drop this.

"Give me a name."

"There's no name to give." I swallow hard as I feel the tension emanating from him. "It was a long time ago," I press.

"Tell me who touched you when you were a child."

I want to ask why he cares so much just to be petulant, but I stop myself. "I don't remember his name," I whisper, suddenly feeling self-conscious. If he knew how many men touched me, and how far it went, he'll look at me differently. Like he already is now. "My mother dated some sketchy guys." I pause and he doesn't let up. "There was always a new one."

"There was more than one?" His voice rumbles with deathly low cadence. He even looks like he's growing in size as the power sizzles around him. "If you don't give me names, Vivian, then I will get them from your mother," he menaces.

My eyes widen in panic as I look up at him. "What? No! Don't you dare go near her!"

"Why do you care? She brought child molesters home!" he roars right in my face making me recoil. The tight grasp on my hair releases and my eyes dart down to the floor in shame as I start trembling, wishing to be anywhere but here. Why did I have to open my mouth? I could've made something up. Anything.

I hear him take a deep breath in then feel his breath against my face when he releases it. "Vivian," he says softer but there's still tightness in his voice. "I didn't mean to yell." He tilts my chin up and I find him frowning in concern. "You will give me some names though. Or I will find them myself."

"I honestly don't know, Sasha. I was young and there were many men that were in and out of my mother's life." *Or bed.* "It was a long time ago and I've moved on. Please." I look at him pleading. "Don't make me rehash old wounds. They've long since healed." They may have left scars, but they're mended and forgotten about. It's taken me years to stomach being touched by anyone, but with his help, I feel the last of my wounds healing and I'm finally coming to terms with my abuse.

"Sasha." I reach up and cup his cheek with one hand. His jaw like granite and stone. "Please, let it go."

"For tonight." Then he slants his mouth over mine and his fingers move between my legs once again.

TWENTY-FOUR

I have no idea how much time has passed when he carries me out of the bathroom. He brought me to an earth-shattering orgasm then he kept me pinned against the wall as he kissed me until my lips were raw. In between kisses, he kept whispering words in Russian that I so badly wanted to understand.

"Can I ask you for something?" I ask as he lays me down in his bed like I'm made of porcelain.

"Hm." He pulls the covers over me.

"Would you get me a book to help me learn Russian? I'll hide it under my mattress or something."

He doesn't answer as he rounds the bed to the other side then drops his towel to climb in with me. I don't hesitate to ogle his manliness first though. "I can do that."

I smile and turn over to my side to face him. But he has other plans as he slides an arm under my body and pulls me into his side. I try to keep the goofy grin off my face as I snuggle up to him. This is new for us. For me, really. Only a couple of times we've fallen asleep together and we were still partially embraced from having sex. This cuddling is intentional. He sought me out, bringing our bodies close together.

His heart is beating at a steady pace as I rest my ear over it. His hard chest rising and falling with mine. I've never felt so cherished before. To think that Sasha Rogov, son of the scariest man ever, is the one to foster such warm feelings inside of me. To help allay the painful scars of my tragic past.

I let out a yawn and begin to struggle to keep my eyes open. So many questions on my mind, but they'll have to wait. I'm drained.

"When I was four, I found a dog running loose in the dead of winter."

I'm suddenly wide awake at the start of this conversation. Startled by his words. "Not too far from here. I could still see the estate." He takes a breath, but I hold mine, afraid to make a sound. "It was below freezing with over a foot of snow. The dog did not even hesitate to come to me, seeking solace from a complete stranger. The way he pleaded with me with his eyes. As if he really had emotions like we do. So, I did what most normal children would do. I took him home with me.

"Even at a young age, I knew how cruel my father truly was. Evil at his core. I knew he would not let me keep the dog, and he would hurt it in some way. So, I tried hiding him on the other side of the estate until I could get one of the maids or servants or even one of my father's men to help me figure out what to do with it. Everyone was too terrified of my father to help me.

"He, of course, found out about the dog. He always does." His voice is vacant of emotion.

"What did he do?" I whisper in the dark. Knowing whatever it is he's about to tell me will leave my gut churning.

"He tortured it." He pauses. "In front of me." I think he's going to leave it at that, but he gives me the story in detail. "His men beat on him and kicked him around as my father physically made me watch." I squeeze my eyes shut fighting back the agonizing tears, and silently beg for him to stop. "Then he finished him off by prying his mouth open until he broke his jaw, and the dog finally went limp," he says as flatly as he started.

I lose the battle and tears leak down my cheeks and onto his chest. "I'm so sorry," I say in a shaky voice. He was just a little boy. My heart weeps for the blonde-haired child whose innocence was crushed so early on. My arm tightens around his midsection, but I don't look up.

"From then on, I knew I would not be allowed to care for anything. Grow attached to anything. Enjoy anything. He's always searching for a weakness from me that he could use."

I press my lips to his chest, tasting my tears there. "So, you really haven't ever loved someone? Had a girlfriend?"

"A couple years later, when I was eight, I made a friend at school. Up until then I had kept to myself. Not only did *I* know I was different from the rest of the kids there, but *they* knew it too. They were afraid of me. Until Brita."

I peek up at him through my wet lashes and find him staring up at the ceiling. His face matching the tone in his voice. Empty.

"I figured she was clueless as to who I was. So, I tried scaring her off by embodying the young mobster I was labeled as." He snorts, as if reliving those memories. "It didn't work. And she *did* know who I was. She said she didn't care." Of course, my mind goes to the worst place possible, conjuring up gruesome conclusions for this story. "I thought that maybe if we were only friends at school, she would be safe. How could my father possibly know who I talked to at school?" My arm tightens around him again as I bury my face into his chest, bracing myself for what's to come.

"I don't know what I was thinking that day when I mouthed off to him. I guess I was overly confident, thinking I had nothing he could take away from me. That he could only threaten me and my own well-being. And my confidence only grew when Brita was still at school over the next week." He pauses. "Until she wasn't. She didn't show up for three days before I asked the teacher where she was. All she told me was that she wouldn't be coming back."

"What happened to her?" I whisper around the mournful mass built up in my throat.

"I don't know." I look up at him again. "I never asked my father about her. I didn't want to give him the satisfaction of confirming that I cared. I will always be inferior to him, until I rightfully become his successor."

"What do you mean by that? Rightfully?"

"Until he dies."

"And do you want to? To continue this life?"

"It's not a choice."

"If he's gone, how so? Who would make you?"

"It's not something you could understand." The sternness in his tone makes me drop it and change the subject.

"What about your sisters?"

He doesn't answer right away and I'm nervous that I may have overstepped, or that sharing time is over. "Rada, Vera, and I all have different mothers. I was born first and brought here to live at the estate to grow up. I don't know who my mother was, and I know it's best to leave it that way."

My heart somehow breaks even more for him. I may not have much attachment for my own mother, and she was a pitiful excuse for one, but I do know that most mothers are good. That they love their children unconditionally. I wonder if his mother fought for him. What if his father had her killed? No wonder he doesn't even want to know who she is or was.

"I was ten when I had found out that I had two sisters living in the city. I had overheard my father talking with another family, bragging about not financially supporting them regardless of if they're even his. I didn't dare ask my father about them, and knew I had to find out myself."

"How did you find out?"

"It wasn't easy. I was constantly being watched and the internet wasn't like it is now. But I eventually found them." His hand that has been resting on the curve of my waist begins making a leisurely trail up and down my side, leaving goosebumps in its wake. "They were very young, and I didn't intend on ever approaching them."

"What made you change your mind?"

"Watching their mothers struggle to provide for them. I sat back for two years before I was determined to do something."

"What did you do?"

"I began setting aside any money I could get my hands on. It wasn't difficult. Money was handed over to me whenever I asked for it and I knew where some stashes were. It was risky, but I was building more authority within the estate. It took a year to build up a large enough sum for each woman, but when I felt like it was enough to help, I took it to them."

"What happened when you took it to them?"

A smirk creeps up on his face and he tilts his head down to look at me. Amused at my curiosity. "I knocked on their door and handed over the money. They of course were skeptical and demanded to know who I was and where the money came from. They wouldn't accept it right away. I had to assure them my father was unaware of it. That this was my doing and all I wanted to do was help." He keeps his hand moving. "Rada's mother remained apprehensive but thanked me and closed the door. Vera's mother took the money and told me to never come back and to stay away from her daughter." He grins then faces up to the ceiling again. "After I came back a year later with more money, and the fact that no one had bothered her in that time, she was little less skittish, but still asked me to stay away from Vera. It took quite a few years for me to ever meet her."

"Did they know about each other? Rada and Vera?"

"Not until after I told their mothers. Thought they could find some solace in each other."

"What about Rada? You seem close with her."

"It wasn't until the next year when I was making the annual drop off to them, that she said I could meet Rada. She was almost nine years old at the time when I finally got to meet her. I knew better than to stay long or visit often. Rada's mother, Yelena, understood very well."

"But your father eventually found out."

He stares down at me for a while before answering. His hand never stopping the soothing motions up and down my body. "I decided to go to him. I was sixteen and I knew he would eventually find out. So, it was either I be a man and tell him that I know I have two sisters, or I completely cut ties with them."

"So, what happened?" Obviously, this isn't a story that ends tragically since he still has a relationship with them.

He smirks. "I'll give you the happy ending, *kukolka*." He removes the arm tucked behind his head to brush my cheek with the back of his knuckles. "I was allowed to see them."

"But why did he bring you to the estate to grow up as his child but not them?"

"Isn't it obvious?" He arches one eyebrow.

"Oh. Because he wanted a son, not daughters." He nods once. "Why doesn't he use your sisters against you though?" I know it has nothing to do with his father having any kind of empathy.

"He will eventually. Which is why I stay," he says quietly, his voice far off.

I stare up at his profile and break for the man he truly is inside. The one with compassion and once a child desperate for the real love of a family. I was already trying to evade the burgeoning feelings for him, but now since he has cracked himself wide open for me, I know I am now falling for him. The fall will be catastrophic and leave me fatally wounded, my heart bleeding out, but what if somehow there's a slim chance we can turn this nightmare into a fairytale?

Before I can talk myself out of it, I sit up and climb over top of him to straddle his hips. I have no idea what I'm doing, so I just listen to my body and go with it. He stares up at me with apprehension, but not rejection, his hands already flexing on my hips. Leaning down, I press my lips against his. He responds instantly and my hips roll on instinct. My pussy rubs against his cock, hardening underneath me. I'm already slick and I easily glide over his length. His hands are all over me. Rubbing up and down my body and tangling up in my hair.

I continue to do whatever feels natural and he encourages me to keep going. I've never felt so brave and bold in my life as I reach behind me and wrap my fingers around his thickness and lift myself over it. We're still kissing as I slowly sink down until I'm fully seated. It makes me quiver and pant against his mouth. I somehow feel more full from this angle.

His hand in my hair and his other on my hip both fist, encouraging me to move. I've seen this in movies and on tv, but it's my body that tells me exactly what to do here.

I rise up to my knees, breaking our kiss to stare down at him, and slowly impale myself. He stares back at me with pure interest, his eyes barely fluttering as I repeat the motion over and over. Again, my body guides me, and my hips start to roll so that I can rub myself against him as I ride.

Moaning, I pick up the pace and at this point I feel like I'm just trying to please myself. Desperately chasing that euphoric high, using his body to give it to me. The sound of our skin slapping together spurs me on, and I can feel myself getting close.

Pulling back some, I plant my hands on his chest and throw my head back. So lost inside the sensuous utopia that I wish would never burst like a bubble. His hands squeeze my hips as he helps slam me back down each time. My breasts feel so heavy, and my core has a hot pulse throbbing around his cock.

I tilt my head down and look at him through hooded eyes and I almost come to a complete stop. The way he's gazing at me as if he's in total wonderment, that pull on my heart is stronger than ever.

My mouth falls open on a silent cry and he abruptly sits up to swallow it. My pussy constricts around him, and I ride it out in haphazardly movements. Once my body goes limp, he flips us over in a flash and starts moving inside of me to roll the post-orgasm into another one. It's almost too much to handle as I squirm and whine under him. He isn't having it though. He pins my arms up over my head and the rest of his body weighs me down so he can fuck me harder.

As soon as my jaw is unhinged with a silent cry, he pulls out to rub the soft skin of his cock against my wetness, augmenting my climax until I can't breathe. I can feel his own wetness jetting all over me and still I can't move one muscle. I feel like I am flying, lost in space as darkness creeps around the edges of my vision.

The crash is brutal as I shudder against him and whimper. I'm completely drained, my eyes unable to stay open. Not at all cognizant of when his body abandons mine before he's back with a warm washcloth to clean me up. I just lay there, lifeless. My heart beating and my lungs sucking in air desperately, but everything else is limp.

I faintly hear him chuckle as he pulls me into his arms and covers us with the blankets. I'm too drowsy to be at all embarrassed of my boldness and just press myself into his side.

"I need you to promise me something," he says after a moment.

"Hm?" is all I can manage. My eyes already shut and my body already succumbing to rest.

"I need you to be strong for me." He pauses. "I have a plan to get you out of this."

His words create a small burst of energy inside of me and I'm able to open my eyes and move my head to look up at him. "You do?" He nods but doesn't look at me. His focus is on the ceiling. "What are you going to do?"

"It's best you don't know, *kukolka*." He looks down at me and stares for a drawn-out moment. Then he brushes his fingertips down the bridge of my nose then my cheek. "But I need you to be resilient. You cannot let him break you. Promise me." I nod my head, not sure that I can, but I promise to try. For him. "Everything outside of this bedroom is just a game being played. By everyone. You either become a player, or you'll end up being played. You understand me?" I nod my head then close my eyes when he leans down to place the sweetest kiss on my forehead.

Settling back in comfortably in his side, I'm out like a light.

TWENTY-FIVE

VIVIAN

When I awoke the next morning, he was still there holding me close. I was afraid to move and wake him up and end the moment, wanting so badly to see him sleeping.

Something about people sleeping is such a testament to how human we all are. That at one point or another in our lives, we were all innocent and pure. Then life molds us into the human beings we become, and no matter how much turbulence and upheaval a person might face, at the end of the day, we're able to shut down and enjoy a little bit of peace.

Just as I thought, when I tilted my face up to look at him, I only got to see him peacefully sleeping for a moment before he stirred. It was still early, so he pulled me into the shower with him before sending me back to my room.

"You look good," Nastia says from beside me as we're prepping some food in the kitchen. I look over at her and she makes a circle around her face smiling. "Good," she repeats.

I bite back a grin and shrug. Then I remember what I have been wanting to ask her. "Hey, Nastia. What is *kukolka*?" I know I chop up the word, but I hope it's comprehendible enough. She frowns, so I repeat the word more slowly this time.

Her face lights up. "Ah, *kukolka*." I nod my head eagerly. "It is a…" She thinks of the right word. "A doll."

"A doll?"

She nods her head smiling. "Yes, a little doll."

"*Kukolka* means a 'little doll'?"

She nods again and thankfully doesn't ask me where I heard it from. To my knowledge, no one knows about Sasha and I. Well, other than Greta who most likely suspects it, between the fulfilling meals I get three times a day and the fact that I somehow evade being anywhere near Mr. Rogov. And probably the three men that Sasha briefly introduced to me.

Just then, Greta herself walks into the kitchen and calls everyone's attention. She speaks only in Russian, and I roll my eyes and ignore her as I continue to work. Sasha didn't forget about my tiny request and had Bash deliver a few books to me to help me learn Russian. I'm working on the alphabet first, and it isn't easy.

Greta ends her speech, and everyone seems to go right back to work. Whatever it is, she'll have to come and tell me herself, otherwise, I'm left in the dark and I could care less. I just do as I'm told around here anyways.

I see her coming my way out of the corner of my eye before she stops right next to me. Wiping my hands on my apron, I face her. "Mr. Rogov is entertaining tonight. Everyone is working." I give her a silent head nod remembering how it went last time and for once I see a flash of pity in her eyes like she's remembering it too. I go to turn back to my work and her hand covers the back of mine. I almost snatch my hand away out of shock. "I will try to keep you out of the room the best I can," she says for only me to hear and my eyebrows flinch in surprise with her sudden warmth towards me. "But I cannot make any promises." I give her an imperceptible nod wanting to voice my gratitude, but she spins on her heels and promptly leaves the room before I get the chance.

The day drags on and I'm constantly jumping at every noise, hoping it's Sasha coming to tell me that I won't have to worry about tonight being anything like the other night. But like the past several days, he's been scarce. I know he told me I could use the passageway to his room, but I'm afraid to use it at the wrong time and get caught. I have to trust him though. He says he has a plan to get me out of here, and that it's better if I don't know what's going on, but what I failed to ask is if it meant never seeing him again.

The thought of leaving him and starting a new life, one in which he does not exist, it's gut-wrenching. Almost as much as it is to think about spending the rest of my life like this. In a maid's uniform, a prisoner, my future unclear, always looking over my shoulder.

Would Sasha come with me if I begged him?

No. His life is here. He made that clear. Even without the threat of his father, he was adamant about his life being this. That it's something I wouldn't understand.

Greta put me on cleaning duties, getting all the guest rooms spotless. When it's time to clean Sasha's bedroom, I'm eager to see if he's here or not. To my disappointment, his room is vacant. In fact, it looks like no one has been here for days. The bed, perfectly made, no watermarks in the bathroom sink or even the shower. There aren't even any dirty clothes in his hamper to be washed.

My hackles are suddenly up, and my chest hurts with panic. What if something happened to him? What if his father knew he was planning something, and I don't know...killed him? No, he wouldn't do that, right?

He's his only son, meaning his only heir. He would find some way to punish him, not kill him. What if he sent him back to Las Vegas? No, he would tell me, wouldn't he? Unless he didn't have time to, or it would be too risky.

Until I find out if he's okay or not, it's going to be all I obsess over. If he isn't here tonight for whatever Mr. Rogov has planned, the obsession and concern will drive me mad. I can't ask anyone without raising suspicion, and the men that are supposedly around to keep an eye on me are never in view. Making me doubt if they're even there or not.

Everyone is running around preparing for tonight's entertainment. I'm just keeping my head down doing as I'm told but I'm on the lookout for any sign of Sasha.

I'm placed in the kitchen to help with food preparations. I'm becoming more concerned when a few hours pass and there's still no sign of Sasha. From what Nastia tells me, one of the large entertainment rooms has pretty much turned into a nightclub. I'm curious as to what she means by that, but not enough to go and take a look for myself. Though, Sasha's whereabouts and well-being might have me walking by to take a peek. No, that's foolish of me to even think about doing. Going anywhere near there would risk me being shoved into the room and forced to participate in whatever debauchery they have going on inside.

I'm finishing up some of the dishes when someone comes and shoves a tray of fancy finger foods at me and tells me to go. Flashbacks of last time have me shaking my head frantically and looking around the room for Greta to intervene, but she's nowhere to be seen. *Again.* "I, uh—"

"Go," the cook orders sternly and shoos me away. He turns his back as if expecting me to obey and I don't really think I have a choice in the matter. No one is free to replace me at the moment. Even if there were, what would I say to get myself out of this? To them, I am no one of importance and not entitled to any special treatment.

A massive lump forms in my throat as I walk towards the exit of the kitchen on shaky legs. I'll linger outside of the room, waiting for another maid to come out so I can hand over the tray and never enter the room at all.

What I didn't anticipate was the party being held in an open area of the estate. No doorways to creep behind and nothing concealing my presence. I see exactly what Nastia was trying to convey when she said it looked like a nightclub. What she failed to mention is what kind of nightclub. You have naked women dancing on small platforms and some swinging around poles. Like the other night, there are women giving out sexual favors for men, and fucking everywhere. Tables are set up for gambling and the vulgar smell of it all is suffocating.

I know I need to hightail it out of here. To spin on my heels and wait out in the hall for someone to hand the tray over to, but the need to allay my fears has me scouring the room extensively for Sasha. My eyes land on Greta first and she's giving me a panicked yet partially confused look. Lowering my eyes to the floor, I quickly make my way over to her. "They made me," I whisper, and she accepts the tray from me, giving me a subtle head nod.

Spinning on the balls of my feet, I start making my way back to the exit when I feel a familiar heavy gaze on me that has me glancing up in one direction. When I do, I automatically feel desolate and pained. Staring back at me is Sasha, but it's not at all my Sasha. It's the profane version of him that is abhorrent and wanes those fuzzy and longing feelings I have for him.

It doesn't matter that he warned about the games always being played, and that everything outside of his bedroom is an act. Witnessing him with a naked woman perched on one thigh while another is pressed against his side, sucking on his neck, tears my gut to shreds. He doesn't even have the decency to show any remorse as he holds me prisoner with his eyes and gropes the woman's breast. His lips curl into a conniving smirk and I watch in slow motion as he turns his head to smash his mouth against the woman sucking on his neck. My heart plummets and I feel bile burning my throat.

I don't need to see anymore. I don't need to find out how far he takes it. He made his point. To me or to whomever was watching, I'm not sure. He asked me to promise him to be strong, but how can I when he is the one trying to break me?

My heart and head are at war with one another, anger and vengeance verses heartbreak and despondency as I pathetically stare at the hidden door in my room for hours, waiting for him to burst through and grovel. Reassure me none of that was real. But he never comes.

I'm left alone to my own incessant thoughts and heartache.

TWENTY-SIX

VIVIAN

Sasha has been the only thing making me want to wake up alive the next morning. Even when I was angry with him, he still gave me something else to feel other than depression and self-loathing.

Days went by and he never sought me out. Without him near, I've let my rage make me feel stronger, now feeling cross and vengeful. Ready to take on any of these Russians if I have to. To annihilate the Rogov's and their devoted guard dogs. I know that when I am of no use to these assholes anymore, they'll dispose of me like yesterday's trash. I feel as if Sasha already has.

If there is no escape for me other than death, then might as well decide when I get to go and take a few with me when I do.

I'm busy cleaning up one of the sitting rooms thinking about how I could get a hold of a gun to take out Mr. Rogov before being shot down when I feel that tingly presence hovering nearby. A million thoughts run through my head, but I decide to just ignore him, like he's done to me for the past few days.

He stands stoically near my only exit as I suppress the invective festering and boiling inside of me. So many words of hate I want to throw at him and maybe even give him one good smack across the cheek. To play with me like he does. To bedevil me and fill my head with hopeful lies. The games aren't worth it. The pain he's able to inflict on me outweighs everything.

I finish up what I'm doing and hold my head high as I go to leave the room. As predicted, he stops me. Gripping my upper arm tightly. "It's best you hate me, *kukolka*."

"First of all, I am not your 'little doll.' And second…" I rip my arm from his grasp. "I do hate you. So, mission accomplished. Now, if you'll excuse me," I say with a sardonic smile and bat my eyelashes dramatically at him. "I have more chores to do before I am sent back to my little prison cell where I will surely go mad and either kill myself or do something stupid enough to get myself killed and hopefully take a few of you with me." I keep the bitter smile on my face as he sneers at me and takes hold of my upper arm once again. This time with a bone-crushing grip. He's practically frothing at the mouth with unfettered wrath. "Unless there's something I can do for you, *Mr. Rogov?*" I'm now baiting him, but it serves him right. He's lucky I have a firm leash on my temperance at the moment.

A murky aura invades our space, and a darkened cloud rolls in over our heads. An ominous look takes over his face, and he puts himself right in front of me. Using his size and girth to intimidate me.

"You lied to me," he spits through his clenched teeth.

I literally jerk my head back in bafflement. "Lied to you? About what?"

He opens his mouth to say something, but he's cut off by the devil himself. The rage instantly drains from me, and I find myself leaning into him for protection now that his father is in the same room as us.

Sasha's nostrils flare and his hold doesn't loosen as his father speaks to him, keeping it in Russian so that I am left oblivious to what is being said. Whatever his father tells him, Sasha's body coils thoroughly and I stifle a cry in pain as his fingers flex around my arm even more.

I don't look at Mr. Rogov, but I can hear amusement and mocking in his tone when he says something else, and it makes Sasha's eyes widen in scornful fury. My eyes widen back in fear then his head snaps in his father's direction and he spews Russian at him. I'm still not looking at his father, but I feel the tension cackling through the air, and I wish I could curl into a fetal position.

Sasha speaks again, this time with less animosity and his father chuckles lowly in response. I swear if the devil was capable of laughter, it would sound like that. Everything about the man rattles me and makes me sick to my stomach with disgust and animosity.

Sasha turns his face back to mine, his pupils dilated making his eyes look black. He grumbles something else in Russian which causes his father to release a maniacal laugh that my body reacts to in a way that could have me fainting from fear. Mr. Rogov rambles something, self-satisfaction evident in his tone. As if he easily composed calamity, pulling at his son's strings, then walks away dusting his hands off. I can feel him leave the room, but the tension remains, and Sasha's hostility seems amplified.

Sasha appears ten feet tall as he backs me up, my feet stumbling until I hit a wall, stopping us both. "Sasha, you're scaring me." I frantically glance around the room for help. Not that anyone would ever interfere.

"I told you to tell me if anyone touched you," he vehemently spits.

"What?" My gaze bounces between both of his eyes, trying to seek out the man I thought I knew.

"I gave you direct orders to tell me or one of my men if anyone touched you."

"Gave me orders?" I shriek.

"You don't deny it," he states.

The trepidation morphs swiftly into anger. Once again, I am being called a whore. I am so tired of men. They all look at us as objects and only worth something until they're not. The longer I stay silent, the more riled up he gets.

"My father tells me you have been entertaining some of the men while I've been gone."

What?! On instinct, I want to scream at him for accusing me of such things. That he was the very first and only man to ever touch me and not make me want to puke. That he has room to talk when he apparently fucks other women! But he's not upset that I was allegedly passed around to other men for my sake, or the fact that I didn't tell him. He's peeved that his *little doll* is now tainted. Little does he know, I was tainted long before him.

He seizes my jaw and chin in a harsh grip. "Tell me I'm wrong," he demands. My nostrils flare from the strain of staying silent. I feel my backbone steel, stronger than ever, and I look up at him in defiance. "Need I remind you that the only reason you are not out there *whoring* is because I wanted you here in my fucking bed?" He jerks his hand on my jaw making my head bump the wall, and I wince in pain. My vision dances with spots, but I don't dare make a peep. "Huh!" he roars. "Answer me, *whore.*"

The compulsion to cry has me shuddering in devastation. I stare right through him, dull and spiritless. Not willing to give him any more than I already have. Which was all of me that had yet been broken.

"You don't want to talk?" He glowers down at me, imploring me to speak. He takes a sharp breath through his nose then jerks away from me, my head hitting the wall again. This time hard enough to take my vision from me for a few seconds and cause ringing in my ears, but I refuse to show weakness and I fight through the sudden nausea. "Fine." He takes a step back. "You're on your own, then."

I watch his retreat and as soon as he's out of sight, I drop to the floor and release a painful breath, shaking with the oncoming sob. My hands jitter as I bring them up to my face and press my palms into my eyes, hoping they could prevent the onslaught of tears and nausea.

I was so wrong about him. He's beyond saving.

TWENTY-SEVEN

SASHA

"I'm telling you, Sasha. No one has touched the girl. You told us to keep an eye on her at all times, and we have," Artem argues as I pace the floor. Fumes from the conflagration still coming out of me.

"Every time it was my shift to watch over her, I have never taken an eye off of her," Trip says with his thick southern accent.

Then Bash chimes in. "No one has touched her, and I went through the surveillance to double check, and no one has visited her in her room either," he says with confidence.

It doesn't make sense. I know why my father would try and taunt me with the fabrication, but why would she go along with it? Is she fucking with me? If she is, she'll pay for it. Does she not understand that I am going out of my mind here? Everything I am jeopardizing? The perilous risk I took just to hunt her mother down to track each man that was in her life and punish them for ever touching Vivian. Including her mother. I put that bitch in the whorehouse. I'm sure she's adjusting just fine.

As for the men who defiled a young girl's innocence, Vivian's innocence, they got exactly what they deserved. Before meeting their death, I forced them to confess to all their sins involving young Vivian. The last sack of shit confessed to something I could not bear. Vivian said she was a virgin, but according to Thomas Bayne, she was most certainly not. Not since she was thirteen years old.

Thomas Bayne deserved far worse than the sentence I doled out, but I couldn't stop myself. I beat him to death and continued to beat him until Artem pried me from the bloody corpse.

When I got home, all I wanted to do was confront Vivian, but to abate my father's skepticism, I kept my distance from her and partook in sexual acts with random women for him to witness. Before Vivian, it's something I would normally do.

The wrath I brought home with me has been aimed at her when I know it shouldn't be. And she only added to it when she once again defied me and dangled herself right in front of my father. It didn't satisfy me to see the hurt and devastation in her eyes, I wanted to run after her and punish her for disobeying me. Then get on my knees to beg her to remain patient for me. The thought of me on my knees for anyone is infuriating.

The lies. The deception. The defiance.

Lies. I fucking hate lies. She had ample time on her hands to confess the truth. The other night when I bared my soul to her, expressed vulnerability, she chose to water down her own truth.

I knew that our first real encounter would be unpleasant, so I continued to stay away. To ease my temper. Until I saw her. I couldn't control myself with her so close.

I approached her with festering anger, then when my father fed me some bullshit, I ate it up because I wasn't fucking thinking straight. I haven't been thinking straight. I knew the fallout from my attachment to her would be violent. I should have had better control. It's no one's fault but my own.

"Sasha," Artem calls for my attention. "You need to get her out of here. Get her to your cousin's. The sooner the better."

"Maybe it would have been better if you had just left her—"

I see red as I charge Trip, wrapping my hand around his thick neck and shoving him into the wall. "Don't you dare finish that fucking statement. You hear me?!" I spit in his face viciously. "You do not question me. And you do not talk about her like that. She remains safely here until it's safe to transport her. Understood?" He nods his head as much as he's able. Then I turn to look at Bash and Artem and they stand there calmly, not at all bothered by my outburst. "Do you understand me?" They both nod in silence. "Eyes stay on her every single minute of every day." I jerk away from Trip and storm out of the room.

Finding out she was raped was enough to have me thirsting for blood. Then guiled with the lie of her being taken behind my back, it only feeds the fury inside of me.

I spend the rest of the evening talking myself down from the ledge. From going to her to squeeze the life out of her, sapping her dry. I pace my bedroom so long I leave tracks. I know I shouldn't be taking it out on her, but I have no other catharsis for the madness that is ripping me apart.

She could have assuaged the animosity by telling me herself that no one had touched her while I was gone. That she was sorry for not telling me the truth of her past. Instead, she enraged me with her silence. Spurred me on with her threats of suicide. Her provocation only fueled the fire, pushing me further from sanity.

"I have more chores to do before I am sent back to my little prison cell where I will surely go mad and eventually either kill myself or do something stupid enough to get myself killed and hopefully take a few of you with me."

I rip at my hair in frustration trying to erase those words from my memory. I know the feeling all too well. I don't know how I managed to keep myself here on this planet before her, because I don't know how I will afterwards. She's quickly become my reason for living. Every move I make is with her in mind. Every thought revolves around *her*. All *her*.

Pulling out my phone, I dial Bash. "Yeah?" he answers with sleep in his voice.

"Tell me again that no one has touched her," I snap.

He clears his throat. "No one has touched the girl. I give you my word, Sasha. We have gone through footage and talked it over. Your father was lying to you. He was badgering you."

"Why would she lie?"

"I don't know. Maybe to taunt you too." He's silent as I try not to crush my phone in my hand.

I don't correct him when he assumes I am referring to my father's instigating lie. I was actually referring to Vivian lying to me about being a virgin. About not being completely truthful when she confessed to being sexually abused as a child.

My nostrils flare. "You will tell me right away if you find anything out." I hang up before he can respond.

Tramping back and forth again, I run my hands through my hair and growl. Stopping, I close my eyes and take a deep breath to try and calm myself. I look down at my hands and remember putting them on her. Laying my hands on her in anger. I was so close to striking her or choking her to death. Unleashing the monster inside of me on her directly.

I'm not even aware of my actions as I head in through the secret passageway and for her room. I shouldn't be anywhere near her, but that pull has me moving without permission.

When I quietly push through the doorway into her room, I shouldn't be surprised to find her crying. She's curled up in her bed hidden in the dark and sniffing against her pillow facing the wall. I know she heard the door open and shut, so she knows that I'm here and refuses to acknowledge it.

Going with my instincts, I peel my clothes off and slip under the covers. Wrapping my body around hers, she cries harder. I don't know what to say or what I *can* say to make any of this better. The remorse I feel is ineffable.

I press my lips against her bare shoulder and give her a tender kiss there. Then another and another. My hand begins roaming her body again on instinct, trying to console her with my touch.

She continues to cry as I continue my caress and when my fingers dip into the waistband of her panties, she doesn't reject me. My hand slides back up her stomach then back down into the front of her panties. Pressing my lips to her shoulder, I move her hair away from her neck to gain access to it.

Her crying begins to dwindle as I softly kiss her neck and replace my hand inside her panties. When the tip of my finger brushes against the apex of her thighs, I'm pleasantly surprised to find her wet for me. She whimpers through more tears and arches her back to press her perky ass against my groin and I slip my fingers through her moist slit making her breath hitch.

She squeezes her eyes shut and her mouth falls open as I massage her. She's still so responsive to me. I fucking love it. I should feel guilty for how quickly she abandons all resolve with my seduction. But when she gasps and speedily comes, I feel no remorse.

Turning her over to her back, she blinks her eyes open to stare up at me with her reddened hazel eyes. We stay connected as I peel her panties off slowly. Her bra following quickly behind. Running my hands all over her soft skin, I admire her refined curves.

Covering her body with mine, I take a nipple into my mouth and pull. I'm gentle but I apply just enough pressure to get her to squirm beneath me. A tiny moan comes out of her nose as her eyes shut and her hands find their way into my hair and fists it. A sign that she needs more. She needs me to feed her animalistic desires.

My cock digs into the mattress as I slake myself on her supple breasts, moving from one to the other, pinching them and nipping them. Then I kiss and nip my way down her body, worshipping every inch along the way. Dragging my teeth and taking her flesh between them to give her a zing of pain here and there. Her fingers remain curled in my hair as I make my way to settle my shoulders between her thighs.

Glancing up, I find her watching me through two tiny slits. Her breasts rapidly rising and falling. Opening my mouth, I stab my teeth into the meaty part of her inner thigh. She sucks a sharp breath in through her teeth and hisses, concurrent with pulling at my hair.

Retracting my teeth, I push her legs up and open. I narrow my eyes on her, silently telling her what to do. She receives the lucid message and releases my hair to hold her legs up by the backs of her knees. I give her one more silent command. Daring her to let go.

Flattening my tongue against her wet heat, she sucks in another breath sharply as I make one long swipe upwards. I pause to use both hands to spread her cunt wide open for me, so I can see, smell, and taste every part of her most intimate area.

Latching onto her bundle of nerves, I suck and swirl my tongue around and she flinches. Her head rolls back and she pulls on her legs, hiking her knees upward further, giving me complete unfettered access.

I punch my tongue inside of her leaking cunt and fuck her with it. My nose rubbing and inhaling her. My mouth inches downwards and I lash at her tight hole, prodding it, teasing her. The way she tenses, I can tell she isn't ready for me to fuck her ass yet. I'll need to feed her curiosity first.

I thrash my tongue against her until she cries out and floods my mouth with her juices, and I swallow every drop. It's the tastiest nectar I have ever had on my tongue. I could taste this every day. Wake her up every morning with my head between her legs, and kissing her cunt goodnight every night.

I leave of trail of her wetness up her body with my lips until they land on hers. She welcomes it and opens her mouth for me, and when I wedge my hips between her thighs, she keeps them spread to accommodate me.

My hips begin rocking as I butt up against her soaked entrance, slicking up my length and watching her convulse. She takes me by surprise when she wraps a hand around my cock to direct me inside. Pumping my hips, I thrust inside of her until our hips touch.

Her inner muscles hug me, and I'm reminded that someone else stole her virtue. It was meant to be mine. It *is* mine. This pussy, this woman. All mine. Her muscles are malleable and shaped into fitting me and only me.

But she can't be mine. No matter how much I believe she was made to be, I can't keep her *and* keep her safe.

My body is completely flush with hers, not an inch of space between us. I've never felt so close with someone before. Physically or mentally.

Undulating and sinking in and out, I get that prickling sensation at the base of my spine. My motions deepen and speed up and when I know I'm about to come, I remain snug inside of her and let her milk me dry with her contracting muscles. Sapping me with her pulsing cunt.

I finally come to a standstill with my cock still buried deep inside of her and our mouths still fused together. I don't want to stop kissing her, but once the feverish haze begins to dissipate, I know that I have to get out of here and quick. I shouldn't have come here. I shouldn't have done this. It'll only make things more complicated and painful for us both.

Pulling back to finally come up for air, we stare at one another, out of breath and perplexed as to what's conspired between us. It was without a doubt different from any other time. It felt like a new beginning and yet it felt like goodbye.

Placing a chaste kiss on her lips as I reluctantly pull out of her and stand. Tearing my eyes away from her as she watches every move that I make, I get dressed and silently leave.

TWENTY-EIGHT

VIVIAN

I have no idea what possessed me to let him touch me again. Why I didn't spit words of rancor at him like I had planned to. Instead, I melted in his embrace. I was vulnerable and found comfort in it. I needed it. I needed someone, *anyone*, to hug me and make me feel human again. His amorous touch erased all that anger and resentment as he held my heart together.

I drop the rag and practically fall into the chair a couple of feet away. Resting my head in my hands, I close my eyes to fight the sudden nausea. It's been like this all morning. The random dizziness and nausea making me feel like I might puke or collapse.

"You sick?" A thick Russian-accented voice asks.

Swallowing hard, afraid to find the person that is attached to the voice, I slowly lift my head to find the man Sasha referred to as Bash looking at me with concern. "I was just feeling a little dizzy. I, uh, bumped my head pretty hard on something yesterday, and I think I may have hit it harder than I thought." I chuckle nervously getting back to my feet. "I'll be okay though." Giving him a tight smile, I try moving past him and my vision blurs as my legs give out and strong arms catch me before I hit the floor.

"You need rest. I think you have a concussion," he says in choppy English and helps me stand all the way up.

"I'm fine, really," I slur, the nausea getting worse.

"No. Let's get you back to your room and get you checked out."

Unable to argue or protest, I let him hold some of my weight as he leads me back to my room. I practically fall into the bed and sigh as my eyes close. Already feeling better by blocking out the light. "I just need to lie down for a little while. I'll be okay," I murmur.

"You need a doctor. I'll have Sasha fetch you one."

The mention of his name has my eyes flying open and me trying to push myself up into a sitting position, but I can only manage to prop myself up on my elbows as my stomach flips and my head pounds. "No!" I rush out. "Please don't tell Sasha. It's just a bump. I'll honestly be okay."

He stares at me for a while as if trying to figure something out. Then he says, "You know, you are going to get him killed," he says in all seriousness and my eyes widen in outrage.

"Are you serious?!" Now, I'm pissed. I was going to thank him for his concern, but then he had to go and say *that*! "I have done nothing but exist! You think I wanted to be shipped off to be sold as a whore?! You think I wanted to come here and be a fucking servant and let the spoiled rich boy seduce and deceive me?! Trick me into falling for him?! To constantly have my mind and body toyed with? To constantly be reminded of the fact that I will always be as worthless as a fucking whore to you people? I didn't ask for any of this!"

"I didn't say that," he says calmly, not at all offended by my outburst. "I said that you would get him killed." He pauses. "I just hope it's worth it."

I just stare at him for a hard moment. "Are you talking about me?"

"Who else would I be talking about?" he sasses, and I really don't appreciate it.

"He won't die for me." I cross my arms. "He'd have to care about me to do that."

"He hasn't been himself lately," he says in Sasha's defense.

"Or maybe he's himself more than ever. A heartless mobster that thinks his own shit doesn't stink." I almost cringe at the sound of my own immaturity.

"You and I both know that isn't true." He starts heading for the door. "I'll be back with medicine for your head."

I fall back on the bed and close my eyes. I want to believe Sasha cares about me, but I don't know what to believe these days. The whiplash he gives me has scrambled my brain, making it nearly impossible to get my thoughts straight.

I've seen the deleterious side of him, and I've felt the nurturing side of him. Both of them too believable.

I feel the lights being blocked behind my eyelids and blink them open to find Bash there. He hands over a bottle of water and some pills. I put the smallest modicum of trust in him and swallow the pills and water down. "Thank you," I gasp.

"I have to tell Sasha. I don't keep things from him." There's almost a hint of remorse in his voice and I nod my head. Like all of us here, we have people to answer to, and orders to follow. Bash has been nothing but kind to me, so I don't have it in me to try and make his job any more difficult.

He turns the lights off before leaving, closing the door, and locking it behind him. I roll over and close my eyes, ready to sleep. Even before Sasha showed up last night, I couldn't sleep. Not with how badly my head was hurting. I thought it was from lack of sleep and all the crying I had done. I didn't remember hitting my head so hard.

The sound of the latches on the door stirs me awake, but I'm far too fatigued to see who it is.

I try again to open my eyes, but it's futile. Even when the bed dips next to me, I can't deny it. My eyes fall shut, and sleep consumes me once again.

"Vivian. The doctor will be here soon," That familiar deep voice rumbles near my ear. "I need you to wake up, *kukolka*." *Mmm, little doll.* I love the name he has for me. "Vivian. Please, wake up." I feel him begin to pet my hair gingerly. Moaning, I snuggle into the blankets more and I hear him chuckle. "I need you to let the doctor check you out, then you can go right back to sleep."

"I'm okay. Just let me sleep," I murmur.

His rough hands carefully cup my face, and it makes my eyes begin to cooperate. His handsome face and messy blonde hair begin to come into view. That dark gaze full of worry makes me stare up at him in a stupor. He looks worried. *Why?*

I rapidly blink my eyes and try to sum up the events which led to this, but for some reason it feels a bit hazy. I stare at him in confusion until reality finally hits me.

The dark gaze turns hard and cold as he watches me sit up and scoot away from him. Recoiling from his touch. He's blatantly offended by my retreat. What did he really expect? A warm greeting and a kiss?

"The doctor is waiting outside to check you out," he murmurs and looks away. That muscle in his jaw twitching as he grinds his molars. I stay silent, swallowing down the caustic words I have for him. He looks back at me again and his frown has deepened as if he's restraining himself from his rancor and it almost makes me break my vow of silence. I am not the enemy here. "I'll send him in and wait outside." He pauses for a moment as if I'm going to thank him. When he realizes he'll be getting no words of gratitude from me, he gets up and walks out of the room.

Moments later, an older man comes in with a friendly smile, but I know better than to trust it. I know not to trust anyone, especially if they seem friendly. I fell for Sasha's adorable smile. I obviously have terrible judgement. And even if he were someone who would be willing to help me, like everyone else, he's powerless against the Rogov's.

The doctor says I may have a mild concussion and I have some obvious stress, causing my symptoms to feel a lot worse. After a few days of rest and some pain meds, I should feel much better. When I asked about the pain meds, he said he would leave them with Mr. Rogov and I pray he means the younger of the two Rogov's, Sasha.

He leaves, closing the door behind him and all I want to do is sleep, but no such luck when the quiet creaking comes from the door for the passageway. He comes to the side of my bed and we just look at each other.

"Are you hungry?" I shake my head no. We're both somber as we silently stare at one another. It isn't as uncomfortable as tension is thick. "I'll stay away from you, Vivian. But I'll make sure you're still protected." I want to laugh in his face. *Still protected?* I've been violated, mocked, humiliated, toyed with, and slammed against a wall giving me a concussion. All by *him*. And he wants to keep me safe? He is out of his goddamn mind!

He grinds his teeth again, obviously getting frustrated from my lack of response or reaction. "I'll have one of the guys check on you in a little bit. You should get some more rest." He pauses and clenches his fists.

His lips thin and his nostrils flare as he breathes out heavily. Then he turns and storms out of my room the same way he entered. *Wouldn't want daddy dearest knowing that he's checking in on one of the house whores.*

TWENTY-NINE

VIVIAN

I wake up to dampness on my pillow. Rapidly blinking in the dark, I wipe the drool from my mouth and stretch. I was out. Getting some much-needed sleep, so deep I didn't even dream.

A light catches my eye and I turn to find Sasha sitting on the floor with his back against the wall and bent knees. The light from the screen of his phone illuminates his face. He hasn't noticed my alertness yet, so I take the moment to study him. His golden brows are drawn in and the tension of his face isn't unusual. But his eyes look heavy as if he hasn't slept in too long.

It isn't long before his eyes snap up to mine. He shuts his screen off taking away the only light, but I can still feel him looking at me.

"How are you feeling?" His deep voice carries through the dark and caresses me.

The pride in me urges me to stay quiet, but I make the decision to break my vow of silence. No longer wishing to quarrel with him. "Okay." My voice is scratchy coming out. I clear my throat and push myself up to sit. "How long have I been sleeping?" I rub at my head that's slightly bothering me and I hear him moving.

The sound of pills in a bottle intensifies the pain in my head. "Here."

I squint towards his voice and lean over to turn the side lamp on. The light causes me to wince, and forcing my eyes to adjust. Sasha holds out a couple of white pills in one hand and a glass of water in another.

"Thanks," I murmur and take them. I chug the water, chasing the pills down. "You didn't answer me. How long have I been asleep?" There's a strong bite to my tone though I'm feeling frail.

"Eleven hours." He ignores my attitude.

We're quiet for a solid minute. "Won't people notice my absence?"

"It's taken care of."

"Okay…" I look away and keep the blankets around me.

"What would you like to eat?" he asks out of nowhere.

"I don't care," I mutter, feeling stubborn again.

"You can have anything you want. What. Would. You. Like." Now, he's the one with the attitude and it infuriates me.

"What the hell is your problem? You treat me like dirt, yet you're acting like you care about my well-being."

He clenches his fists at his sides and grinds his teeth. "What do you want to eat, Vivian," he growls.

"I said. I. Don't. Care. Stale crackers for all I care," I sneer.

"Vivian. I'm warning you. You are treading on very thin ice."

My eyes bulge and I'm on my feet. "Me?!" My voice is shrill. "I—" I glance around and pick up the glass of water from the side table and hurl it at him. His eyes widen and he has to dodge it because my aim was on point. It shatters against the wall and he gawks at me in shock. "I've had enough of you assholes! I refuse to play any more of your games! Do whatever you want because I. Am. Done! I won't fucking clean." I start stripping out of the maids uniform I'm still in. "I won't keep my mouth shut." I struggle with the dress and end up ripping it then balling it up and slam it on the floor with a scream and stomp on it like a psycho. "And if anyone fucking touches me, I will fight. I will fight to the fucking death."

"You have no idea what kind of fire you are playing with," he threatens with a dark look.

"I don't give a shit, Sasha! I have taken too much from men like you!"

He jumps forward to close the gap between us and I stand my ground. Not at all afraid of him hitting me. "Yeah, I know you've taken too much," he says through his teeth, and I rear back in befuddlement. "You said you were a virgin." I narrow my eyes at him, wondering where the hell he is going with this. "Thomas Bayne."

And just like that. The wind is taken right out of my sails, and I retreat back a step, hugging my midsection. I haven't heard that name in years. And to this day, it still has the same painful effect on me. Flashbacks immediately begin to surge to the fore of my brain. Forcing me to relive those disgusting memories.

"Tell me," he snaps, and I shake my head vigorously. Begging him not to make me talk about it. "Tell me what he did to you."

"Stop," I plead in a strained voice. I rub my arms, feeling ashamed and dirty.

"Thomas Bayne."

"No, stop," I whisper and back up again, the bed behind me ending my retreat.

"So, you *do* know his name." I sniffle and stare at the ground wishing it would swallow me up. "Another lie."

That snags my attention, and my head snaps up. "Excuse me?"

"You said you were a virgin—"

"No!" I shout, anger again seizing control over me. "I never said those words. You insinuated, and I didn't deny it."

"You—"

"Stop it! Just fucking stop it!" I bellow out and pant in frustration. "Yeah, I let you think I was a virgin because *what*? You think I was going to tell you it was taken from me by an older man when I was still practically a child?! That my mom blamed me and called me the whore?! That I went to the police and my mom somehow convinced them that I'm always making up lies?!" I swat away the falling tears. His eyebrows twitch. "Why on earth would I tell you, a fucking mobster about to have your way with me, a thing about my past? Huh?"

"You could have told me when I asked you about the men who touched you. You said you didn't know any names."

"So fucking what!? Why do you care anyway?!" I throw my arms out and he falls silent. "Is it because your little *whore* was already damaged goods when you thought she was pure? Because you weren't the first and only man inside of me?"

The way he's confronting me about omitting the full truth about my past trauma like it was my fault is exactly why I didn't want to ever tell him. It reminds me of my mother and how she reacted to her dirtbag boyfriend raping me. I ran to her, broken and afraid. And she made me feel like it was somehow my fault. Then only months before my eighteenth birthday, her new flavor of the month tried to force himself on me and she caught him. She again disappointed me by reacting out of jealousy rather than a poked mama bear. That's when I finally left.

I'm not idiotic enough to think any of it was my fault, but I do still feel dirty about it. Like I will never be clean again. Sasha began to expunge those feelings from me, until now. I'm dirty to him too.

He jumps the gap between us again, his body bumping into mine. He looks like has a million things to say, but he doesn't voice a single one. He scowls and sneers and breathes fire down on me, but he holds his tongue. His hands twitch at his sides like he wants to choke the life out of me, and I welcome it.

"Do it, Sasha. You're no different from any other man in or out of my life. No point in pretending you are," I taunt. "Go ahead. Hit me. Choke me. Take me against my will proving you are above me."

"Don't," he bites out.

"Don't what? Call you out on your delirium? Daring you to take a good look in the mirror?" He says nothing. "Come on, Sasha. Don't you want to slam my head against the wall again? Maybe this time, smash my head wide open?"

He brings his hands up in a blur and I tense up in reaction, waiting for the blow. His hands land on either side of my face, but the landing is soft aside from the firm hold he has me in. My eyes are squeezed shut on instinct, and I flinch when his forehead falls to mine. Both of our breathing is labored and ragged, sending it back and forth.

"I didn't mean to hurt you, angel. I lost control and was not in the right mind." His voice is pained but I'm still on high alert, expecting a bludgeon to the head. "I had no idea how hard I hit your head, I swear." I swallow hard, not at all cognizant of what is truly happening. "I don't ever want to hurt you. I only want to protect you. You're right though." He pauses. "I am no better than them. I've hurt you, and I will continue to hurt you. Whether I mean to or not. It's what we do."

I keep my eyes tightly shut and sniffle.

"Soon, angel. Soon, you will be free of us. I know my word has no meaning for you, but I promise you. I will get you out of here and away from all of this. You'll be able to live a better life. All I ask of you is your patience. Please, do not get yourself into any trouble before then. Keep your head down and mind yourself. Promise me you will." I sniffle again, and he applies more pressure. "Vivian. I need you to promise me. I won't ever ask for anything from you again."

I swallow again, my throat dry and soar. "I promise." My voice cracks and his hold on me lightens with an exhale.

"Thank you," he rasps, and I shudder on a sob when he places his gentle lips to my forehead. Breathing me in and lingering.

Then he's gone.

THIRTY

SASHA

Kazimir meets me in the foyer of his home when I arrive. He's clearly anxious to learn of whatever information I have collected for him, and I don't blame him.

The past few weeks have been toilsome and mentally straining. Between the information I discovered about Vivian's past, to the shit that is about to hit the fan from what I am about to divulge to my cousin.

Usually, we greet each other with a cheeky grin and some kind of mock-insulting comment, but he can sense the calamitous tension I'm carrying with me, so we hardly say a word and he escorts me to his office.

He heads right over to the chilled box to pour us each a glass of vodka with a heavy hand. I accept the glass and he leans his hips back against his desk, too anxious to sit. For me, I'm too anxious to stand as I sit down in a chair facing him.

We salute, then take a nice sip of our clear liquor, and I wait until I hear the doors behind us seal shut to speak.

"You were right to be suspicious of my father." He doesn't move a muscle, and patiently waits for me to elaborate. "I've had my guys do some digging, and although there is no concrete evidence, it's enough to say he was possibly in on the attack." Waves of hostility radiate from Kazimir, though he's still unmoving which is more unsettling. "Transactions prove he had been spending more time than usual with the Semenov's in private locations. Having meetings that no one, including me, ever knew about. Deals and shit." I pause. "And we both know my father would benefit from taking you out." He would pretty much be entitled to the Kalashnik empire given the family relations. Every family thought Kazimir was vulnerable enough to either take him out or take advantage of his youth. But they were all wrong. Kazimir is not a force to be reckoned with. He's smart, tactful, and resourceful.

The silence creates a thick smoke of pent-up rage the longer we sit there. He's gone completely still, I'm not even sure if he's breathing. I know my cousin to remain cool on the outside, but there's always that violent fiend that surfaces when provoked.

I stand to my feet cautiously, prepared to restrain him from flying off the handle at any given moment.

"You will not stand in my way, Sasha," he says gravely. His face granite and his body beginning to quiver.

"I know you want to—"

He abruptly smashes his glass down on his desk, liquid and glass flying everywhere. "You have no idea what I want!" he roars, his voice booming off the walls. "She almost fucking died!" He jumps forward, but I remain rooted. The sound of the door swinging open doesn't distract me from facing my cousin. "I will fucking kill him! I will lock him up along with my own father and give him the fucking treatment he deserves!" Spittle flies everywhere as he comes closer. I frown at him wondering what the fuck he's talking about when Maksim comes in to mediate. He wraps his arms around Kazimir to pull him back.

I know he doesn't mean to direct his anger at me, so I take a step back and stay quiet while he spews words of violence and hatred at me in Russian while Maksim tries to get him to calm down. Maksim is clueless at first as to what is going on. But he's filled in after a minute of Kazimir's tirade.

Maksim speaks to him calmly, telling him he needs to have his head on straight. That he can't do anything rash, endangering Marta again. The mere mention of her name has him snapping his vengeful gaze at him. "You have to put your emotions aside to do this right. To keep her safe," he says, and I can see the immediate affect Maksim's words have on Kazimir.

"I'll help in whatever way you need me to," I say, snagging his attention.

He frowns at me. "Why?"

I snort with a smirk. "Why the fuck wouldn't I? I told you that I would."

Maksim removes his arms from Kazimir, and he studies me closely. Most likely trying to discover if this is a trick or not. I have nothing to hide, so I stand there and let him come to his own conclusion. I told him I would get the information he was seeking, but I didn't explain that I would take his side and aid him in his declaration of war on my father.

"The girl," he states.

I look away. "She is a great incentive, but no." I look at him again. "I'm doing this because you're my cousin."

"But he's your father."

I shrug my shoulders. "And Vladimir was yours." I pause and raise a questioning eyebrow. "Or *is*."

"I'm not going to elaborate."

I smirk. "Didn't think you would," I murmur and sigh. "I'm on your side, Kazimir. I came to you for help getting Vivian out and safe. I still expect you to do that for me, so if I need to help you take revenge on my father to do it, then so be it."

He's still unsure of my true intentions as he continues to survey me. "Do you love her?" I rub at the back of my neck feeling antsy all of a sudden. My defenses shooting up into place. "And don't give me that bullshit that you don't know. You fucking know. Especially if you're willing to have your father *murdered* for her." I give him an offended look. "What did you think I would do with this information?" He's right. Of course, he'd want to kill my father if he was found guilty, it's just a brash statement to hear aloud. No one speaks about my father that way and gets away with it.

"Sasha," he says with less venom in his tone. He relaxes slightly and leans back against his desk again, but I stay standing. "Do you want the girl?"

"I want her safe."

"But do you want her?"

"It doesn't matter," I growl.

"It does matter. If you want the girl, you should be able to have the girl." I snort and shake my head. Are we really all this entitled? "Our fathers make the mistake of trying to mold us into replicas of themselves, but neglect to realize that it can bite them in the ass in the end. Take a page from your father's book, Sasha."

"Meaning?"

"We talked about this. What would your father do if he wanted something, but someone was standing in their way? Even if it was his own son." I sigh and rub at the scruff on my jawline. "You're being given the same opportunity I was."

"Your father was also a cocky bastard and didn't think you would ever attempt to take him out. My father... he's paranoid, he can smell deceit miles away."

"So, that's it. You are just going to roll over and let him take away something you want."

My fists clench and my molars grind. "I am not rolling over, Kazimir. I am trying to protect her," I bite out.

"What if you can do both?"

I sigh again and run a hand through my hair. Feeling stressed and weighted. I said I was on his side, but plotting my father's murder has me restive. I thought we'd fuck him over some other way, not kill him. "Do tell me, cousin."

"I will take the girl in, keep her safe and hidden. You have my word." He pauses. "And I will take your father out. With your help."

I sit back down in the chair and ponder on this idea. This opportunity. Is this even possible? Could we take him out?

"If you let her go, you will soon regret it."

"She'd be safe and be able to live a life she's never had."

"With someone else." I look up at him. "You want her finding another man? One she'll marry and have children with?" I grit my teeth, tasting blood from biting down on the inside of my cheek. "Belong to someone else…"

"She's mine," I snap.

"Exactly. She's yours and no one should be able to take her away from you. It's time for you to think like a *Pakhan* and not a soldier."

Getting advice from my little cousin is almost laughable. Getting good advice from my little cousin is outrageous. But he's right in every single way. I can't roll over for my father. I won't let him deny what belongs to me. It's time for a new *Pakhan*. Out with the old and in with the new.

"You take Vivian before any kind of retaliation."

Kazimir nods his head.

"Tell me what you need from me," I say, signing my soul over.

I invite Bash inside with me out of fairness since Maksim is staying put, and we begin to go over strategies. My old man is smart. No one can hear of this plan but our most trusted. That is until it's time to actually fight and take sides.

An hour goes by, and we have something cunning now in the works.

"I think it's time for another drink," Kazimir says and pours the four of us a glass of cold vodka.

"How's Marta?" I ask after we salute to a drink.

"She's recovered well," Kazimir replies with tightness in his voice. "I will have to inform her of our new guest though. I don't want her thinking I have another woman with another child of mine staying here." We both chuckle. "Plus, Marta could keep her company. And vice versa." I nod in agreement. "I'd like a moment alone with my cousin," he announces.

Both Maksim and Bash take their leave without a fuss.

"Will you tell her you're coming for her?" he asks, assuming I'll take his advice.

"I don't think it'd be a good idea."

He grins. "If she were to find out, would this become a hostage situation?" he muses causing me to crack a smile. "What would you like me to do if she finds out and tries to escape?"

"Don't let her."

"And what can I expect if that were to happen?"

"She's becoming quite the fighter," I say with some pride. She's grown so much stronger from when she first came to me.

"Good to know."

"And she's smart."

"Understood. I'll be sure to have her safe and secured."

"And unharmed."

"You have my word, Sasha."

Letting Vivian go completely would be the right thing to do. The unselfish thing to do. But I'm not a good man, no matter how much goodness she saw in me.

I'll let her think she's on her way to a brand-new, bratva-free life.

But that angelic woman belongs to me.

THIRTY-ONE

VIVIAN

It's been weeks without any sign of Sasha. No sight and no word from him. Not since our argument ending with a promise to get me out of here.

The thought of never seeing Sasha again is poignant and painful. I wish so badly to live in a world where I could have both. Both a new life and Sasha. That isn't our reality though. Our reality consists of tragedy and angst. Neither of us able to get what we want, nor live the way we desire.

He made me promise to stay strong and to keep being inconspicuous. He *begged* me. The desperation and despair in his voice was heart-wrenching. It was enough to dissolve the resentment I possess towards him, reminding me that we do have something real between us. That it was not all in my head. It was real. He's real. I finally recognize which side of Sasha is the true side. His anger may have gotten the best of him, but with the pressure he has been constantly put under, he was bound to break.

Sasha has been the single person able to make me feel whole again and not so dirty. Yes, he's hurt me more times than I can count, but it doesn't change the way my body and mind react to him. In a perfect world, he could be the one. But perfection is a myth. And happily ever after's are for dreamers.

I wait for what feels like hours after dinner in my room. Waiting to sneak in through the passageway to Sasha's bedroom. I need to say goodbye before it's too late. To catch a glimpse of that tenderness he momentarily reveals. Even if I have to surrender my body to him once more. I will spend the rest of my life wishing I had if I do not. I've had enough of my time wasted.

I slide into the slippers he brought me as well as one of the t-shirts I took from his closet that no longer smells of him.

The air is stale and cold as I slink into the dark. As if it's been a while since anyone had occupied the elongated space. I shuffle towards the rod iron spiral staircase and peer over the twisting rail. Down into the dense opaqueness. Curiosity pulls at me.

The catacombs.

From my understanding, the catacombs are an underground cemetery, like a tomb of some sort. Though I'm sure it isn't dead people with lavish burial chambers down there. It's a place where they meet their cruel fate.

Thoughts of Sasha shake some sense into me, and I ascend the steps instead of feeding my curiosity. Heading towards the alternate unknown.

I track the lights as they continue to gradually illuminate my way. They reflect off the pale dust covering the floor, and I can make out shoe prints. I guess from Sasha, whenever he walked through here last.

I get to the end of the hall and I'm shaking with nerves. Pressing my palm flat against the hidden door, I stand there for several moments. I don't know if I'm waiting to hear something on the other side or trying to tell myself to turn back around. But there are no noises from the other side and I'm pushing through the door before any more reluctance can stop me.

The desk blocking it forces me to use my full body weight to make enough of a gap for me to squeeze through. No lights are on and it's dead quiet. The eerie aura has me pausing. The darkness seems to cloak me like a second skin.

Ignoring every warning in my gut, I walk further into the room. My first location; the bed. The sheets are crinkled, telling it's been slept in recently. But it could have been nights ago if I go by the recent instructions to the staff to not enter his room.

I run my hand over the spot where he sleeps and it's cold to the touch. I have the urge to crawl up in his place, but I divert my attention to more investigation, heading to the bathroom next.

The sink and countertop are dry, but the shower has some condensation left from whenever it was last used.

I scan the shower and grab his bodywash, opening the bottle to inhale his scent. It has me yearning for him more.

Moving on, I investigate his closet. Turning on the light, I walk the length of it and run my fingers along the soft fabric of his clothing. His smell is unmistakable and everywhere. Grabbing a plain black t-shirt, I peel the one I'm wearing off and slip the clean one over my body and relish in the familiar fumes.

I should go back. I should slip back through the doorway as if I were never here. I tried. But he wasn't here. Maybe it's a sign. It just wasn't and isn't meant to be.

But my stupid heart tells me to enjoy the memories a bit longer. My feet involuntarily moving, leading me to his bed again. This time I don't even entertain the alarms coaxing me back to the safety of my bedroom. Instead, I slide under the soft sheets of his bed and close my eyes, content with my poor decision.

Although I dreamt about Sasha, I slept well. Better than I have in weeks. When I wake, I'm still alone, the bed still cool around me. Disappointment stinging.

I still have almost two hours before I need to be ready for my daily chores, but I can't lay here and pathetically wait for something that is clearly not going to happen. I did it though. I tried. I sought him out, and I put myself out there. What else could I have done? At least I can say that and not regret being too proud to do so.

I'm still clad in the black t-shirt, and I'm keeping it. Not for nostalgia, but for the fact that I'd like something else to wear other than underwear and my skanky maid's uniform. I honestly don't know why I haven't thought of it before. Why haven't I thought of using his room to escape? Oh, right. Because I wouldn't know what the fuck to do after that. But I could have been stashing things from his room this whole time.

My mind has the same thoughts and memories playing on loop as I make my way back to my room to ready for the day, but I'm inured to it now. I have to be, or I'd be walking around in a state of dysphoria. I'm choosing strength and valor. They cannot always win. If they want to break me, destroy me, taunt me, they'll have to try a lot harder.

"You're going to rub a hole in that table if you keep it up," an unfamiliar voice comes from behind me and I'm ready to test my intestinal fortitude.

Relief gives me reprieve when I turn around to find Artem. One of Sasha's minions. He's got a slight smirk on his face, but I'm not at all amused. I don't join in on his antics and go back to wiping down the table with vigorous circles.

He clears his throat. "I need you to come with me."

I still and think about my actions before making one. Sasha asked me to keep my head down, and to not make any trouble because he's getting me out of this place, but where the hell has he been? For all I know, things may have changed.

"Where?" I ask then turn my head to look at him.

"Please," he says lowly, but with patience.

"Do I really have a choice?" I mutter and collect my things to throw into my cleaning caddy. "Lead the way."

Artem ignores my sour attitude and turns to begin the journey down the hallway. We seem to travel the entire length of the estate, passed bedrooms, offices, through the foyer and down another hallway until we come to the end and stop at a closed door. No latches or locks, just a plain bedroom door.

It's unlocked when he turns the knob and I follow him into a bedroom on the small side compared to the other rooms in this place, but still much bigger than mine. It's less luxurious than the other guestrooms, but it lacks the personalization of being someone's private room.

I flinch when he closes the door behind me and throws the lock into place. Swallowing hard around the trepidation growing in my throat, I rigidly swivel my head to vigilantly watch him. He doesn't look at me as he breezes by and heads towards what looks like a closet.

He only stops to turn back to me when he realizes I'm no longer following him. "I'm not going to hurt you, Vivian. I promise. I'm showing you where to go if there were something to happen."

I frown. "What do you mean?"

"Please, come."

I set my cleaning caddy down on the floor and sigh. Steeling my spine, I cross the distance to meet him at the threshold of the closet. He turns on the light and we go through the empty walk-in and stop at the large vault-like door at the back wall.

"This is a panic room," he states, and my eyes widen in fascination. "To open it, you have to enter this code." He types in six numbers and looks at me. "Do you need me to repeat it?" I shake my head, already having the numbers memorized. *It wasn't hard since it was my birthday. Not going to dissect that little fact right now though.*

He pulls on the knob sticking out and cranks open the heavy door. Lights begin automatically turning on inside and it's not at all what I expected when he said panic room. He steps inside, but I linger in the doorway, still weary of his intentions.

He doesn't seem bothered by it though as he begins to explain everything I'm seeing inside. "If anything were to happen, you come straight here and close yourself inside. Do not hesitate, and do not tell anyone. Once that door is shut, it's locked. Only those who have the code can enter, unless..." He points to a red button on the control board. "The wrong person might have access to it. That's when you would push this button."

"What does the button do?"

"It'll make it inaccessible to anyone on the outside."

"Anyone?"

He dips his chin once.

I look up at all the screens that make up most of the wall in the small room that's about the size of my bedroom, but it includes a toilet, sink, and a small cot from what I've already observed. I'm still focused on the screens though as they display what looks like live feeds of the interior and exterior of the house.

"When you say 'if something were to happen'," I say, and look over and up at him. "What exactly do you mean by that?"

"If something were to happen to Sasha, one of us would come to make sure you get here safely."

"And then what?"

"Then you stay in here until it's safe to come out."

I shake my head, not fully understanding. "But what if something happens to you guys too? How will I know to come here? And how will it ever be safe for me to come out?" I ask feeling panicky, thinking about the worst-case scenario.

"If something were to happen to all of us, it would mean we're under attack, and you would know. And if that were to happen and none of us survive, Sasha's cousin would come for you."

"Sasha's cousin?"

"Yes. His name is Kazimir. He promised to look over you."

"But I don't know what he even looks like."

He sighs and squeezes the back of his neck as if it helps him maintain his patience with me. "He's young, dark hair, scar on his face." The permanent frown on my face deepens. Is he serious right now? "No one knows about this arrangement, so it's not like anyone would try to pretend to be him to get you to trust them." Arrangement? What the hell is he talking about now? "I know this is a lot to take in, but it's vital you understand. If you feel like you are in danger, come here, close yourself inside, and do not open for anyone but Sasha, Bash, me, Trip, or Kazimir."

"Sasha's cousin with a scar on his face," I stupidly repeat.

He smirks and nods his head. "Yes. And..." He heads over to a metal cabinet and opens the doors. I bravely make my way inside, curious as to what he's now showing me. "These are all loaded." I gape at the guns hanging inside. Two handguns and three big guns that I guess you would call rifles. Not that I know anything about guns. "If for some reason someone gets inside of here, you shoot them."

I start vehemently shaking my head and back up. "I have no idea how to shoot a gun."

"The safeties are off and they're all loaded. Aim, and pull the trigger."

I shake my head even harder. The thought of killing someone has my knees wobbling and my head dizzy. I hug my midsection in self-comfort. I can't believe what he's suggesting. I'm not like these people. Murder isn't so inconsequential to me. Life has meaning and taking one is not up to us.

"Vivian." He faces me with no amusement. "I know this is all scary, but it's important. It's life and death."

"I know it's life and death," I rush out in a high-pitched voice.

"You do not want to be taken by someone that is not us. You shoot to kill, and you keep shooting."

"I don't think I can do that."

He studies me for a long moment. "You'd be surprised of the fighter deep inside of you. You've made it this far. There's no stopping you. You prevail time and time again. You can do this."

I gawk at him. "You don't even know me," I say quietly.

"I know enough, and I know Sasha. If he has faith in you, then so do I."

"But I thought he was—" I cut myself off, remembering that I'm not supposed to breathe a word of what Sasha told me last. "Never mind," I murmur and look down at my feet.

"He still plans on getting you out of here." My head snaps back up. "This is just in case of an emergency." All I can do is nod my head. "There's also plenty of food and water to last you."

I don't ask for how long. The thought of being stuck in here by myself, not knowing who to trust or what to do, has me speechless.

I follow him out of the panic room and back into the hallway on autopilot. The stress from all this is going to kill me. Or at least age me ten years.

Before we exit the hallway to arrive in the grand foyer, he stops and turns to me. Then he hands me the cleaning caddy I'd forgotten to pick up on the way out. "Oh. Thank you," I mutter and accept it. "Will I see Sasha again? Like before…"

He glances around and I look down in embarrassment for being so careless. He steps in and lowers his head to speak for only me to hear. "He will come to you."

And just like that, warm hope blooms inside my chest.

THIRTY-TWO

VIVIAN

I'm assigned to lunch duty, but when I hear the boisterous cackle that belongs to the evil sultan of the house coming from the dining room, I try to pawn it off to someone else. The other maids have already filed out of the kitchen, and I have no way out of it. *Again.*

Whatever. I'm supposedly out of here soon. What could Mr. Rogov possibly do to me before then?

The back of Sasha's blonde head is what I first spot. I almost falter in my steps, my breath taken away and my heart racing just from being in the same room as him. Especially because it's been so long.

The other women already served Sasha and his father, along with most of the other men at the table, their plates. I try not to make eye contact with any of them as I try to figure out who does not have a plate in front of them yet.

My eyes clash with silvery-blue ones and before I can look away, I notice the scar on his face. The way he's holding my gaze, it's safe to assume that this is Sasha's cousin, Kazimir. He looks much younger than the rest of the men here, but he seems perfectly comfortable and content sitting with them in his sharp suit. His inky hair reminds me of Sasha's the way it's on the longer side and lightly styled, yet you can mess it up with a single ruffle.

One black eyebrow arches, and it shakes me out of my stupor. I go behind him and serve him his plate. My eyes bounce up to Sasha's, but he isn't looking at me as he talks to the unfamiliar guest across from him.

Moving onto the man next to Kazimir, I find him with his upper body twisted so that he can face me. He's handsome enough, and his little smug smirk on his face says that he's well aware of it. His eyes roam the length of my body, and he might as well announce his lewd intentions. I give him a tight smile and place his plate down. As I go to step around him to drop off the last plate, a rough hand grips my elbow.

"Where are you running off to, beautiful?" I avoid looking him in the eye as the man holds me hostage, still giving me a pompous smirk, showing off his perfect teeth.

"*Kukolka*," Sasha says, demanding my attention. I feel the air shift as everyone quiets and looks my way. His eyes bore into mine, as if he's physically pulling me in. "Come," he orders casually yet firmly.

"Oh, I didn't know she was already claimed," the man touching me muses and let's go. His hands up in mock surrender.

I don't hesitate to run to Sasha after I drop off the last plate. Mr. Rogov's laughter still sickens me as I make my way around the table. "My son's *pet*," he goads, and I hear a few chuckles around the table.

As soon as I reach Sasha, I gasp when he yanks me into his lap, my legs draped over one side. Thankfully, with my back to his father. A subtle sign of protection from him.

I ignore the chatter and degradation around me and stare at him with pleading eyes. Begging him not to humiliate me in front of all these men. His dark eyes dance around my face with mock delight, then he disconnects with me to join the other men in conversation, as I sit there like the 'little doll' he's named me. But I'm grateful to be a silent prop rather than the center of attention.

There's a strong pull from a heavy gaze across the table, but I tell myself to tune it out. I do my best to ignore it, but something about the demand for acknowledgement has my eyes peering up to meet captivating ones. I feel like prey caught in a spider's web, already paralyzed by the venomous bite. The face that belongs to the man holding my gaze is flawless. Like, preternaturally perfect. And there's something about the hint of a smile on his lips that creeps me the fuck out. Not in a creepy pervy way, but a serial killer way. He isn't at all abashed to be blatantly staring, though no one says anything and feigns ignorance. Including Sasha as he continues to speak with whomever.

The name Cedric is called, and he bores his eyes into me for a split second longer before severing the connection and turning his focus elsewhere. I'm finally free to look away and breathe again. The hand squeezing my upper thigh tells me Sasha was not at all ignorant to the attention. I wish I could tell him it wasn't what it looked like. I wasn't ogling the man. I was frozen with fear.

A finger is tucked under my chin to turn my face, my eyes colliding with Sasha's. He moves my hair off my cheek then leans in to whisper, "Come to my room tonight. And do *not* come back out here." Then he trails his lips along my cheek and to my mouth. I'm stunned when he kisses me. It isn't crude or punishing. It also isn't appropriate enough for an audience.

He pulls back to give me a cocky grin, his gold teeth gleaming, then swats my butt. Hard enough to make me jump a little in his lap. He chuckles, but it's a taunting sound. "Run along, *kukolka*." He jerks his hips up, launching me to my feet. I don't delay.

I walk out of the dining room quickly, but I don't head back to the kitchen. Sasha told me not to go back out there, so I need to avoid the kitchen altogether and hope my absence isn't noticeable.

I'm still shaken up when I turn the corner and almost run right into Greta. I squeal and slap a hand over my chest in fright. She frowns up at me. "Where are you going?"

I take a deep breath. "To get the cleaning stuff from the closet."

"You're on kitchen duty."

My shoulders sag. "I just came from there. I helped serve Mr. Rogov and his guests lunch."

Her stern look deflates, awareness registering on her face. "Go ahead. Stick to the guest rooms on the east wing while they are unoccupied."

I nod my head and as usual, she doesn't stick around for me to thank her.

Grabbing a cleaning caddy from the supply closet, I make my way upstairs to do a sweep of the guest rooms in the east wing like she said. The rooms all have luggage and various personal effects. When Greta said unoccupied, she obviously meant momentarily.

I finish up cleaning one room and move to the next, trying not to think about seeing Sasha tonight. I'd be lying if I said I didn't miss him, but that doesn't make me any less nervous. I know it'll be goodbye. I have no idea how I will react to it.

My steps falter as I enter the next room. It looks unoccupied with the bed perfectly made, and when I make my way into the bathroom, the only sign of occupancy is the meticulous way the items are placed on the vanity. No water stains or little hairs from shaving. But it's the navy hand towel that catches my attention. I turn and find its match hanging on the hook. Also clean and pristine, both not belonging to the estate.

The bathroom smells fresh with some kind of sanitizer. Then I notice the copious disinfectant wipes placed throughout the space. The back of the toilet, both sides of the sink's vanity, a pack next to the faucet. Is this guy a germaphobe or something?

Curious, I head into the closet since there isn't much to clean in the bathroom. *Holy shit. Who is this guy?* I bet it's Cedric. Each piece of clothing is sealed in a garment bag and hung up. And I mean *every* piece of clothing. Even the hangers aren't even ours. Only a serial killer would be this thorough and bringing all of his own things, and Cedric screamed creepy serial killer, the germaphobe part was unexpected, but not particularly surprising. I can picture him now dismembering someone like Dexter. But all the tarp and plastic aren't so that he doesn't get caught. It's because he's afraid of germs.

Not wanting to stick around much longer in case he comes back, I leave the closet and double check the bed. I didn't notice it at first, but those are definitely not our sheets. Probably not our pillows in those cases either. If

I'm right about my suspicions, I'm sure he wouldn't be too keen on someone in his room touching his things.

Time to leave and act like I was never here.

The next room is a total contrast to the last one. Whoever this guy is, he's a fucking slob. It looks like he's been living here a week and I know he couldn't have occupied this room for more than one night so far. But the sheets are crumpled and hanging off the bed, the chairs in the sitting area are all rearranged, a suitcase lies just outside of the closet with clothing hanging out of it and scattered around the floor.

Sighing, I quickly get to work.

I tackle the bathroom first, then I tidy up the closet, and hang the rest of the person's clothing up and place the empty suitcase inside. Whoever the occupant is likes his dark liquor. A decanter of it with only half its contents left is in the sitting area along with a dirty glass. With my personal experience, men who drink dark liquor excessively always turn into a depraved miscreant. The dark memories has me scurrying along to get this room over with.

The final chore is making the bed once the sheets are changed. I closed the door so I would be alerted when someone entered, and it fulfilled its purpose as I hear it open.

Composing myself, I turn around to address the intruder and come face to face with the man that touched me in the dining room. He seems pleasantly surprised to find me in here. *Alone.*

His grin has me wanting to run, but I give him a friendly smile instead. "I'm just finishing up, sir. I'll be out of your hair in a second." I spin around to give my back, praying he leaves me alone now that Sasha openly laid claim to me. Even if he let them think I was his 'favorite pet,' as Mr. Rogov so nicely put it.

"I see why Sasha has some kind of fondness for you," he says, hunger in his tone. "You are a sexy little thing." I ignore him and hurriedly iron out the crinkles on top of the comforter with my shaking hands. "But nothing too special." His voice is now closer. I start putting all the pillows into place. "Must have a sweet pussy." Closer… "Or can swallow a good dick," he says from right behind me. Not touching me, but close enough to feel the heat from his body.

I fluff the last pillow, but I'm terrified to turn around. "Uh," I clear my throat, "I'm all done in here." I pretend to iron out more crinkles. "Is there anything I can get for you, sir?"

The heat from his body intensifies and I can now feel his breath moving the back of my hair as he breathes down on me. "Collin," someone interrupts, and I exhale in relief.

"Pity," the first intruder, who is apparently named Collin, mutters, and I feel like I can take a breath when his heat dissipates. "I was only looking," he muses.

I bend down to gather the dirty sheets. "Right," the other man I haven't faced yet responds curtly.

I put my head down and move towards my only exit. "See you around, beautiful!" Collin calls out in a derisive tone, mocking my skittish state.

That feeling of someone demanding my acknowledgement pulls at me again. I don't have to look up to know who it is. But my eyes involuntarily move to the dark ones locked on me. Cedric. His intense stare and mysterious smirk…it's chlling.

It's only a second as I walk by him and able to break the connection, but it's one long second, intense enough to rattle me and have me practically running out of there.

When I turn out of the bedroom, ready to bask in freedom, I almost run right into someone. I screech and jump back, still jumpy from my most recent encounter.

The large combat boots block my way. I timidly roll my eyes all the way up the massive figure. He was at the table with the other men, standing out like a sore thumb. Not only was he one of few not wearing a suit, but because he looks more like he should be in a motorcycle gang than hanging around the bratva. He looks like he's close to seven feet tall with the brawn to match. The sleeves on his thermal are pushed up his thick forearms revealing colorful ink. The auburn-colored hair that matches his thick beard is long and tied up in a knot behind his head, and his emerald eyes are cast downwards on me. There's no smirk or malice to his face, but it's no less intimidating.

I literally gulp and try not to swallow my tongue. "I'm so sorry, sir. I didn't see you there."

"It's no problem." His deep voice rumbles. Then he steps to one side, giving me clear passage.

Don't have to tell me twice, Thor.

I breeze past him and go as fast as I can without running. After tossing the sheets into the laundry, I make a beeline for my room. For the first time, it feels like a safe place, and I couldn't be more grateful.

THIRTY-THREE

SASHA

The stress of today and *every* day weighs heavy on me as I sit and wait for Vivian. It's stressful enough meeting with other eminent families. The stress of wondering who's plotting against you is stifling.

But I was even edgier from having to sit with Kazimir in the same room as my father. I know it was most difficult for him. Not only did my father disrespect Kazimir by scheming his demise behind his back, but he almost succeeded at killing what means the most to him. Marta.

For him to sit there as if he were oblivious to his uncle's deception was an award-winning performance. The word underestimated is underrated when it comes to my cousin.

If roles were reversed, and Vivian had almost died, in *any* situation, I'm not sure if I could sit there outwardly unperturbed and possess the same remarkable amount of poise.

In order for Kazimir to get away with obtaining his innocence in his father's deplorable decent, he managed to make ties with one of the biggest names in the entire underworld. Alejandro Martinez. Cuban born with strong connections with practically every country in the world, he's the strongest ally you could wish for, and the worst enemy to ever acquire. Their new friendship isn't something that was publicly announced, so Kazimir flew right under the radar. Alejandro took complete ownership for my uncle's death.

When Vivian entered the pit of venomous snakes, I was more than miffed. Then Collin O'Ryan laid his filthy hand on her, and I was murderous.

Fortunate for Collin, his brother, Cedric, saved his life by anticipating his brother's unstable impulses and keeping a close eye on him. Artem informed me of the incident between my Vivian and Collin in his room after I had issued my warning. I was already spitting mad from the first encounter. He had to all but physically restrain me until I calmed down.

I'm drained from today's adrenaline rushes, but the prospect of seeing Vivian tonight gives me enough fuel to keep going. This could be goodbye for us. I plan to make it out of this alive, and if everything goes as planned, I will be able to have Vivian in the way that I yearn for most. But my father has bested me at everything thus far. Always remaining one step ahead.

Kazimir advised me to take a page from my old man's book, but it's hard to outwit the inventor. There's a very strong chance my father has already calculated a collapse in his kingdom.

As long as I can get Vivian out of this before my father takes action, it will be a victory for me.

I'm sitting on the edge of my bed with my head hung and my hands clasped between wide knees. I'm so lost inside my own head that when two pink fluffy slippers appear in my peripheral, my head pops up on high alert. I failed to hear her approach.

She stands there meekly wearing a shirt of mine that brushes the tops of her thighs. Seeing it on her brings out this unfamiliar feeling, but it isn't unwelcome. It's a feeling that's been suppressed and buried deep inside of me to lay dormant.

"You didn't hear me come in?" she asks in her soft angelic voice.

So many things I need to say to her, but every single word dries up on my tongue. I straighten to my feet and take one long stride to close in on any space between us. Cupping her beautiful face in my hands, I slam my mouth down on hers. Unwilling to waste even one second of my time.

She's slow to react, but when she does she's almost as feral as me. Our most primal urges surfacing, burying our pride and judgement. Pretending the world can desist and put a pause on turning.

Her hands are all over my naked torso and she moans when I grind my erection through my pants into her. When she digs her nails into my back, dragging them down over the mangled scars, I chomp down on her lip. She doesn't whimper in pain; she whines in salacious greed. Begging for more. My little cat is always begging for more.

Picking her up in my arms to wrap her strong legs around me, I spin us around to crash down on the bed. Pinning her underneath me, I grind into her more and she moans and pushes her perfect curves into me.

Her shirt comes up over her head revealing her perfect naked form. I shuck my pants and briefs off, my cock butting against her slickness. We're both groaning through our vicious attacks with our mouths and our hands. I impale her with a single yet brutal thrust. Stealing her breath and filling her up. She whines into my mouth, but doesn't let up. Continuing to delve her tongue into my mouth to explore it and wrestle with mine.

Spearing her savagely, I alternate between rocking and rolling my hips. "Sasha," she hoarsely whispers.

"Yes, angel," I murmur into her mouth.

"I—" she arches her back and cranes her neck back so I can attack her neck with teeth and tongue. "This can't be it."

Growling, I rut into her. The malediction of our fucked-up fate drives me to a place I avoid. Reaching a hand between us, I pinch her clit. She yelps and tries to wiggle free, but it only makes me direct more pressure.

She starts crying but she's pulling at me, not letting me go anywhere. Only trying to get closer. She starts chanting my name like a prayer, all the way up until her cunt flutters around my cock and chokes it. Her muscles lose its strength and I twist our bodies to have her straddling my lap with my ass perched on the edge of the mattress.

Everything seems to slow down, yet becomes ardently heightened. She rocks her hips in my lap and I can feel every single point of contact. Our foreheads are pressed firmly together, arms banded around one another like the only thing keeping us alive is the shared breath between us leaving a dewy sheen on our skin.

I thread my long fingers into the back of her hair to separate us. She lazily peels her eyes open and looks me in the eye. Not once skipping a beat. I press my slack lips to hers and we indolently move them, too lost inside a sensual haze to give it more physical effort.

The buildup is as intense as it is when I'm fucking her until she bleeds, but it's a different kind of eruption. It's leisurely and drawn-out. She mewls and her kisses turn sloppy, confessing to me that she's teetering on that euphoric cliff's edge. It has my body chasing its own high.

Her moans double and her energy becomes more aggressive. My hands grip her ass cheeks with a crushing force. I don't pull out. I should, but fuck that.

She quivers as I spout warm ropes inside of her. Not giving a flying fuck about the possible consequences. Not right now. Later I can beat myself up about it.

Her hips come to a stop, and she drops her head to my shoulder. I embrace her body in my arms and we breathe heavily as silent moments tick by.

We only move to get comfortable under the sheets, her head on my chest and my fingers trailing up and down the silky-smooth skin of her backside.

"What now?" she whispers.

"In two days, you'll be removed from the estate and placed at the Kalashnik estate." She looks up at me, but I can't look at her until I get my words out.

"Kalashnik?"

"My cousin, Kazimir."

"Oh." I can feel her eyes leave my face. "He was at the table earlier, wasn't he?"

"He was."

"The one with the scar on his face," she says quietly.

"*Da.*"

"Do you know how he got that scar?"

I smile a little at her curiosity. Unabashedly asking questions. "His father gave it to him."

She looks up at me again. "His father?" I nod. "Oh, my God. Are all your fathers that horrible?"

I snort, finding more humor in it than necessary. From an outsider, it *would* be surprising. "Most."

"Why?"

"Having an heir is paramount. But they always fear being usurped by them."

"Like Kronos," she murmurs.

I grin up at the ceiling, delighted she knows anything about Greek mythology and the comparison she found in it. "Yes, *kukolka*. Much like Kronos."

They procreate to birth heirs, keeping the empire as a legacy handed down from generation to generation. But our fathers tend to envy us and our youth. Knowing that their time will one day run out, and we'll overthrow them without much effort. That we'll one day become greater than them. They're so accustomed to holding all the power, they don't ever want to give it up. They eventually see us as their biggest threat for the crown, rather than their closest ally.

"So, how long will I be at your cousin's? And where will I go afterwards?"

I turn on my side and gather her in my arms, our faces hardly an inch apart. "I can't give you answers to everything just yet. But I need you to trust me. I know I haven't earned it, but I need you to trust me now more than ever."

Her hands rest flat on my chest as she searches my eyes. "Only if you tell me one thing." I wait. "Why are you doing all this?"

It's a repeated question, but a tightness still constricts around my throat. I feel jittery, like I did when Kazimir asked me if I loved Vivian. It's an unwelcome feeling of vulnerability. I don't know why this question is so hard to answer. He's right. I do know if I love her, but it wouldn't be fair to her to give her hope where there might not be any. Where there might only be grief.

She boldly stares back at me, silently demanding some kind of answer. She licks her lips and asks, "Will I ever see you again?"

I brush back some of her dark hair and shake my head. "It wouldn't be safe for me to see you," I lie.

There are two possible outcomes from this. I either succeed and take out my father and can go back for Vivian. The false hope. Or my father will outwit me and kill me. If the latter happens, Kazimir knows not to tell her of my death, and to safely set her up with a new life somewhere far away.

"Then come with me." She pushes her body into me, as if trying to tempt me.

"You know that I can't."

"Can't or won't?"

"Both." She darts her eyes away and I see her swallow hard. Gently tilting her chin up with my fingers, my nostrils flare when I see the tears welling in her eyes. "I can't, because this is the life I was dealt." I pause. "I won't, because I will not risk your life. You disappearing… he might not even try to hunt you down. You could start a new life. One where you can be anyone and do anything. If I were to come with you, we would spend the rest of our lives on the run, because he would never stop hunting me. I won't risk your life, and I won't spend my life running like a coward."

"So, you'll spend it here, desolate, alone and miserable?"

"Knowing that you and my sisters will be safe? Yes. I will. And I will find some sort of peace in that."

Even though my father would most definitely use my sisters' lives to try and draw me out, the idea of leaving with Vivian is still tempting. Then I think about what would happen to her if he found us, and I realize again that it's impossible.

My father has to die, or I do.

"I'm so sorry." She shakes her head and takes a long blink. "I wasn't thinking about your sisters. That was selfish of me."

My lips slightly curl up at the corners. "My angel," I rasp.

"I wish I'd gotten to meet them."

"Me too, *kukolka*." I press my lips to her forehead and leave a kiss there, burying my nose in her hair to savor the scent.

Rada is the warmer of the two. Vera is harder to crack. She's jaded with a huge chip on her shoulder. But I have no doubt they would grow to love Vivian.

Almost as much as I do.

THIRTY-FOUR

SASHA

"Sir, your father wants to see you," I'm passing through the foyer when one of my father's dogs stops me.

"Now?"

He nods his head. Sighing, I pass him and head straight for my father's office, eager to get whatever this is over with. Today is the day I'm smuggling Vivian to Kazimir's estate. She'll be transported to a few different locations as a decoy, then make it to Kazimir's as her temporary destination.

I'm not aware of my surrounds when I walk into my father's office until it's too late. My father stands behind his desk, but something catches my eye when I stop in front of it. Looking to my left, I find Trip. Bloodied and beaten, tied to a chair.

Before I can go for my gun, I'm restrained. My arms bound by two large men as I curse and thrash. "What the fuck is this!" I bellow out.

The men aren't much of a match for me as I'm able to free one arm. Before I get to grab at my gun another two men jump in. I'm overpowered and forced into a chair as they make quick work of tying me up.

I'm deranged with madness and frothing at the mouth as my father stares back at me, unfazed at the display. I taste blood in my mouth from the struggle and spit a mouthful out onto the floor.

"I'm so sorry, Sasha," Trip croaks out weakly next to me, but I keep my eyes locked with my father's cold ones. "He swore he'd kill my mom and my sister." Although Trip is estranged from them, he still doesn't wish for any harm to come to them. He hasn't spoken to them since before he came to work for us, but of course my father had him thoroughly cased out, scraped up any useful information or possible incentive.

"Tell me what you have been planning behind my back," my father says evenly.

"Didn't he already tell you?" I sass, referring to Trip.

"I want to hear it from you," he growls, the arrogance rising to the surface.

I stare back at him, unwilling to admit to anything. Trip didn't know everything, and neither does my father. Vivian would be in here tied up as well if he had.

He gives a dip with his head, and I hear a gun cock. I slowly turn to face Trip and he's looking back at me, eyes already dead. The gun is pointed right at his head, and he and I both know he's not making it out of here alive.

"He doesn't know—" *BANG!*

I don't flinch or react as blood explodes from the other side of his head and his body almost flips back in the chair from the impact. Seemingly cool, I turn back to face my father. Acting as if his life meant nothing to me. Now isn't the time to mourn my friend. Even though he betrayed me in the end, he's been close to me for years. Loyal for most of them.

I watch prudently as my father rounds the desk to stand in front of it. He doesn't tear his eyes away from mine as one of his men comes to hand him his revolver. He accepts it without even blinking.

"You've been given everything," he starts. "One day you would've inherited everything." He glances down to check the chamber, spins it, then snaps it back into place. His eyes come back to mine. "Why the fuck now?"

I don't answer and I see it coming before my head is rocked to the side with the punishing strike. It feels as if it were a blunt object, but it's just Ox's fist. We named him Ox for a reason.

"Why?" my father demands again.

I brace myself for another blow. He's merciless as he hits me in the same spot. Spots dancing in my vision and I spit more blood out before recovering. My head up and my eyes fearlessly locked on my father's.

His eyes jump up over my head when the door opens and the clamorous sounds of a struggle sound behind me. If he had already rounded up Trip and turned him, I'm sure I know who he has now. But the fear of one of them being Vivian...

I don't let the intense relief show when I see only Artem and Bash being dragged in. Bash is already bloodied up, I'm sure because it took several men to beat him into submission before being able to restrain him. I wouldn't be surprised if he took at least one man out in the process with his hands alone.

They're both forced into chairs and bound to them. All the while they curse and spit and fight. Artem sees Trip's corpse first and stills. Bash then takes notice, and he visibly vibrates with scorching rage. Seeing Bash angry will make a grown man piss himself. To see him irate, it sends a shockwave through the room that every person in here can feel down to the bone. He's fucking menacing.

I look back at my father again and he now has a venomous smirk on his aging face. "What have I taught you about caring for things?" he taunts. "They're weaknesses."

He turns to my men and I strain every muscle in my body, but I'm helpless. "I'll give you each one chance to tell me what my son has been up to," he instructs. "I'll start with you first Bash." He pauses. "What is my son planning?"

I hear Bash hock up a ball of spit and blood which he launches it at my father. It lands right at his feet. "*Chlen tebie v rot,*" *take a dick in your mouth,* he sneers.

The offense is evident on my father's face as he raises his gun and cocks it. There is no protest from Bash as he stares down the barrel of the gun without fear. I remain facing forward, planning all the ways I'm going to rip my father into pieces.

The door bursts open behind me, giving my father pause. "Sir, you need to come to the surveillance room. It's urgent," the man rushes out, the panic in his voice lucid.

My father takes a deep breath and lowers the gun. His eyes bouncing to mine for a moment then back to Ox. "Stay with them," he orders. "If they manage to get free," he looks at me. "Shoot them."

We're all silent as he leaves the room, leaving us armed with only one man. Though that man has the strength of three, and we're utterly defenseless.

There's no point in trying to convince Ox to free us. He's as loyal as dogs come. He's not even capable of going against orders. Like a programmed, robotic soldier.

A boom in the distance has us all silent. The invasion on the estate wasn't supposed to happen for two more days. My father was going to find out about the missing maid and be distracted. That's when Kazimir's men would invade.

Ox's phone goes off and he fishes it from his pocket. He frowns as he listens, then he tells the caller that he'd be right there, and asks what to do with us before nodding and placing the phone back in his pocket. Bash lunges at him, taking him down with Artem right behind, throwing himself at the brawl of heavy fists and muscle rolling on the ground. I pull and yank at my restraints, wondering how the fuck they got out of theirs, but mine don't even budge.

Another rumble comes from the distance, this time rattling the walls. Then the sound of a gun goes off in the brawl in front of me, and I pray Ox is on the receiving end of the shot. I release the breath I was holding as Bash and Artem kick Ox's massive body off of them and help each other to their feet.

"What the fuck is going on?" I growl as Artem heads for me, and Bash starts collecting any guns he can find.

"I don't know," Artem murmurs as he cuts the ropes from my wrists. "We couldn't get a hold of you or Trip, so we knew something was up." My wrists are freed, and I go to rip at the restraints around my ankles myself. "We strapped up and prepared for the worst." He holds up a knife. Obviously the one he used to cut himself free.

"Vivian," I say as I soon as I jump to my feet. Another boom goes off, this time much closer. I look to Bash as he hands us each a gun. "Find her and make sure she gets to the panic room." He nods and leaves without needing further instruction.

"What do you want me to do?" Artem asks, prepared for anything I ask of him.

Rapid gunfire grows louder as the intruders breach the property. "We're going to play one last game with my father."

I have enough faith in Bash to get to Vivian and get her to the panic room to allay my worries for the time being. Vengeance on my father drives me to finish this now.

We replace Bash's chair with Ox's body, restraining him, and we jump back into our own chairs, pretending to still be tied up. I'm sure whoever Ox spoke to gave him orders to shoot and kill us. I know my father enough to know he'll come back to his office for a few things before fleeing the estate. Survival being more vital than pride.

Artem knows to take down anyone who accompanies my father. But the old man is mine.

It's not long before the door opens and footsteps approach. We hang our heads as if dead, and the ruse is a success. My father instructs someone to make sure we're dead and there are no hard feelings for my father's callousness. No sentiments or nostalgia breaking my heart. Only revenge flowing through me.

As soon as someone comes close enough to me, I strike. Even though Artem and I are both armed, we're immensely outnumbered. Two to six. I use the first guy I took down as a shield and fire back at my father's men while scanning the room for him.

Another boom rattles the floors, causing our ears to ring and I faintly hear my father shouting as the two men left standing cover him. Artem and I take them down, but my father slips out.

We hastily collect their guns and strap up, ready to join the fight and hunt down my father. Bash appears right outside the doorway, out of breath. "I think she made it to the panic room."

I'm instantly furious. "You think?!" I shout over the gunfire and chaos.

"I can't find her anywhere and the panic room has been recently sealed," he rushes out and we all duck when another loud noise hits and debris from the ceiling rains down on us.

It's hardly comforting, but the only way I can make sure of her safety is to find my father and finish this once and for all.

"Remember." I check the magazine of my gun. "My father is mine to kill. If you find him, take him down if you must, but do not kill him."

They both silently agree, and we walk right in the direction of the bloodshed.

Unless my father was able to tell all of our men that I am now the enemy, they won't shoot us. And Kazimir's men know not to shoot us as well, giving us a pretty clear passage.

I won't rest until I have my father's blood pooling at my feet.

THIRTY-FIVE

I'm just finishing up changing the sheets in a bedroom when there's a clamor in the distance. It sounds like a bomb just went off. The anxiety and fear immobilizing me.

I hear commotion below me on the first floor, but I remain frozen to my spot. Not having a clue what to do.

Another loud booming sounds, closer this time and my fight or flight instincts kick in. The panic room. Is this the 'in case of an emergency' Artem was talking about? It sure feels like the potential attack he cryptically described, and I remember his instructions including that they may not be able to reach me.

I don't think it's necessary to stand around and debate whether or not that time has come.

But what about Sasha? What about Nastia and Greta?

He also told me to tell no one and run for it.

Fuck.

I poke my head out of the doorway and I see men rushing past with large guns strapped to them and shouting in Russian leaving me completely clueless. Loud noises begin sounding off one after another like gunshots. Really *big* gunshots. There's a temporary break in the gunfire and I hear shouting coming from all over the house. I have no idea what's being said, but if the bomb-like noises are any indication, something is very wrong.

Oh, God. What the hell is going on?

Another boom blasts through the estate and it rocks me on my feet and rattles my chest. I cover my head afraid that pieces of the ceiling will crumble on top of me.

"Vivian!" Nastia comes out of nowhere in a panic. Tears streaming down her face and hyperventilating.

"Nastia, what's going on?"

Now gunshots begin going off and they're coming from right outside the house. She screams and jumps into my arms. Sobbing and hugging me close as if I could somehow protect her. Actually, maybe I can.

"Come on." I grab her hand and begin pulling her.

We head for the stairs but stop when a man with a gun runs past the landing. Fuck, we need to get downstairs to get to the panic room at the end of the hall. What about Greta though? I should find her.

More gunshots explode and bullets fly over our heads, peppering the wall behind us. *Fuck, now they're coming from inside.* We jump down and wait for it to pause. There's obviously no time to go on any rescue missions. But it's too risky to go down these stairs. We'll most likely catch a bullet before we even hit the bottom.

"Nastia." I turn to her, and she's crouched in a tiny ball, her one hand squeezing the life out of mine and her head buried in her other. "Nastia, I need you to think." She sobs and shakes. "Nastia!" I yell. She flinches and only curls up tighter. "Nastia," I growl through my teeth and try prying her face out of the obscurity of her arm. I yank my hand out of hers to grip the back of her blonde hair and pull it up to meet my gaze.

"Nastia," I say more calmly but with sternness. "I need you to think." I chop my words up slowly hoping it'll help her to understand. Her English is coming along much quicker than my Russian, though she had a head start on me. "Is there another way downstairs?" She cries, her chin quivering and her eyes squeezed shut. "Nastia," I say with tenderness, trying to coax her out of her hysteria. "I know where we can hide. Where we can be safe." She rapidly blinks at me, trying to depict my words. "How else can we get downstairs? Is there another way to get us down that way?" I point towards in the direction we need access to. She sniffles and tries to hide again when more gunshots go off, but I keep a hold of her hair. "Nastia," I grit out, trying not to shake her again. "We need to get downstairs and go that way. Do you understand me," I demand firmly.

She swallows and blinks vigorously again, trying to clear her mind. Then she nods and I exhale heavily. The adrenaline pumping through me has me cool and collected, driven by determination. I smile to reassure her. "Good. Where?" She meekly points down the hallway. "Come on." I have to drag her to dart across the top of the steps. Once on the other side and out of sight, she gains more confidence and leads the way.

If there wasn't another path to take us downstairs without taking our chances walking through the line of fire, I thought about using the secret passageway through Sasha's room located up here. We could've taken it to my room and then went down the hall through there, but if my door was for some reason locked, we'd be fucked. The only other place to go would be the catacombs, and I don't know what would await us down there. For all I know, whoever is attacking us might end up down there and we'd be sitting ducks.

We get to a stairwell I've never seen before. I've never ventured this far in the east wing. We quickly descend the stairs hand in hand, trying not to trip over ourselves. It's dark, but the noise of the gunfight now seems distant.

Once at the bottom, I know where we are and take back the lead. Luckily, we don't pass anyone as we run through a room with doors on both sides, the other ones leading into the hall we need to get to.

More gunshots pop off and Nastia jolts forward with a horrendous scream. She falls to her knees, stopping us. "Nastia!" I crouch down and she pulls her hand away from her left shoulder, covered in blood. She tremors at the sight of it, and I know she's about to either go into shock or freak the fuck out. Neither would do us any good.

"You're okay, you're okay," I chant and pull her to her feet. "We have to keep going." I wrap an arm around her waist, taking most of her weight. She sobs loudly, but she lets me pull her along. "You're doing so good. Just a little further."

We get to that bedroom at the end of the hall. I close and lock the door behind us for good measure. Moving swiftly towards the closet, Nastia stumbles, but I keep her upright and force her to keep moving with me.

My fingers are shaking as I lift my hand and enter the passcode. "Fuck." I accidentally pressed two buttons at once and the keys light up red. "Shit. He didn't tell me what to do if this happened," I mutter and wait a few seconds for the red light behind the buttons to turn off. Taking my time this round, I punch in the code, and the door clicks.

I don't hesitate or linger. I crank open the door with my one arm, still holding up a wilting Nastia with the other, and I pull us inside. Giving the room outside one more glance, I shut the door and seal us inside. The locks click into place as soon as the door closes and the sounds of battle fade as the lights flicker on.

"Come on." I propel us to the cot and let her fall onto it.

There's metal shelving full of food, water, and supplies. I rummage through it frantically looking for any kind of first-aid kit. "Yes," I hiss when I find what I'm looking for. I don't have a clue of what I'm doing, but I know her wound needs to be at least cleaned and covered.

I spin around holding the supplies and the screens distract me, pulling me in. There's no sound to the monitors, but I can see men gunning each other down. I can't even tell who is who. It's not like they're wearing jerseys or a certain color to make a distinction.

I frantically search for Sasha but can't find him. The anxiety overwhelming as the adrenaline courses through my veins. I get even closer to the screens where my nose is almost touching them as I keep looking for him. My stomach sinks with gut-wrenching fear. The physical toll it can have on your body is unthinkable.

I continue scouring the monitors as I finally find Sasha. I press both palms around him on the screen and send a silent plea to God, beseeching him to keep my Sasha safe. He didn't ask for this. To be brought into his fucked-up world. He has a good heart. A heart that's been stifled from acknowledging all the positive things he's done in his life. From saving a cold animal, to caring for his sisters when their father abandoned them… and saving me. He doesn't deserve to go out like this.

Nastia moans behind me, reminding me I'm not alone. She's writhing in pain when I rush to her and empty the supplies I'm carrying onto the cot. "I know, I know," I utter under my breath and push her onto her good side so I can see the wound. I find the entry and exit wounds and sigh in minor relief. "Well, good thing is, I'm pretty sure the bullet went right through. So, I don't have to try and fish it out." I give her a tight smile, but it's evident she doesn't have a clue what I'm saying. I give her a brighter smile. "You'll be okay, Nastia. I'm going to clean this and bandage you up." She nods her head, and I get to work.

I work quickly, cutting the fabric away from her shoulder to be able to clean it thoroughly and pack the injury with gauze to maintain the pressure until we can get her some proper medical attention. I'm anxious to get back to the monitors to find Sasha again.

"Here, this should help with the pain," I say giving her a few small pills and a bottle of water.

"Thank you," she says quietly and accepts them from me.

There's nothing more I can do for her at the moment, so I rush back to the wall of screens and search for Sasha. I find him quickly this time, not much further from where he was last. He looks like a warrior. Right in his element. I should be terrified, but instead I'm filled with pride.

"No!" I scream when I see something hit him, jerking him back. He's still on his feet as he aims his gun and shoots it. "No!" Something else hits him, hurtling him back several feet and to the ground. He goes down hard, and I watch in horror as he lies there unmoving. "No!" I choke out and slap one hand over my mouth and the other over my stomach. Despair and anguish ripping at my insides.

I back away from the screen slowly as I wait for him to move. Something. Anything. A foot, a finger, his chest. *Move, goddamnit! No, Sasha. You can't do this. You cannot do this to me.*

I knew when we said our goodbyes that we wouldn't be together in this life. I had accepted that I would be forced to mourn a love lost. But I hadn't planned on having to mourn the loss of his life.

"No," I cry and drop to my knees. Tears pour from my eyes and I feel like part of me is dying with him. I feel like I just lost the other half of my soul. My life no longer has meaning. I'll walk around a desolate planet living like a ghost.

"Vivian, what is it?" I hear Nastia from behind me, but I can't right now. She wouldn't understand. "Vivian?"

"Rest, Nastia," I say flatly with my back still turned to her. "You'll need your strength." She silently settles in, still shaken up and crying. I turn to pull the sheet over her body and watch until she closes her eyes.

We both need rest. But I'm not tired. The adrenaline is waning, but anguish and vengeance replace it. Getting to my feet, I go to the cabinet where I know the guns are. I grab them all, having them ready to use. Sitting on the floor with my back against the cot, I sprawl out the guns. I was told they're loaded, and the safeties are off. All I have to do is shoot. Nothing feels real anymore. I'm in a panic room, surrounded by weapons, ready to kill or be killed. My eyes betray me and stray to the screens. My breath stutters when I see that half of them has lost signal, including the one where I last saw Sasha's final resting place.

THIRTY-SIX

SASHA

"Sasha," a familiar voice brings me into consciousness. "Artem! Over Here!" he calls out and I make an attempt to open my eyes. "Get up, Sasha. You're not dying here," Kazimir says loudly, his voice as monotone as always.

"Sasha," Artem says, slapping my cheek and I let out a groan. "Come on, you bastard. Open your fucking eyes," he hisses and slaps me a little harder.

"Vivian," I mumble. Her face is all I can see behind my closed lids.

"I don't know where she is, but you're not doing her any good by lying here dying. Now, get up. We need to finish this," Kazimir pushes.

It seems to do the trick as my eyes crack open. My vision is skewed, my ears are ringing, but I dig deep for some strength.

"Come on," Artem says in a strained voice as he pushes me up into a seated position. Several parts of my body scream in agony, reminding me I'm alive.

I look around at the motionless bodies scattered around me. "My father?" I rasp.

"Injured, but alive," Kazimir states.

"Bash?" I question as they both help me to my feet, my left leg in excruciating pain.

"Alive when I saw him last," Artem murmurs.

I notice it sounds less like a war zone. "Where is he?" I ask, referring to my father.

They try to help hold my weight, but I bat them away. I hold back a groan from the unenduring agony that has my head spinning and my stomach rolling with nausea as I steady myself on my feet. I look at Kazimir and he points down the hall.

I look down and check my gun to make sure I have enough ammo. "Start taking care of things. It's time to clean house." I hold my gun up and look between them. They both have injuries of their own, but nothing serious, from the looks of it. "I want anyone loyal to my father taken out." They nod their heads, and we part ways.

I'm sluggish as I make my way to my father's office where he decided to take cover like a coward. He most likely tried to make it to his chopper first but lost his crew shielding him on the way.

The door is closed and locked, most likely barricaded as well. Knowing how close I am numbs the pain like morphine to where there's hardly any, allowing me to move more freely.

Rendering the lock useless with bullets, I give the door a good shove. It only moves slightly. But I'm determined to get in no matter how much physical pain it'll cause me later. *This. Ends. Now.*

I crash through the door, almost catching a bullet when I stumble forward. I use the momentum to throw myself to the ground. No more gunshots sound off and I look around. The only place he could be hiding would be behind his desk.

A gargled, acidic chuckle comes out from behind it. "Didn't think you or Kazimir had the fucking balls." He pauses and I army crawl closer. "Tell me why. I know you don't give a fuck about any of this, so why? Kazimir promise you something?"

"You made an enemy with him." I check my gun while he chuckles then starts hacking. "You don't sound so good, father."

"That *boy* shouldn't have been given his position."

"Says the man who's hiding behind his desk like a fucking pussy." I slowly rise to my feet. "That *boy* has everyone underestimating him. Making him lethal."

I don't hear any movement, only his ragged breathing. I stealthily circle the desk with my gun raised. My father looks up at me from his sitting position on the floor. Face pallid and close to death's door as he relies on the desk to hold him up.

He doesn't even attempt to hold his own gun up as he laughs, revealing his blood-stained teeth. "This is all for the whore, isn't it?" I don't bother with an answer. "Always over a whore," he says dryly. "You've learned nothing from me." He looks at me with such disappointment.

"You've taught me plenty. I wouldn't be the one standing and aiming the gun if you hadn't, so thank you for that."

He makes the mistake of raising his gun and opens his mouth to speak, but I make him swallow bullets. I vehemently pop off round after round until there isn't much left to shoot. I don't feel guilt. I feel nothing for the man who I called father for thirty-two years. The only thing I feel as the weight of my father's oppression falls away is freedom.

Without him, I can be my own man. I can have whatever it is that I want. No more hiding. No more paranoia of constantly being watched.

I know any remaining gunfire is just the guys finishing off the final members of my father's crew as I limp out of the office. We'll start over and build up our own. Fresh meat with no ties to my father.

It feels like it takes me forever to get to the bedroom at the end of the hall. The door to the bedroom has already been broken into, hopefully from Bash making sure she got to safety. I stumble my way to the closet. The door is still tightly sealed when I get there. I'm hardly able to stay on my feet as I attempt to enter the code through the pain and the blood dripping in my eye obscuring my vision. I use the last bit of strength to pry open the door.

When I do, I come face to face with Vivian holding up a gun, aiming it right at my head. Her hands are shaking, but she looks fierce and determined. Like an ascending angel, doing God's bidding.

Even knowing that it's me, she doesn't lower her weapon. Tears trail down her porcelain face and my instinct is to wrestle the gun from her, which would be easy even in my fragile state. But if she wants to, she should shoot me. She too should be able to take what she wants. She's earned that right, and I would die happy knowing that she's safe. My father is gone. Artem, Bash, and Kazimir know not to harm a single hair on her head. Even if she does kill me, she's safe to start a new life.

Flashbacks of our first moments together start reeling through my head as we have a standoff. Including the very first time I saw her. It was before she started working at our casino. I saw her walking out of the deli after making one of her weekly payments towards the debt she brazenly took on with us. She stirred things up inside of me that I was convinced were dead and was instantly significant to me. I spent the next week trying to shake her from my mind, but I found myself right back at the deli the very next week, just to catch a glimpse of Vivian James. And I continued to do so for almost two years.

If she never missed that payment, never came to work at the casino, I would've stayed away. Every part of her was meant for me, but in this life, I was not meant to have any kind of happiness. I only find it to lose it.

THIRTY-SEVEN

VIVIAN

I stare at the door with a gun at the ready. The coolness of the metal now warm in my hands. I don't know how much time passes, but the majority of the screens are still dark.

I hear Nastia stirring on the cot next to me. "Vivian?" I don't answer her. I can't. I can only think about keeping us alive. If I speak, I'll fall apart. "Vivian, are you okay?" I hear her sitting up and see her legs swinging off the bed, her feet landing on the floor next to me. I bob my head up and down. "How long have we been in here?" I shrug my shoulders. She goes quiet for a while. "What do we do?" she asks quietly.

I take a deep breath in then slowly let it out. "For now, we stay put. Here." I pick up one of the small guns next to me and stretch my arm out. "If someone gets that door open, we'll need to shoot our way out of here," I say in a dead tone.

Her eyes widen. "No. I don't want it."

"Take it, Nastia," I say evenly when lamentation and sorrow try to crush me. "Here." I place is next to her on the sheets and she starts vigorously shaking her head.

"No, no. I cannot."

"Yes. You can. Sasha is dead, and I don't know who else is, but if the wrong people find out we're in here, we're going to have to fight our way out." She continues to gawk. "I know you're scared. So am I. But we are not going to just hide in here until we rot away. Nor are we going to let those men take us and sell us or kill us." I point to the screens without looking. "If someone opens that door, and I say shoot, you shoot." I look at her solemnly. "Aim. And. Fire." I hold the gun up, aim it at the door, and put my finger on the trigger. "Please." My voice cracks and that mournful lump tries to choke me.

She looks at me with remorse and gingerly picks the gun up like it's a ticking time bomb. "All you have to do is aim," I aim at the door. "And pull the trigger." I give her a nod of encouragement and she shakily lifts the gun up and aims it at the door. She sniffles and swallows hard, and I watch as she begins to squeeze the trigger. "No!" She drops the gun in surprise, and I jump back the same time it cladders to the ground. Thank God it didn't accidentally go off.

I drop my head to my knees and close my eyes. Trying to conjure up serenity. Collecting myself, I pick up the gun and face her again. "Do not put your finger here," I lightly tap on the trigger. "Unless you are ready to shoot." I point it at the door and she nods her head with enthusiasm. I place the gun on the cot next to her and swivel the gun on the mattress so that the barrel isn't pointing at either of us.

I don't mean to be short with her. She's injured and scared. But I'm holding on by a thread here.

Sasha's face haunts me. His messy blonde hair, soft to the touch. Those dark eyes full of hope. His sexy smirk, showing off his pearly whites and his shiny gold caps.

I squeeze my eyes shut and drag my nails against my scalp, wishing I could pry those visions out of my head. It hurts. It hurts so badly. I should have looked for him. Begged him to forget about defending the place and just come with me to the panic room. I could've saved him.

The walls and door are soundproof, but I can feel the energy being drained from the estate. The life bleeding out of the cold floors and the stale walls. Not that there was much life in them to begin with. Always so cold and bleak.

I don't know when Nastia started to cry again, but I tuned her out some time ago. Living in my own head. Ignoring her sniffles and blubbering in Russian. She's sweet, but pretty much useless to me right now. She'll only get herself killed if Sasha's cousin doesn't come to our rescue like they said he would.

I fall in and out of consciousness. I know I need to rest at some point to recharge, but I can't risk it. I need to stay alert until I figure out whether or not we're safe.

I perk up, instantly sober and energized when there are noises coming from the door. I look at the panel with buttons and switches and know I need to get to the red button. The camera surveilling the door to the panic room is one amongst those that went out. Leaving me blind to whoever approaches.

It's too late though. Metal on metal screeches and Nastia begins to panic. But I'm solely focused on the door and armoring myself with indomitability and retribution for whatever comes next.

I rise up to my knees, hoping that by remaining low it'll give me some kind of advantage, and I point the gun. My arms are extended, elbows locked, shoulders tense. Not one little shake or shiver. I'm steady and wired.

I take a speedy glance over at Nastia and she's failed to arm herself like I told her to. "Pick the damn gun up, Nastia. Now," I command. I snatch up the gun up and shove it at her. She presses her back against the wall and shakes her head crying. Refusing to touch it. "Take the fucking gun!" I shout and she obeys with clumsy hands.

Awesome, she'll probably end up accidentally shooting me.

It's all I can do because we're out of time. The door is being cranked open and adrenaline bursts through my veins like a drug. I feel like I'm having an out of body experience.

The door is ungracefully opened, and everything dulls. Sound, smell, touch. The gun begins to shake in my hands as tunnel vision kicks in giving me blinders to anything around the bloodied, vengeful god standing at the threshold. A rifle hangs limply at his side and his chest raggedly expands under his torn and soiled shirt.

I'm frozen in fear. Terrified it's my mind playing tricks on me. I saw him die. He went down, and he did not get up.

"Do it, Vivian," he says, sounding like an exhausted version of himself. "I deserve it. Everything I've done to you; you have the right to pull that trigger." My chin trembles and fresh tears run down my face. "I'm warning you right now," he growls. "If you don't kill me, you're stuck with me. You're mine. So, if you don't want that… if you don't want me, then you have to kill me." He takes a large step forward and the gun shakes harder in my hands. My shoulders begin to burn with intensity as I slowly rise to my feet. "Do it," he pushes. "You know you want to. You'll be free of me. Finally, be free of this place." *It's him. It's really him.* "Free yourself, angel." He expands his arms out wide to give me a bigger target. "Be free. Pull the fucking trigger," he says calmly. It shakes me back to reality and I'm slow to realize this isn't a dream or a hallucination.

I'm only still holding the gun because I'm stunned. Why would he think I would shoot him? Why would he think I *could*?

Something shiny invades my peripheral and I remember Nastia. "It's okay, Nastia." My words are barely audible as I carefully put down my gun.

Sasha and I stare at one another. I'm disappointed to see that he's at all surprised that I would put my gun down.

A teary smile takes over my whole face and it only takes a few large strides to get close enough to launch myself into his outstretched arms. He releases a grunt, but his arms automatically close around me, holding me close and hard enough to make breathing a little difficult. I don't care though. He's real. He's alive.

"Fuck, baby," he grumbles into my hair. Then he starts murmuring in Russian and I bury my face into his neck more. A sob wracks through me and he pets the back of my hair gently. "I promise things will be different. We're safe. He's gone." His voice is low and emollient as he holds me tight. "You're safe with me."

I peel my face away to look him in the eye for a heated moment. Saying things with my eyes that I don't have the guts to put into words before I slant my mouth over his and kiss him deeply.

"I thought you were dead." I cry, tasting blood from his kisses. "I saw you go down and you weren't moving and I—"

"Sshh, baby. I'm here." He strokes my hair back. "I mean it, angel. I'm not letting you go. You were made to be mine."

I nod my head sniffling and place another teary kiss on his lips. "Okay," I say quietly. Resolute intentions behind it. He blinks lazily at me, and his eyes visibly begin to droop as if he's about to fall over. I climb down from him, and he lets me. "Sasha, you're hurt." I inspect his body with my eyes and see all the blood. Not sure where it's all coming from, or how much of it actually belongs to him.

"I'll be alright, angel." He presses his lips to my forehead, and I close my eyes to savor it. "I need to take care of things though."

He peers around me and gives me a grave look. "She came to me before I ran for the panic room," I rush out knowing he's upset that I saved someone rather than only worrying about myself. He nods his head, knowing now isn't the time to argue. "She got shot, but I think she's okay."

"I'll have her looked at." He looks down at the length of my body. "Are you hurt at all?"

I shake my head. "No."

"Good." He stares at me for a moment, and I want to demand he sit down and let me go get help. "I'm going to take you to my bedroom, where you'll remain until I come back. Understood?" His words aren't tender, but his eyes remain soft. I nod, willing to comply with anything he asks of me right now, still high on relief that he's alive.

He takes my hand in his and I gesture for Nastia to follow as he leads us out. "Sasha, are you sure you're okay?" I say, noting the path of blood he leaves with every limping step.

He removes his hand from mine to wrap an arm around me, tucking me into his side. "I'll be fine, angel. Just need to get patched up."

I gasp at the horror scene when we reach the end of the hallway leading us into the grand foyer. "Don't look, Vivian."

I dart my gaze away and stare at his feet as we make our way towards the stairs. We come to a stop, and he calls for Bash. I don't know the man, but I know he's someone Sasha trusts, so I look up and I'm happy to see that he's alive as well. Although he looks even worse than Sasha.

I catch a few words of what Sasha says to him and watch as Nastia goes to Bash. He said something about a bed and food. Nastia looks back at me and I give her a little smile. She returns it and Sasha starts taking us up the stairs. I divert my gaze once again when I see more blood.

Sasha's limp only worsens by the time we arrive at his bedroom. Once inside I pull away from him. "I think you need to sit down. I can go—"

"No," he says firmly, with more strength than I thought he could.

"You're not stepping foot outside of this bedroom until the house has been cleared."

"But, Sasha. What if you can't—"

"I mean it, Vivian," he says with finality. "I'll be alright, I promise." He kisses me sweetly on the lips and I lock my arms around his neck to deepen it. "Stay here, okay?" I nod my head with tears in my eyes, clinging to him. Wishing he wouldn't leave me. "I'll be back as soon as I can."

"Okay."

He looks just as reluctant to leave as I am desperate for him to stay. I drop my arms from him and watch him turn and walk out the door.

THIRTY-EIGHT

VIVIAN

I'm curled up in his bed when there's a knock at the door. I sit up and clutch the covers to me. Shortly after Sasha left, I showered and washed up. Then I grabbed a t-shirt of his and crawled into bed to fall asleep to his scent.

"Just a second," I call out and swing my legs off the bed.

The door opens and I can't explain why, but to see Greta standing there, I'm overwhelmed with relief and glee. "Greta!" I shout grinning and jump out of bed. She freezes with wide eyes as I run and throw my arms around her almost knocking the tray she's holding in one hand out. "I am so happy you're okay!"

She stands there rigidly for a moment, then lifts a hand to hesitantly pat me on the back. I don't take offense to it. She's not exactly the warmest person I've ever met. And we have never embraced before.

I retract myself from her and she stares back at me as if she's afraid of what I might do next. "The young master told me that you need to eat."

Food is honestly the last thing on my mind, but I could surely use the company.

"Come in." I open the door all the way and move aside for her to enter and directing her to the small sitting area. "Sit. Please."

She wipes her hand down the front of her crisp maid's uniform after putting the tray down. "I don't think so, Miss James."

Miss James?

I frown at her. "Please, still call me Vivian. And I insist. I want to make sure you're okay."

I plead with my eyes, hoping to somehow convince her to stay for a little while. I have no idea what's going on out there, I need to learn something about the situation.

She relents, but not without reluctance. She takes a seat across from me and I can tell from her posture how uncomfortable she feels. This would never have been permitted before, and everything about her says she's out of place.

"So, what'd you do when the attack began? Where did you go?"

"I was in the kitchen when it started. We hid in the wine cellar."

I nod my head. "Is everyone else okay?"

She looks down at her clasped hands in her lap. "I'm afraid not," she murmurs. "Those who were not in the kitchen with us got caught in it."

"I'm so sorry." I chew on my lip feeling guilty for not trying to take more people into the saferoom with me.

She looks up at me. "Nastia says you saved her." Now it's me who looks down. I nod my head, not exactly feeling like a hero. It was pure luck on Nastia's behalf. "She said you were brave."

I snort and shake my head, still feeling slightly ashamed. "I wouldn't call it brave," I mutter.

We're both silent. I can't take credit for accidently running into her. Although I thought about Nastia among the few others when I knew I needed to get to safety, I wasn't planning on going in search of her. Sure, I was aware of the fact that it would've been a suicide mission to do so, but bravery belongs to the fearless. I was terrified.

"You should eat while it's warm," she says, standing to her feet. I meet her eye and I have so many questions to ask her, but I see how anxious she is to leave, so I let her.

"Okay, thank you."

She leaves, taking her company with her. Lonesomeness engulfs me and I feel like I'm on the brink of shutting down. I hug my knees to me and stare at the food, the peace that surrounds me is offensive.

People died today. Innocent people. They were murdered and I'm sitting here completely unharmed with a warm meal served to me on a silver platter. I had a hot shower and a luxurious bed to curl up in feeling safe. Greta is already formally addressing me as Miss James. I don't feel right about it at all. I wish I could be out there doing something. Helping in some way.

I let the food go cold and curl back up in bed to wait for Sasha. A million questions fester inside of me. I feel like I might go crazy if I don't get answers soon.

I try to get some sleep, hoping it'll pass the time, but all I can do is toss and turn. Glancing at the time on the clock thinking more time has passed than actually does. Sasha has been gone for over three hours. Three hours that feels like three days.

I'm giving it one more hour. If I don't hear from anyone by then, I'm going out there. I'll stomach the heavy stench of copper in the air to find someone who can find Sasha for me. If they can't do that, then I can at least offer my help to anyone that needs it.

Sasha must sense my restlessness as he comes back before the hour is up.

I bolt from the bed and meet him halfway. His battered shirt is gone, but he's still covered in dried blood. "Hey," I say as I visually inspect his body. Most of his wounds are stitched up but not bandaged.

He places his hands on my hips and kisses my forehead. I'm afraid to touch him, hardly an inch on his body is unharmed. "I'm sorry I had to leave you for so long." He sounds almost as tired as he looks.

"It's okay. I know you have a lot to deal with. Are you okay?"

"I'll be fine." He kisses my forehead again then releases me to walk towards the bathroom. "I need to shower off before seeing the doctor again. Didn't want him to bandage me only to have to do it over again."

He disappears into the bathroom without closing the door and I stand there, unsure of what to do. When I hear the water in the shower turn on, I feel like I should go offer him some help. I have no idea how to do this. Without the threat of his father, I don't know what we are.

As I awkwardly stand there, all I can think about are the newly stitched areas of his already scarred torso. I don't care if he doesn't want the help.

I peel the t-shirt off my body and toss it next to his ruined pants. The bathroom is already steamed up and the limited visibility gives me courage.

After I wrap my hair up on top of my head, I slide into the warm air. Sasha sits on the bench with his knees wide, head back, and eyes closed. It doesn't look like he cleaned anything off yet, the exhaustion overpowering him as soon as he sat down.

He cracks one eye open without moving, then shuts it again. "Angel," he says on an exhale. "Come here."

"Can I help get you cleaned up?" I ask as I close the short distance between us. He snorts and reaches out without looking, tugging me into his lap. His smirk drops and he grunts in pain. "Sasha—" I push lightly at his chest but his arms constrict around my waist. "I'm hurting you." He rolls his head side to side arguing. "We need to get you washed off so the doctor can properly fix you up."

"You worried about me, *kukolka*?" he muses, slurring his words.

"I am." I lick my lips and stare at him. The left side of his face is one big bruise and looks a little swollen. Obviously needing ice on it. "Come on, Sasha. Let me help you."

"Just give me a few more minutes," he murmurs sounding like a teenager trying to snooze an alarm clock.

I watch him for a moment then gently lay my head on his shoulder, careful not to disturb any of his stitches. I give him ample time to close his eyes and rest, but what he really needs is to get some proper rest. In a bed. In order to do that, he needs to get this blood off of his skin and let the doctor dress his injuries. I need some real sleep too.

I carefully untangle his arms from my waist and place them at his sides. He doesn't protest. I get up from his lap slowly and still he remains peaceful.

A smile twitches at my lips at how adorably spent he is. I'm pretty sure I love him. The crippling grief I felt when I thought he'd died. The strong urge to nurture him back to health. Every emotion squeezing at my gut screaming he's mine.

But I'll digest these feelings later.

I don't want to put anything on his injuries that will irritate them so I take to gently massaging the crusted blood away.

He hums at the contact, bringing a smile to my face.

Fucking adorable.

I drop to my knees and get to work on washing away the remnants of the battle we've survived. He finally peels his eyes open when I move on from his legs to his torso. They're only partially open when he looks at me. The white in his eyes stained with red and pink. His apparent exhaustion feels contagious, it rolls off him in waves and the weight of the humid air works to pull me further under the spell.

He stares at me through two tiny slits as I scrub away the crimson stains, watching the red water run off his sculpted body, forming a red river to the drain.

"Can I get your back?"

He cracks his eyes open a little wider and weakly sits up from the wall. I go through the same ritual across his muscled back as he hunches over with his elbows on his thighs and his head hanging down. When the water finally runs clear, I work my fingers through his hair before I'm satisfied that he's thoroughly cleansed.

He lifts his head up and tries to twist his upper body to face me. "You need to take it easy."

He ignores me and pulls me into his side, draping my legs over his. "Thank you, angel." There's a twinkle in his droopy eyes as he stares at me.

"You're welcome," I whisper.

Using one hand, he cups the side of my face then slides it to the back of my head to bring my lips to his. Every cell in my body lights up with stars and sizzles. I'm the one to deepen it and moan when his tongue licks mine.

His hands begin to slide all over my thighs, inching their way to my greedy pussy, but I pull back and dodge him when he tries to dive back in. "Sasha, you're going to hurt yourself. You need bandaging, and we both need some sleep. There will be plenty of time for this later."

Groaning, he drops his head to my shoulder in surrender.

THIRTY-NINE

SASHA

I wrap a towel around Vivian, trying not to ogle her curves. She admitted to not being able to sleep while I was gone, so she needs rest almost as much as I do.

I wrap a towel around my waist and we head out of the bathroom with her dainty hand in mine. She's been quiet, but I can see the questions brimming her brain. There's so much curiosity in her beautiful eyes.

I leave Vivian sitting on the bed and step away to make a phone call. Before I can hit the call button, Vivian finally speaks. "So, what happened? Who were those people? Why did they attack us?"

I eye her over my screen with my head tilted down. She's antsy, twisting her hands in her lap and squirming. "I promise to answer your questions after I see the medic again." Before finally making my call, I notice the untouched food over in the sitting area. "You didn't eat," I plainly state.

She shakes her head and looks down. "I'm not hungry."

"Hm," I reply, determined to rectify that.

I call Artem telling him that I need the doctor up here to finish dressing my wounds and for two hot meals to be sent up. Other than the wounds he earned from the struggle of being dragged to my father's office, he was lucky not to have any bullet holes in him. Bash is perhaps worse than me. Nothing fatal for either of us, but he'll need more time than me to completely recover.

I toss my phone on the bed and look down at Vivian. I can't get a read on her right now. I know she's traumatized from the incident, but something else is plaguing her. She seemed pleased when I told her she was staying with me, but she's had a lot of time alone to change her mind.

My fingers itch to touch her. To pluck the thoughts and fears from her pretty head. Crack that intelligent brain wide open.

When I left her here almost four hours ago, I succumbed to my pain and injuries as soon as I left the room. I collapsed and woke up later during a minor blood transfusion. In my disorientation, my only thought was of Vivian. She was, and will always remain, my number one priority. That includes her happiness.

What if she can't be happy here? Can't be happy with me? Will I really hold her prisoner here if she's unhappy and wishes to leave?

A knock sounds at the door and I tell them to wait. I head into my closet to throw on some sweats and I grab a shirt for Vivian to wear. She thanks me sweetly and slips the shirt over her head as I take the towel from her.

"Get comfortable, baby." I pull the covers back and let her swivel her legs up. "It shouldn't take long." I press a kiss to her forehead and go to let the doctor in.

I stare at Vivian's back, her precious body buried under the covers while I let the doctor check my stitches out and bandage everything. She doesn't stir the entire time, even when someone comes with the food I asked for.

The little bit of innocence she had left has been tainted. If she stays, I'll only destroy it. She's too sweet for this world. Especially too sweet for mine. If I keep her, will I be the one to finally break her?

The doctor leaves and I walk around the bed with a limp in my step. I hate to disrupt her peaceful slumber, but she needs to eat.

I sit at her side and lightly brush away a fallen lock of hair. Her skin has started to pale, being away from the suns rays. Something that'll have to change. But Russia isn't the best place for that. Only seldom would she feel the warmth from the sun on her skin here.

That gut feeling tries to sink in, but I shove it back. Ordering it to wait.

Weeks ago, she snuck into my bedroom one night and made herself comfortable in my bed. I don't know why. She should've hated me. It was best that she did. But there she was, sleeping like an angel in a demon's chambers.

The temptation to slip inside the bed with her was torturous to deny. But I forced myself to leave my room, then leave the estate for assurance.

She isn't the only one that thought I had died today. After I caught a few bullets and barely clung to life, I was sure I had too. When I did, there was nothing. No thoughts, no bright lights or scorching fires. No angelic face to give me comfort. Nothing. Just floating around in darkness. Numb and mindless. I'm still shaken from it.

I don't have the heart to wake her right now. Food will have to wait. My exhaustion heavily outweighs my hunger at the moment.

Pulling back the covers a little to see her in my t-shirt, it reminds me of the first time seeing her wearing one of mine. It shifted my heart. It was the most domestic sight I had ever experienced before.

She can toss out her maid's uniforms, she'll never have to work a day in her life ever again. I can't wait to spoil her rotten. Take her shopping and buy her everything she could ever want. A whole new wardrobe and fancy jewelry to adorn her dainty fingers and slender neck and edible earlobes.

Peeling my sweats off, I slip into bed with her, molding my body to hers and breathing her in. She moans and wiggles against me, causing my cock to stiffen.

"You awake?" I murmur into her delicate shoulder with the softest skin.

"Kind of," she says in such a feminine voice. I kiss her shoulder, and she rolls to her back. Her eyes jump around my torso. "Are you alright?"

I toy with a chunk of hair and study her in wonderment. "I'm fine. Nothing serious."

She frowns. "Nothing serious?"

I smirk. "Nothing that can't heal on its own."

She lightly pushes back some of my unruly hair. "You almost died," she whispers, exuding genuine sorrow.

"I'm sorry if I scared you."

"Are you ever going to tell me what happened?"

I groan a little as I lay back, my body too sore to remain hovering over her. She repositions herself to turn into me and prop herself up on one elbow. "I'm not exactly sure where you'd like me to start."

"Start with telling me who attacked the estate and why?"

I tuck an arm under my head and sigh. "Kazimir."

Her dark and perfectly arched eyebrows pinch together, causing two creases to form between them. "Your cousin? I thought you could trust him."

"I can."

"I don't get it. Why would he attack the estate then?"

I grin. "To help me take out my father."

Her eyes widen. "You planned this?"

"Not entirely," I sigh and turn to stare up at the ceiling. Hoping I can appease her curiosity quickly. "It wasn't supposed to happen for another two days, after I had already gotten you to Kazimir's."

"So, what happened?"

I swallow the sliver of grief that pierces through me. Trip was a good soldier. I'm partly to blame for the position he was put into. Knowing he had any kind of family, I should have kept him out of everything. So, his life is on me.

"My father found out," I say giving her the short and less grievous version.

She doesn't need to know that I was bound and beaten at my father's command. That he was going to kill me if Kazimir didn't have a guy notify him of the dire situation.

I didn't give him shit for it when he confessed to that, but we will be having a talk about it. I should've been aware that we had a rat. Even though it wasn't to be used against me, I should have still been in the loop. He can't pull that shit with me if we're going to trust each other.

She's quiet for a while, but still sitting up. Not quite ready to delay her questioning. "Were you the one…who killed him?" she asks quietly.

I refuse to lie to her. Whether or not she stays with me, she should get the truth from me. "Yes."

She waits a moment. "Was it hard?"

I'm shocked by her question, but also pleased she doesn't seem upset. "No."

Another silent moment drags by. "Was he ever good to you?"

"I grew up never wanting for anything." *Other than companionship.* "And he could've been worse. But, no. I can't remember a time when he was good to me."

"I don't know if I could ever do that. Like, if I were given the chance to kill my mom, I don't know if I could actually do it."

I turn to her. She stares back at me with doe eyes. So pure and seraphic. "No, you wouldn't. Because you're better than that. But…" I run a finger down the side of her face causing her eyes to flutter. "If she was aiming a gun back at you, I know you wouldn't hesitate. You have competent survival instincts. You're much stronger than you give yourself credit for."

She finds joy in my small praise, trying to hide her smile.

"Now, let's get some sleep, angel."

FORTY

VIVIAN

The smell of deliciously warm food wakes me from my deep slumber. I sigh and stretch before sitting up. Sasha is nowhere to be seen, but the platters of food over in the sitting area takes my full attention.

Not willing to wait around for him, I climb out of bed and follow my nose. I snag a pastry and take a bite before I even take a seat. Moaning around the sugary bursts of flavor that tingle my tastebuds, I exhale in contentment.

I glance around the room, not used to seeing it in the daytime like this. I've cleaned it a handful of times during the day, but I'm now looking at it from a different angle. Nothing personal adorns the walls or shelves. He does have a good selection of books I noticed the first time I was here. Most of them are in Russian, but they all look well-loved.

The clock reads noon, and I can't believe I slept in so late. It was after midnight by the time I got into bed, but I've always been an early riser, no matter how little sleep I get. I guess given the circumstances of yesterday's events, I was out cold.

I'm chewing around another huge bite of the pastry when Sasha enters the bedroom. He still has a limp, but he's dressed as if it's just another day. Not at all visibly carrying the trauma or penance for what conspired… For every person that died… For him ending his own father's life… For him almost losing his own. I know he yearned for his freedom. To be released from the shackles his father kept him in, but Sasha has softness to his heart. He didn't let his father break him into the soulless creature in which he attempted to mold him.

Which has me thinking… Sasha can have anything he wants. He can love if his heart desires to. The thought of it stabs me in the chest. Now that he can be free to care for whoever he wants, will he still want me? Was our connection only out of convenience and proximity?

He frowns as he approaches me. Squatting next to me, he studies me with solicitous intent. Concern creasing his forehead. "What's wrong?"

I force a little smile. "Still kind of tired, I guess."

He lingers for another moment and drags the tips of his fingers down the side of my face making my eyes feel heavy. His touch always so efficaciously potent. He tucks his fingers under my chin and gently coaxes me forward to meet him for a tender kiss. He moves his lips gently with mine before pulling away.

I'm left dazed and disoriented as he stands up and takes the seat next to me. The blood splits between my cheeks and my legs. I'm too embarrassed by how simple it is to have me on the edge by a single chaste kiss to face him. I distract myself with another pastry.

"Would you like some coffee?" he asks after shoveling some food in his mouth.

"I would. Is there any juice?"

He pours me a glass of orange juice and a cup of coffee loading it with milk and sugar as I request.

He looks at me with amusement when he hands me my cup of coffee. "Anyone that drinks coffee black is psychotic," I tease. He sits back down with his own cup of coffee that he added nothing to and smirks over his mug to drink it. "Case in point."

We're quiet while we both eat like we're starving. The silence has me overthinking everything and obsessing over my earlier thought.

Will Sasha still want me now that he can have anyone he wants without consequence?

What if he really gets to know me and realizes it was just a fixation and it'll fade?

And what if he loves me? Will I really be happy with a bratva leader? In Russia?

"I need to talk to you about something," Sasha says breaking me from the tumultuous path I was leading myself down. I try to come across as aloof when I face him. "I want you to know that you have a choice." He pauses. "If you do not wish to stay here, you may leave at any point in time." A golf ball forms in my throat. *But he said…* "You have options."

"Like what?" my voice fails me by shaking. I don't let the hurt show though.

"If you chose to leave, you can go anywhere you want. Start over new anywhere." *How?* He must see the question in my face. "I'll give you more than enough to live off of." I start shaking my head, not willing to let him support me. I've taken care of myself my whole life. I may not have always done the best, but I'm still here. "That part is non-negotiable, Vivian. I'll set you up with an account and if you truly wish not to use the money in it, that's your choice. But it's okay to accept help sometimes."

I hate how much he gets me. It stings that much worse hearing this.

He said that if I didn't pull that trigger, I was his. What happened since then?

When he told me weeks ago he was finding me a way out, I was sad about never seeing him again, but hopeful for a brighter future. Then when the time came closer and he opened up to me, revealing the man that lives deep inside, it pained me to leave him. I wanted to beg for him to come with me. Then when I thought he died, I realized I couldn't live a life without him. He gave me a choice already. Shoot him and be free. Or stay and be his. His solace and his to cherish.

"Vivian?" I blink away the burning in my eyes and throat, and look up. "Do you understand?" I nod my head silently, but he doesn't seem convinced. "Eat up. I have a few surprises for you today."

I give him a timid smile, but it's forced. I don't want surprises. I don't want money given to me for a new life. But I also don't know what I *do* want.

He's implying I have the choice to stay, but he's not saying he still wants me to. Is this some kind of test?

After I'm full, he tells me I can go wash up. While I was sleeping, he moved all my toiletries in his bathroom, only confusing me more and filling my head with more questions I'm too scared to get the answers to.

When I come out of the bathroom, I find him still in the sitting area. The plates have been cleared and he's sitting in front of an open laptop.

"Do you mind if I borrow another shirt?"

His eyes darken when he looks up at me from the screen. He watches drips of water run down my chest and bare legs. "Come here, *kukolka*." He leans back in his seat and the pet name fills my belly with butterflies.

I walk to him, but he might as well have me tethered, pulling me in with his intense gaze. His shadowy eyes only grow darker the closer I get. Most women feel a little self-conscious from gaining weight, but the way he worships my new curves, I have never felt more womanly and beautiful.

Stopping in front of him, he looks up at me and peels away my towel, letting it drop to the floor. His eyes are ablaze as he peruses my body closely. My skin pebbles with goosebumps and my nipples peak at the attention.

He looks up at me again with a smirk. "You cold, angel?" I shake my head and his smirk grows.

His rough hands gently land on my hips and he explores them before venturing to my butt. He makes leisurely circles around on the soft globes there, then abruptly lifts me to straddle his lap.

"Sasha," I squeal making him grin. "You need to be careful, you might rip open your stitches."

He ignores my concerns and cups one of my cheeks and soothes the skin there with his thumb. Staring at me as if he's in admiration. All I can think when I stare back at him is if he wants me to stay… If he loves me like I love him.

"You're beautiful, Vivian," he rasps, making my cheeks burn and my chest ache. He says it so solidly I have no choice but to believe him.

Before I can thank him or tell him how beautiful I think he is too, he leans in and presses his parted lips to mine. It starts out slow, but so sensual. The kind of kiss I could linger in for hours. We're in no hurry.

His phone starts to ring but he ignores it. He threads his fingers through the back of my hair with his other hand, holding me close, and deepens the kiss. My hips rock on reaction, butting against his erection through his pants.

The sound of his phone sounds again and he growls into my mouth before pulling away. I'm a panting mess as he pulls his phone out with his eyes locked with mine.

"*Da*," he snaps, agitated. His nostrils flare and he takes a deep breath. He rattles something off in Russian then hangs up. "I have to go. But I want to show you something first. Something you can do while I'm gone."

I frown, hating that he's leaving me again. "How long will you be gone for?"

The corner of his mouth twitches. "Should only be a couple of hours." I nod my head and look down. He tilts my chin up with his hand grasping in. "I promise, things will settle." I nod again and climb off his lap.

Sasha goes on to show me that I can order some clothing and other essentials. He had a couple of stores pulled up online saying they aren't too far away and that everything could be picked up today.

I didn't even bother asking if we could go to the stores in person. I'm sure he'll be too busy to take me shopping.

Right before he leaves, he kisses me until my eyes rolled to the back of my head and then adds, "Get as much as you want, *kukolka*. There's no budget."

FORTY-ONE

VIVIAN

I feel spoiled by Sasha already. He insisted I buy a whole new wardrobe and anything else my heart desired. And the stores he let me choose from were not modest in price. But my heart desires only one thing. And something I cannot find in any high-end boutique. *Security.* And that security can only be found in him. All I've ever wanted was to feel cared for and secure.

The only time I feel like I belong is when I'm with Sasha. And when I'm with him, I feel more at home than I have ever felt in my life. But lately, I don't see a lot of him.

It's been a week now, and neither of us has brought up the elephant in the room. Will I stay, or will I go? Does he want me to stay, or does he even care?

I know things are still hectic from the attack on the estate, so much so that he had me couped up in his bedroom until yesterday, saying there was a lot of construction going on and it wasn't safe for me. So yesterday, he finally let me venture out of the room.

He took me to their indoor pool that looked like something at the Playboy mansion. He admitted that he hasn't been there for over a decade and I couldn't believe it. Knowing I now have access to it, I will be in it every day. Too bad they don't have an outdoor pool.

So far, I'm not finding Russia the most beautiful place to live in. Not that I have seen anything outside of these walls, but it's always snowing! I grew up in Southern California then lived in Las Vegas for four years. I am not a cold weather girl.

I spend most of the day alone at the pool. Laying there on a raft with a frozen cocktail wishing I had someone to share this with. A girlfriend or two for companionship.

I've never had problems making friends. When I still lived at my mom's, I tended to gravitate to the troubled teens like myself but we had ourselves a good group of friends. When I fled to Vegas, I kept in contact with a few, but then life happened, and we drifted apart.

Living in Vegas I had a lot of friends. Having so many different jobs gave me the opportunity to meet a lot of people. But I wasn't particularly close with any of them. I don't think I've had an actual best friend since middle school, and that hardly lasted through high school.

I don't even know how I would make any friends here. I don't have a job, I don't go to school… *School.* Sasha said that if I left, I could do anything. Go anywhere. Meaning I could go back to school. Get some kind of degree in social work and be able to help young women like I dreamt of doing.

Would he let me finish school if I stayed?

I'm lying in bed trying to read a book, but it's useless. I read the same page over and over again. Sasha didn't have dinner with me and it's now after midnight and he still isn't here. Last time I saw him today was for breakfast. Things seemed fine, but his mood has oscillated more than usual lately. I'm never sure which Sasha I'm going to get.

The one that looks deeply into my eyes before worshipping my body and making love to me. Or the surly man that doesn't speak before practically ripping my clothes off and fucking me until I can't take anymore.

I'm not sure which one I prefer. Both of them seem stressed. He holds so much back. I miss him and the possession to the point of insanity he showed me when I pointed a gun at him. I want that obsession back, that feeling like he'll never let me out of his sight. To fervidly demand that I stay. Proclaim me as *his* and that I am never leaving. Basically holding me prisoner here.

Being alone is worse than being a captive. Having so much time by myself only flourishes those fears of mine. Has me conjuring up new ones. Rethink and overthink to feed my insecurities, making me doubt if our connection is genuine or not.

The door flies open in a way that startles me. I sit up and watch as Sasha literally stumbles in, slamming the door behind him. I turn on the bedside lamp and take him in. His hair is all over the place, and he kicks his shoes off haphazardly.

I'm speechless at his temperament. I've only seen him drunk once before, but this is different.

"Hey," I say quietly.

He stops several feet from me, looking at me with his chin tilted down. "What are you doing?" I don't answer, confused by his question. "Are you staying or leaving?"

"I—"

"You need to make a decision," he snaps, immediately hurting my feelings. He's bringing up what we've both been avoiding, and he's doing it vehemently drunk.

"Sasha, I—"

He cuts me off again. "Are you leaving? Yes or no," he demands harshly.

I stare at him aghast. Is this the passion I was looking for? Because if it is, it allays none of my doubts or fears. It feels like he's kicking me out. Why didn't I give him an answer right away when he first asked me? Would things be different? Or would they be better? This is all so fucking mind —*fucking*!

"And what do *you* want, Sasha?" I shout.

He steps forward with flaring nostrils and points a finger at me. "I asked *you*." I glare back at him defiantly, refusing to join him in this little game. Or am I playing it too? "You have until tomorrow."

"For what?" I jerk back.

"To give me your answer."

I throw the covers back and angrily climb out of bed. "And what about you! Don't I deserve some kind of answer!"

"I don't need to answer to you," he seethes. "I answer to no one."

"So, that's how it's going to be now? You're the big bad boss now." I stalk forward. "A king sitting on a fucking throne of lies, deception, whores, entitlement." I stop only a foot from him, jutting my chin out. "And most of all, cowardness."

"Are you *trying* to provoke me, little doll?" he warns.

"If that's what it'll take."

He stomps forward, his body bumping into mine, forcing me to retreat back with every advance he makes. "For what? Huh?" He grows more agitated by the second. "You looking for attention or something?"

"I'm looking for something truthful from you."

He literally shoves me back, placing his hands on my shoulders and giving me good push. My eyes widen thinking I'm about to fall to the floor, but the bed is right behind me, so I land on the softness of the mattress.

I stare at him wide-eyed and indignant. "Did you seriously just push me?"

"Something truthful?" He peels his shirt off and throws it. "I've been nothing but truthful with you."

"Yeah?" I watch as he slips his belt off and tosses it on the bed. "Then why did you tell me I was yours and I wasn't leaving, then turn around and tell me I can go whenever I like?"

"And what does that have anything to do with being truthful?" I gulp as he pulls his pants and underwear down, his cock already bobbing in the air.

"You..." The words dry up on my tongue. I can't think like this. Not with him naked and his hard cock only inches from my face. "You aren't telling me what *you* want," I say halfheartedly.

"No, Vivian." He grabs my legs so that my upper half falls back, and he goes right for my panties. Pulling them down and off in one swift movement. "It doesn't work that way. You're lucky I'm even giving you a choice."

My mouth pops open in outrage. "Are you serious?!" He leans over me and yanks my bra down. I kick at him and try to cover my breasts up. "Stop it! What the hell are you doing?!"

He easily enough dodges my kicks and catches both of my ankles and uses them to flip me over on my stomach. "Sasha!" I thrash and squirm but he has me pinned down. "Sasha!" He readjusts himself so that he's straddling my hips. "Sasha," I growl in warning.

"That was very naughty of you, little cat," he tsks. He wrestles my arms behind my back, and I feel him binding them with something. I'm pretty sure it's his belt.

"Sasha. I am not kidding. Let me go," I demand, and he has the audacity to chuckle. "Sasha!" I fight to free my hands, but they're tightly bound and he's still sitting on my ass, pinning me down to the mattress.

"We're going to play a little game," he taunts.

"I am so over your fucking games," I seethe.

"I'm not sure that you are, *kukolka*." I purse my lips refusing to play along. "We're going to see how much you can really take."

I frown, afraid of what he means by that. He removes his weight from me and I don't move. "Tuck your knees under you." His voice has gone cold, taking the heat from the room. He smacks my ass good and hard making me yelp. "Now," he barks.

"Sasha—" *Smack!*

He spanks me again in the same exact spot. It stings as I grit my teeth in anger. "Do I need to tell you again?"

I'm pissed as I ungracefully tuck my knees under me. Trying not to lose my balance with my hands tied behind my back.

He grabs the tender flesh on my ass. "Good, little doll." Then smacks the same area again. "You're going to stay like this unless I say otherwise. You move, I will bring you to the edge of orgasm over and over, but I won't let you come."

The air rushes out of me and I feel the need to squeeze my thighs together, but I don't dare to move. His hands start roaming my bottom, teasing me with swiping just barely between my legs with his fingertips. With my ass spread wide like this, I can feel the air hitting every damp part of me, adding to the sexual anticipation. I'm still furious, but just as aroused.

He mutters in a mixture of English and Russian, rubbing my ass, teasing the heat between my legs and ass cheeks. "Fucking perfect, *kukolka*. So fucking mouthwatering."

I bury my face in the covers and squeeze my eyes shut fighting back a moan. He wants to play, then so will I. I will not let him know how much I am enjoying this.

The mattress dips as he moves around. My eyes pop open when I hear him spit and I feel it hit my butt crack. I sit still and he rubs the new moisture around my tight hole. He's teased it with his tongue before, but that's as far as it's gone. I'm curious, but still a little reluctant about it.

He uses his thumb to put a little pressure of the tight ring of muscles as his fingers start playing with my pussy. Every muscle in me tenses and I squeeze my eyes shut again. Strenuously, I fight the twitches and moans my body naturally wants me to release.

A low growl comes from his chest, and he presses the tip of his thumb inside and two of his fingers dip inside my pussy. The sound of my wetness is vulgar to my ears as he pumps his fingers and his thumb. My breath stutters over and over. My body struggling to remain staid. It's a wonderful intrusion. Different from everything else I have experienced so far with him. It only furthers my curiosity. But right now, I'm supposed to mad.

He picks up the pace and slams his hand into me, making a slapping noise and taking the air right out of me. I can't hold back anymore. I moan and try arching my back to expose more of myself to him, but the position I'm in prevents me from doing so. He speeds up more and I scream into the mattress. He groans through his teeth as my body ejects an excessive amount of wetness, splashing against his hand and stars dance behind my tightly shut lids. My body convulses and I rock and twitch.

His hand doesn't stop. He fucks me with it through the entire experience. "Sasha," I rasp through my heavy panting. "I can't. I need—" I moan again and squirm.

Smack!

He smacks my ass hard but doesn't stop. I whine and grit my teeth and clench my fists. "No, no, no," I chant in a breathy voice. My voice pitching higher and higher. "Oh, my God," I gasp as I come again, squirting and convulsing.

It's torture. A sweet torture, but torture nonetheless. I want to beg him to stop, but I'm incapable of words. All I can do is leave my jaw unhinged and breathe heavily out of my mouth.

He somehow forces another orgasm from me, and I want to collapse. Close my eyes and pass out. His thumb remains inside of me, but he pulls his fingers out and doesn't waist a second to shove his cock inside.

"Sasha, I can't," I cry weakly.

Smack! Smack!

I scream through my clenched teeth into the mattress. His thumb pumps in and out with jerky thrusts and he fucks me hard with his cock.

Smack! "Up," he orders.

I push my ass up into the air and when I do, he hits me at a different angle and my back bows. I'd spread wide for him if I could. Feeling him as deep as I can.

"Want me to fuck you here?" he asks, thumbing me and stretching me.

Yes!

"You'll have to ask me for it."

What?

"You want something, you ask." The adamancy in me has me biting my bottom lip, refusing to speak. "From now on. If you want to come. If you want my cock. If you want me to eat your cunt until you're gushing. You will have to ask for it."

Is he seriously trying to use sex as a weapon?

"I was hoping I could fuck the stubbornness out of you but looks like I'll have to wait it out instead."

He's right about that. The thought of him abstaining from touching me until I cave and ask for it? It's infuriating. Two can play that game though.

We can definitely see who can hold out the longest.

He fucks me harder, twists his thumb around and uses it to pry my tight hole open. The sting from the muscles being stretched has me rolling to the edge. I scream into the mattress again, combusting and shattering.

His cock pulls out abruptly and thumps against the crease of my ass. Warm strings of wetness splatter all over my back, ass, and hands still restrained. I can't help but to rock my hips as he slides his cock up and down to release every drop.

I'm still seeing stars and gasping for air when he yanks at the belt around my wrists and my arms fall to my sides. I feel his body heat hovering over my entire back side and his breath appears in my ear. "Tomorrow, little doll. I want your answer tomorrow, or you will spend the next several days fighting the urge to beg me to touch you. And when you do, you will get on your hands and knees to do so."

I'm utterly speechless as his body heat leaves me. A minute later, the bedroom door slams shut, and he's gone.

FORTY-TWO

VIVIAN

Sasha hasn't come to bed for three nights now. I've roamed around the lifeless estate hoping to run into him in my skimpy outfits. Or that someone would tell Sasha about my lack of clothing, and he'd come find me to reprimand me for wearing such things in front of his men. But it isn't working.

I don't even know if he's been to his room to shower or change at all. If he has, he waits until I'm either asleep or when I'm out of the room. Is he afraid he'll be the first to give in or something? Because he has no idea how deep my stubbornness runs. I've been poked and prodded all my life. I've been taken advantage of, toyed with, demeaned, degraded, violated. It's only made my resolve stronger.

All these fucking games. How old are we anyway?

I've had enough of it. If he wants to be petty and hide from me, then he can do so. I'm done. He's the one who will give me an answer. And he'll give me one tonight.

I ordered a bottle of vodka with my dinner tonight, but I won't take the cowardly way out. I don't need to be inebriated to confront him. Yes, a couple shots for a little liquid encouragement, but I want to be clear-minded and level-headed. I'm prepared to say exactly what I have to say. Fillet my heart and demand him to do the same.

It's getting late and I'm finally amped up enough to do this. Instead of looking for Sasha, I plan to seek out Artem or Bash. Or even Greta, who remains the head of the maids.

I debated on wearing something sexy again and doing something to my hair and applying a little makeup, but fuck that. I'm not going to try and convince him to want me to stay or try and seduce him. He either does, or he doesn't. I'm not going to give him my stupid answer that he demanded I tell him days ago but decided to evade me instead. He's being a pussy right now, and I'm not going to stand for it.

I eye the bottle of vodka as I stand there, still hyping myself up. "Just one more tiny sip," I mutter. Picking up the bottle, I toss back less than a mouthful and slam the bottle down and wipe my mouth with the back of my hand. "Let's do this."

I'm wearing a simple matching PJ set with my hair on top of my head in a messy bun and my face free of makeup as I bound down the stairs, beginning my search. Stopping anyone that I pass asking if they know where Artem, Bash, or 'the young master' is. He still refuses to be called Mr. Rogov. But 'the young master' sounds a lot cooler in Russian. And none of us care to be reminded of his late father.

I hit the foyer and I catch Bash walking through it coming from the direction of the office. "Bash," I snap and he stops. I cross the distance with a swift pace and plant my hands on my hips when I stop in front of him. I have to crane my neck back to look up at the tall motherfucker. "Where is he," I demand.

His eyebrows both arch, surprised at my brazenness. "Well, hello to you too, Vivian," he mocks, but I'm not in the mood.

"Where is he, Bash?" He releases an exasperated sigh. "You might as well tell me where he is or I'll just follow you around until you're inevitably forced to bring me to him."

His eyebrows rise up his forehead even further, and then he shocks me with a deep chuckle, his shoulders bouncing up and down. He coughs into his fist then points in the direction of the office. Amusement still clear in his expression.

"I'm glad you find this funny," I utter under my breath and stomp away.

The door to the office is closed when I arrive, but I don't bother knocking. I burst in and his head snaps up from his chair behind the desk. "Let's get this over with, Rogov. No more playing hide and seek or who can withhold from sex the longest."

He gives me a dry look and I finally notice the man sitting in the chair in front of him. I don't pay him any mind though as embarrassment heats my cheeks. Sasha better tell him to leave, or I will.

He looks to the man and says, "We'll have to continue this tomorrow, Franki."

"Alright," the American sounding man says standing to his feet. "Elijah does want it settled right away, though."

"First thing tomorrow," Sasha confirms.

I don't even look at the man once as he breezes by and leaves the room, closing the door behind him. "So?" I say. He stares at me, drumming his fingers on top of the desk. Not willing to respond.

I walk forward, affright seeping in and depleting my grit. But I cannot live like this anymore. Living in the unknown, falling further into despondency. Chipping away at what little I have left of me. All these stupid *games*!

Now or never.

"You're demanding that I give you an answer that I have already given you. To make a choice that I had already made." My emotions slam into me out of nowhere. My vision blurs and my chin trembles, no matter how hard I try to steel it. I came in here with such valor, what the hell happened? "You told me to pull the trigger, or to stay. I stayed. I chose *you*. I don't need to make the same choice again, because it will be the same answer," I say with my voice cracking.

His demeanor doesn't change, and it's infuriating. "Sometimes I wish we could go back." I swallow around the agonizing lump. Feeling like I'm doing this all for nothing. But why stop now? "Go back to me being a maid, terrified of your father using me to hurt you." I choke up and have to compose myself. My eyes too blurry to make out his face. "At least then, I felt *something* from you. Now, you're giving me nothing."

He doesn't speak, he doesn't move.

"Say something, goddamnit!" He remains irritatingly still. "If you want me to leave, then at least have the balls to say so!"

Behind fat tears, I see him rise to his feet. Squaring his shoulders and fortifying like a statue. "You think I don't want you here?"

"Do you?" He can't avoid the question forever.

"I thought I had made that clear."

I growl and grit my teeth in exorbitant frustration. "No, Sasha. You have *not* made that clear. You had at first, then you revoked it by saying I could leave. Acting as if you couldn't care either way."

He moves quickly. Rounding the desk with powerful strides. "Why," he demands when he places himself right in front of me. "Why do you want to stay?"

We've locked horns. We're either both too stubborn or too afraid to be the first to display our vulnerability. But I made a promise to myself that I wouldn't hold back. I'll give him the contents of my heart, and it'll be up to him what to do with it.

"Because I love you." There. It's fucking out there. My heart is splayed wide open to dispel any lingering doubt.

Everything about him deflates. I blink away the tears so that I can lucidly see the astonishment on his face.

FORTY-THREE

SASHA

No one has ever told me they loved me. I've never felt loved, or the desire to love someone else. I've cared for others: my sisters, my men, my cousin, Brita. But I've never felt anything for anyone nearly as strongly as I feel for Vivian. Fervid and an overabundant urge to please. Her proclaim has me fraught with overwhelming emotions I have no idea how to interpret.

"It's okay, Sasha," she says truthfully and ending her tantrum. "I didn't say those words because I needed to hear them back. I said them because I need you to know how I feel. Whatever happens, you deserve to know how I feel. All I ask is that you tell me if you want me to stay or if I should go. Please," she begs, her hazel eyes still brimming with unshed tears. I know my silence can also be taken as dismissal but I'm so overwhelmed by her confession, I'm incapable of sound.

Her shoulders sag and she shakes her head in disappointment. "You said that I was yours and—"

"You *are* mine."

Her eyes jump up, and the longer we stand there, the more her bottom lip quivers. "Then tell me what you want," she says with exasperation.

I step forward and slide my hands across her cheeks and cradle her head like she's a delicate flower. "If you chose to leave, I don't think I would actually let you go." Her lips slowly curve upwards in a teary-eyed smile. "Because I love you too."

Her smile drops, and her glossy eyes go wide, bouncing back and forth between both of mine. Trying to actually *see* the truth in them. Her delicate hands slide up to my shoulders and rest there. "Say it. I want to hear you say it."

I grin, knowing she doesn't need to hear me say it. She wants to win. And if that's what my baby wants, that's what my baby will get.

"Stay, Vivian."

She grins back. "Do I actually have a choice?" she teases, making me chuckle and shake my head.

"No, you don't."

"Good." She jumps up to her tip-toes and crushes her lips against mine. "Because you'll have to physically remove me if you ever want me to leave," she warns in a breathy voice.

"Is that so?" I murmur in amusement.

But the amusement quickly fades as the kiss deepens and she presses her hot body into me, her hands pulling and tugging my hair as she tangles her fingers into it. My hands roam her body, groping every soft handful of flesh.

"Don't you dare make me ask for it, Sasha," she cautions.

I grin against her lips. "I already gave you one victory today, *kukolka*." I taunt her and make no move to take it further than kissing.

"Sasha," she whines in frustration and grinds herself into my erection.

"Are you going to always make me let you win?"

She giggles and kisses me harder. "There can only be one stubborn person in this relationship."

Chuckling, I scoop her up and turn to take the few steps to my desk and set her on the edge there. I pull her shirt up over her head then remove mine. She wasn't wearing a bra so I'm able to dive in head first.

"Sasha," she rasps as her fingers comb through my hair and she arches her back. "I want you to fuck me in the ass."

I growl and yank her body closer to me, her ass on the edge of the desk. My mouth gorges and I overindulge myself on her heavy breasts. "You sure about that?"

"Yes," she says quickly.

"My sexy *kukolka*."

I back away from her and she pants heavily with her legs spread, wearing only small pajama shorts. Her large breasts rising and falling, her cheeks and chest vibrant with color.

I unbuckle my belt and trousers, then shove them down and take a seat right there in the chair facing the desk. "Take the rest off, and come here."

Her eyes light up with delight and she hops down to her feet. Slipping her thumbs into the waistband she shimmies out of her shorts and panties. When she approaches me, she stares down zealously, waiting for her next instructions.

Her eyes catch on my cock as I stroke it. "Do you like it when I touch myself, little cat?" Her lips twitch as she shyly looks up at me then nods her head. Her curious gaze jumps back down to watch me more. "We can explore that later. Right now, you're going to turn around and sit on my cock."

Biting her lip, she turns around and backs up between my spread thighs.

I help guide her by her hips until she's sitting in my lap. I take her wrists and plant her hands on the armrests. "Hands here."

Next, I hook my arms under her knees, hoisting her up. "Put my cock inside your cunt, then put your hand back."

She does exactly as she's told. Wrapping that small hand around my cock, she leads it to her cunt, and I don't dally. I let gravity take her all the way down until her ass meets my groin.

"I need you to make a mess of my cock, baby." We work together raising and lowering her down on me. She throws her head back with heavy panting. "It'll be easier for my cock to fit inside."

"Will it hurt?" she asks with her eyes closed and still using her arms to help her bounce up and down.

"Yes, *kukolka*. But you'll fucking love it," I rasp against her cheek.

She moans and rolls her pelvis every time she slams down on me. All too eager for me to stretch that tight rim of muscles, to feel her limits being pushed. To explore more of what her body is capable of.

"Touch yourself, baby. I got you."

One of her hands leaves the armrest to rub herself. Her chin drops and she tries to drive her hips down harder. "Yes," she hisses.

I kiss her neck and nip at her earlobe. When her breath hitches, I make a suction on her neck with my mouth, pulling the skin taut and not letting go until she is done convulsing.

"Fuck, baby."

I lift her so my cock pops out and sit her back down to glide it between her globes. Moistening her up and keeping her stimulated. Once I'm satisfied in preparation, I hike her up again and press my mouth against her ear.

"Now, put my cock in your ass, little doll."

Her breathing picks up expressing her nerves, but she wraps that hand around my cock, and she guides it to her tight little hole. I love watching her boldness and bravery soar. The way she stormed in here and demanded my concession. I don't do well with authority. My father was the only one I ever answered to, and I despised him for it. But with Vivian, I revel in the fact she can break me. She said there can only be one stubborn person in this relationship, and if she wants to claim that role, I will let her.

Sometimes. Old habits die hard.

"That's it, baby," I rasp as I begin to lower her, and she relaxes her muscles for me. Welcoming my entrance, obliging the new intrusion.

I hiss through my teeth when she sinks lower and her muscles give way, allowing me past the tip and hugging me tight. She whimpers then shivers from pain and pleasure. I plan on taking the first entry slow, allowing her only a moment to accommodate me. Because as soon as her ass touches my thighs and groin, full seated, I rage.

Lifting her up, I slam her back all the way down extracting the air from her lungs. I pant and do it again and again. My cock never feeling so fucking good before.

Her knuckles turn white gripping the armrests and she's losing strength in her arms, but her head cranes back more, pushing her breasts out and arching her back. She cries up to the ceiling as I continue my spree. Her ass slapping in my lap and her breath hitching with a whimper behind it.

She needs more. *I* need more.

Lowering her legs, I have her rise to her feet. I stand and spin her around. Latching my mouth to hers, I back her up to my desk and prop her back up on it. "Lay back."

She heeds my order and lies back, looking up at me with glazed over eyes. I crank her legs up and push her knees back. Without having to tell her, she hooks her hands behind her knees to hold them up.

Spitting in my hand, I rub it over my cock and spear her. Burying my cock back inside her ass deeply. My groin meeting her ass. I slam into her over and over and watch as her tits bounce and her face contort in ecstasy.

"Fuck your pussy, *kukolka*." I suppress the grunt that threatens with every thrust. "I want you dripping and blushing for days, thinking about the mess you'll leave on my desk."

She moans and slips her fingers through her tender flesh. I'm pleasantly surprised when she uses three fingers. She's not at all shy when she begins fucking herself.

My chest rumbles with an animalistic growl and I wrap a hand around her neck. I don't apply much pressure, just enough to hold on and use it as leverage to be able to pound into her harder.

"Fuck, Vivian. Fuck," I rasp under my breath, barely audible.

Cream covers her fingers and leaks down onto my cock making it almost unbearable to hold out. I know she's close, but I might be closer.

Her back bows and she moans loudly, her hand slowing. I pull out and stroke my cock to ejaculate in and around her gaping hole. The muscles convulse and spasm until it begins to close up on its own, swallowing some of my cum.

I'm drenched in sweat and struggling for air. My body aches from overexertion and from still healing in several places. With the little strength I have left, I help sit her up and I take her in my arms.

We embrace with our moistened skin sticking together and our hearts bumping loudly through our chests.

This, right here, is where our life begins.

FORTY-FOUR

VIVIAN

After having that breakthrough, Sasha and I have no secrets between us and I've embraced my life with him.

I always thought I would never want to be taken care of and pampered and pranced around like some trophy wife, but the fact that I am no longer afraid of one of my mom's pervy-ass boyfriends sneaking into my room, or being able to survive, or having to live in my car again, its freeing. I have no worries, and I have never felt so carefree in all of my life.

It's been only a few weeks since Erik Rogov was dethroned, but things around here haven't been brighter. I'm even closer with Nastia now, and Greta has finally warmed up around me. Not sure if she feels like she has to, or if I finally worn her down.

When I came into the bedroom to shower off after being at the pool, I found a package I've been expecting with some new clothes I ordered. I tore into it feeling like a kid on Christmas morning. I've never really had brand-new clothing before. I've always had to shop at thrift stores or had some kind of hand-me-down clothes. Even when I was out on my own, I had to shop second hand. To have brand-new clothing and shoes is surreal.

I'm twirling around in my new dress in front of the floor length mirror of the closet when Sasha appears in the background out of nowhere. I gasp and spin around in surprise. "Oh, my God, Sasha! You scared me." He doesn't smile or smirk as he casually takes in the full length of me. "Damnit! I didn't want you to see me in this," I pout.

He arches a brow and slowly approaches me. "Why the fuck not?"

"Because I didn't want you to see me in this until there was a reason to wear it." I continue to pout and cross my arms.

He snorts and wraps his arms around my waist, yanking me into him.

My hands land on his broad shoulders, our faces only an inch apart. "Then I guess I should give you a reason to wear this," he murmurs. "I'll have to take you out tonight."

"Really?" My voice rises.

He nods his head then presses his lips to my neck and starts exploring my body with his large hands.

"Aren't you still supposed to be taking it easy? You did get shot a bunch of times and almost had one side of your face smashed in," I say lightly.

He snorts and lifts his head grinning. "*Kukolka*, if I can fuck you multiple times a day, then I'm pretty sure I can stand to go out for a few hours."

I bite back a smile. "I guess you're right." We're going to have our official first date.

Sasha pulls me into the shower with him to fuck me against the wall before showering up for our dinner date. He doesn't take long to get ready and says he has some work to do before we go and leaves me to get dressed.

The dress I'm wearing is tight and comes down to just below my knees, putting my hips, ass, and breasts on display. I began a routine at the home gym we have about a week ago. Not to lose weight, but to be healthy and stay somewhat toned. Also, to have something to do.

I'm a little nervous about tonight. Not about the date itself, but about the few topics I'd like to bring up. I've been selfishly basking in our new relationship and enjoying our intimacy for the past few weeks. It's time to discuss my life here now that it's been decided that I'm staying.

I take one last look at myself in the mirror. Even though my hair doesn't hold a curl very well, I still put in the effort and put on a little makeup too. This will be the first time Sasha has seen me dressed up. Well, he's seen me dressed up when I had to work at the casino, but this time I don't look like a hooker.

When I hear the bedroom door open, I take a deep breath and walk out of the closet to meet him. He stops mid stride in the center of the room and devours me with his eyes. It's the exact reaction I was hoping for.

I make the decision to go to him, meeting him halfway. "*Krasotka*." *Gorgeous*.

I smile and wrap my arms around his neck. "And you look pretty hot in a suit."

He grunts with a dry look. "Don't get used to it," he mutters.

Bash drops us off right in front of the entrance of the fancy restaurant and we're immediately greeted at the door and escorted back to a secluded area. I squirm a little in the seat, suddenly feeling a little out of place. I've never been anywhere this fancy before. Sitting at the dining table back at the estate was a culture shock for me. This is another level. I really went from rags to riches.

I'm quiet while we're served wine and Sasha orders for us in Russian, and I'm waiting for Sasha to ask me what's wrong.

"What's wrong, angel?" He asks as soon as we're alone, as if on cue.

Taking my hand in his and bringing it to his lips to kiss the inside of my wrist. His eyes fixated on me the entire time.

I can't let him distract me with arousal. Focus.

"Nothing's wrong. There're just a few things we need to discuss." He kisses my wrist again then places my hand back in my lap before letting go. He gives me his full attention, propping his elbows up on the table and clasps his hands together.

I clear my throat. *Here goes nothing.* "I want you to shut down the brothel," I rush out before losing my nerves. He arches one eyebrow and his mouth twitches. "I don't feel right about it. All those women…it could've been me. I can look past everything else that you do, but I cannot look past you trafficking women."

There. I said. I stated my case.

Silent minutes tick by. All he does is continue to stare at me with slight amusement, as if I'm adorably clueless to him, but this is real life we're talking about. Real people.

"Okay."

"What?" I splutter, choking on my wine as I was taking a sip to fill the awkward silence. I cough a few times and Sasha hands me my water. I take a couple pulls on it to soothe the irritation in my throat then gasp. "Thanks," I mutter and he stifles a smirk. "I'm sorry, but did you say…okay?" He nods his head then takes a sip of his own wine. "Okay…as in you'll shut it down?" He nods. "You'll stop selling women?" He nods. "Just like that?" I say flatly, unsure if I believe him.

"Just like that, *kukolka.*"

Really? I thought I would have to argue with him and throw a temper tantrum and threaten to hold out on him until he did.

"Is that not the answer you were hoping for?" he teases.

I rapidly blink and shake my head, trying to absorb his reaction, or lack thereof.

"You said there were a *few* things you wanted to discuss."

"Right," I murmur and squirm in my seat. He kind of threw me off here. I wasn't expecting to move along so quickly. "The other thing I wanted to talk to you about was my mother."

The lightness and delight drains from his face and a dark cloud comes rolling in. "What about *her*?"

Wow, I thought he'd be upset about the first request, but he was pleasantly receptive. I did not expect him to be upset about the brief mention of my mother, but he's livid.

"I kind of wanted to track her down."

"Why?" he snaps.

"I don't know. Maybe to make sure she's okay. I mean, people can change, and—"

"She did not." I frown. "Do you not remember how I met with her to get the names of every boyfriend she ever had while you lived under her roof?" I swallow hard and start rubbing and squeezing my hands together in my lap. Yes, I remember. But it's something I try to forget. As if it never happened. "She didn't ask about you or your life or your health or anything. She blamed you, Vivian. She blamed you for—"

"I know," I snap harshly. "I know, Sasha, okay? I don't need to be reminded. I just thought that maybe..." I trail off, trying to abate the onslaught of tears.

"*Kukolka*," he says gently and runs his fingers down the side of my cheek. Giving me instant comfort. "I don't mean to be so brazen, but she is not worth it. It will only bring you heartache." I look down and nod my head, knowing he's right. It was stupid of me to think four years would magically change her into a good person. "Vivian." He tilts my chin up to look at him. His eyes hold so much sympathy, and it reminds me that I already have someone who loves me beyond measure.

I give him a reassuring smile. "Okay." He studies me for a moment then drops his hand. "So, the last thing I wanted to talk to you about was school."

He returns my smile, and my estranged mother is already forgotten.

EPILOGUE

VIVIAN

A year and a half later…

Today is the day, and I am freaking the fuck out. I'd like to say I know Sasha fairly well now, but men in general can be so unpredictable. Especially moody mobsters.

About a year ago, I asked Bash for a favor. Well, two. One, a dog. I asked him to take me to the shelter to get a dog for Sasha's birthday. It wasn't until the third shelter till I found the perfect one. He's a huge pittie with inky black fur, ears cropped, and missing one of his green eyes. He looks like a stocky black panther pup. They say he was rescued along with others from some backyard breeders that bred them to fight. I was tempted to tell Sasha that piece of information when I presented him with his new furry best friend, but I refrained from doing so. He would have them killed for sure. A part of me was okay with that, but I can't lose too much of myself here.

The second thing I asked from Bash was to track down Sasha's mother. He was hesitant, but he caved. Most men around here eventually cave for me. I'm sure it's because they're afraid I'll go tell my big scary bratva boss fiancé.

Artem assisted Bash in the search for his mother and it didn't take them long to find her. When they told me, I demanded to meet with her myself before breathing a word of it to Sasha. We had to be extra sneaky. Good thing Bash and Artem are mainly in charge of escorting me around when I leave the estate. I was touched that they risked keeping something from Sasha for me. I know they both hate lying to him about anything.

The meet-up with his mother went better than I could have hoped for. Sasha deserves the family he's yearned for. And his mother deserves it too.

"No, Loki," I scold him when he tries to stick his big nose in the plate of appetizers I have sitting out on one of the coffee tables. I ruffle his boxy head and smile.

The argument between Sasha and I over naming the dog was hilarious. His inky hair reminded me of Elvis Presley, so I went ahead and named him Elvis. When I introduced him to Sasha, the first thing he said was he wasn't calling him that. I swallowed my censure and ignored the fact that he didn't say "Thank you" first, and gave him a few suggestions. He hated them all. Until probably the hundredth one. Loki.

It took him some time to warm up to the dog, I'm sure it mostly had to do with painful memories from his past, but now you hardly see one of them without the other. Loki is only tailing me right now because of the food I'm putting out.

I chose a sitting room because the formal dining room is a gaudy monstrosity. Coming to the estate is enough of an intimidating experience and I wanted something more cozy for Sasha's family.

And today is even more exciting because we finally get to meet the newest addition. His sister, Vera, just had a baby with her new husband only a couple of weeks ago, and I cannot wait to hold the precious little girl. But more than anything, I'm interested to see Sasha's reaction to the little bundle.

I'm honestly not sure if I ever want to have kids. I'm only twenty-three, so I have plenty of years to think about it and Sasha has never pressured me, unlike Marta's husband. He's been tirelessly pushing her to get pregnant, but Marta's young too. I don't understand the rush.

Vera wasn't so rosy towards me at first when I first met her and Rada over a year ago. Sasha told me to not take any offense to it. *She can be bitch.* His words, not mine. But I won her over eventually.

Rada was sweet and friendly from the first greeting. She acted like I was already part of the family and couldn't wait to get to know me. The two couldn't be more opposite. Where Vera seems to attract herself to a domestic life with a husband and children in the suburbs, Rada is free-spirited. She's always traveling the world, taking on random modeling gigs, and she always has a new boyfriend. Sometimes even a new girlfriend.

"They're about five minutes out," Artem announces, and I whip around in a state of panic.

"What!" I glance down at my watch and realize how late it's gotten. "Shit," I hiss. "Where's Sasha?" I rush out.

"Still in his office."

I sigh and straighten up to compose myself. "Okay, I'll go talk to him."

"You still sure about this?"

"It's a little late now, Artem, isn't it?" I mutter as I walk past him and head for the office.

I stand in front of the closed door to the office and take a few more deep breaths to soothe my nerves. Last I heard, he was alone, so I don't bother knocking.

"Hey, baby," Sasha says looking up from his desk as soon as I enter.

"Hi," I say quietly shutting the door.

He leans back in his chair and frowns as he tries to dissect my current demeanor. "Is there something wrong?"

"Um." I lick my dry lips and walk further into the room. I wipe my sweaty palms on the soft fabric of my dress. "I did something," I confess abruptly.

His frown only deepens, and he shows more interest by leaning on his desk and tilting his head down. "Go on..."

Damnit. I hate this. How do people ease into things? I have no idea how to give a gentle delivery with serious stuff like this. Like when I wanted to talk to him about the sex trade, and my mother, and school. There's only one way I know how to do this. And it's like ripping off a Band-Aid.

"I found your mother."

EPILOGUE

SASHA

I don't react right away. I refuse to. Does she think I lack the capability to find my mother if I wanted to? She had no right to. I've never met her, and there's no reason to. I'm almost thirty-four years old. I don't need to be reconnecting with the woman who gave birth to me.

"And she's coming over tonight," she says dropping another bomb. "Her name is Sofia, and she would really love to meet you."

I jump from my chair so abruptly it falls back, the clamor from it causing her to flinch. "Vivian," I say lowly, straining to control my temper. "You had no right to go snooping around behind my back." The more I speak, the more threatening I become. "And you definitely had no right to fucking throw this at me last minute," I seethe. "To invite a stranger into my home, without my knowledge, and to claim that it is my mother. A woman I have no desire to meet." Tears bubble up in her beautiful eyes, but I'm too far gone already. "Tell Bash and Artem that she is not allowed here and then to come see me."

"Sasha." Her voice cracks.

"Now, Vivian!" I roar, and she recoils from the outburst.

A single fat tear falls from her eye, and she sniffles. "Okay." Her chin quivers and she nods her head, looking down. "I'm sorry."

She turns to leave and the wrath sizzles out like a bucket of ice water was dumped on it. "Vivian," I say sternly, but she practically runs for the door. "Wait." I round my desk and jog to stop her. She throws open the door and goes to take off, but I'm faster, catching her around the waist as a sob wracks through her and I bury my face in her hair feeling like a worthless bastard. I never lose my temper with her. She never gives me reason to. "Baby, I'm sorry. I didn't mean to talk to you like that."

I made a vow to only bring her happiness for the rest of her life. To only make her smile and to never shed a tear again. I'm upset she would go and seek out my mother without consulting with me, but my angel never does anything without good intentions. She doesn't understand that I told myself she died a long time ago. So, to me, she's been dead since I was a small child. And I made peace with that years ago.

"Vivian," I say softly and turn her to face me. Tears flow down her pink cheeks causing her makeup to run, and my heart splits in two. "Baby." I cup her face in my hands and level with her. "I didn't mean to be so aggressive, but I hate surprises, especially when it comes to my past."

She sniffles and nods her head. "I'm sorry," she whispers.

"No, you don't need to apologize."

"No, I should've talked with you about it first instead of inviting them all over and—"

"Them?"

She takes in a shaky breath and releases it. "I don't know why I thought this would be a good idea," she mutters, looking at the ground in shame and guilt.

I shove my hands into my pockets and exhale through my nose. *The things this woman does to me...* She takes a tiny peek up at me through her dark eyelashes. "When are they supposed to be here?"

"Now," she mutters, unable to keep eye contact with me. "I'll go tell Bash to tell them to leave though." She goes to turn away, and I stop her.

"No." She looks at me with those beautiful hazel eyes, solidifying my relinquishment. "Go take a few moments to yourself, then go greet your guests." Her face drops and her eyes light up. "I'll come find you in a bit."

She turns her body into mine and my hands automatically go to her hips as she rests hers on my chest. "Are you sure? If you're not ready for this, I understand. It was rash of me—"

"It's fine, angel." I give her lips a soft kiss. "Now, go. I'll see you soon."

She reluctantly peels herself from me and runs towards the stairs, not willing to stick around much longer in fear I might change my mind.

Loki comes up to me wagging his tail. "Did you know about this?" I ask and rub his head. "Traitor," I mutter, and turn to go back into my office.

I pour myself a glass of cold vodka before unbuttoning my suit jacket to take a seat at my desk. *Sofia.* That is the most single piece of information I know about my mother. I have no idea who she was before me, and no idea who she became after, what she looks like, or how old she is. To me, she's been dead.

I sip on the clear liquor, leaving the peppery aftertaste on my tongue. Loki whines and grunts next to me, and his tail starts wagging when I look at him. He stares up at me as if waiting for something.

"What? If you want to go, then go." He wags his tail some more. "I'm not ready yet," I murmur and finish my glass. He whines and grunts again, but I ignore him. I grudgingly agreed to this, but I'm in no rush.

I stare down at my empty glass, watching the condensation drip from it and debate on having one more. But with the stress I'm under, one more will turn into finishing the bottle if left alone too long. I won't do that to Vivian. I can't.

My angel.

After a few months of Vivian going back to school, she came to me with a request. *Another* request. I can't say no to the woman. She wanted to start a charity for young women, to fund homes and shelters for them. She wants the main focus to be sixteen- and seventeen-year-old girls. Runaways and those who are close to aging out of the system that need to get out of harmful situations. Girls who are trapped, like she was.

I sanctioned her appeal to give up the business of the whorehouses, including the one I had placed her mother in. I made sure they were all sent away with enough money to not ever speak about it and some of them I set up at some of our legit businesses. Except for Vivian's mother, that is. I let her walk away with her life. Which was much more than she deserved.

I look up to find Vivian walking into the room with a hesitant smile on her face. "Come here, angel."

Her smile brightens and she comes right to me. Perching herself in my lap and wrapping her feminine arms around me. "Are you okay?"

"I'm fine, *kukolka.*" I brush some of her dark hair off her shoulder.

She eyes the empty glass on my desk. "You sure?"

I grin and wrap my arms around her waist. "I had one glass. Just to help take the edge off."

She nods her head in understanding. "You ready?"

Cupping the back of her head, I bring her lips to mine. Her body molds to mine and I'm tempted to bend her over my desk. But I won't do that to her. Even if she wouldn't protest, I know she set this thing up for me tonight.

Tearing myself from her, I take a deep breath in then out of my nose. "Let's go."

We walk hand in hand out of my office and head toward the sound of people talking. Before turning the corner to make our entrance, I stop and spin her into me. I stare down at my hazel-eyed angel and admire her beauty as if I'm seeing her for the first time.

"I love you, Vivian."

She beams up at me with her radiant smile. "*Ya budu vsegda lyubit tibya.*" *I will always love you.*

The End

Want to see how Sasha reacts to meeting his mother and the additional family he never knew he had? Sign up for my newsletters for extra chapters and short stories about the Men of the Mafia and their women who have tamed them.